# Devouring Kiss

# DEVOURING KISS

DEMONIC PRINCE

BOOK TWO

KAREN KINCY

ISBN-13: 979-8-9899697-1-5

Editor: Laura Apgar

First edition

❀ Formatted with Vellum

# CONTENT WARNING

*Devouring Kiss* is a dark fantasy monster romance. It contains explicit sex scenes (including primal play and male monster anatomy with demonic spikes), fantasy violence in battle, discussions of infertility and non-consensual breeding, memories of childhood abuse, imprisonment and torture in a dungeon, and trauma responses such as nightmares and dissociation. Read with care!

# CHAPTER ONE

## ROOK

A dragon sleeps in my arms.

*My* dragon.

She's still naked after shifting into a woman last night. Not that I'm complaining. My gaze travels over her gorgeous body. Careful with my claws, I stroke my knuckles over her red hair. It feels like silk under my fingers. Her scent intoxicates me—sweet clovers with a hint of smoke like incense, lingering from her dragonfire.

I could hold her like this forever. But Hexfall is nothing but a temporary haven for us, a good place for monsters to hide.

Dawn creeps into the broken tower where we slept. Once, Hexfall was a castle for kings, my ancestors, but this place was cursed long ago and fell into ruin. Enchanted roses choke the abandoned fortress with thorns.

Pyrah yawns, uncurls like a cat, and kisses me on the cheek. She can be unexpectedly sweet when she's not breathing fire or killing knights.

"Pyrah." Gravel roughens my voice.

"Good morning." Her hand drifts down my abdomen. My muscles tense beneath her touch. "Why are you hard already?"

"Always hard in the morning," I mutter, which is the truth.

"I guess I haven't learned that yet. We haven't spent that many mornings together."

I grunt. "True."

Five days. That's how long it's been since I captured her from her cave. All of this is uncharted territory, for both of us.

She curls her fingers around my cock and strokes me in one lazy tug. Fuck, that feels good. I suck in a breath and resist the urge to rock my hips. My balls ache, heavy with unspent seed.

"God, woman, you're relentless."

"Should I stop?"

Rolling over, I pin her down to the blanket, holding both of her slender wrists above her head in one of my hands. I love the look of my black claws against her pale skin. It feeds the possessive instinct inside me.

"No," I growl.

"Why not?" she teases.

"Never tempt an incubus."

She glances at me through her eyelashes, pretending to be coy. "I'm terrified of being trapped by a big, strong demon." But then she can't help smirking, as if this idea amuses her.

"You're bigger and stronger than me," I point out.

"Only when I'm a dragon."

I kiss her neck. My fangs graze her skin just hard enough to make her shiver. I bit her there last night, to claim her as my mate, though the marks have already faded to silvery scars. Before long, there will be nothing left. My bite was not enough to mark her.

Unlike the teeth of a dragon, which left her with far deeper scars.

"You have rose petals tangled in your hair," I say, to distract myself.

"Do I?"

"Such a lovely red."

With a few words of honest flattery, I have her melting in my arms. She looks into my eyes as if she's spellbound by me.

"I wish we could stay here forever," she says.

"We can't." As an apology, I kiss her again, this time on her collarbone.

"Why not?"

"You know why. Hexfall isn't our home."

We don't have a home together. Not yet.

She hides her worry behind her smile, but her eyes betray her true feelings. "Should I drag you back to my cave instead?"

I shrug. "And then what?"

"I could think of a few things you might enjoy." She implies dirty, *filthy* things with the purr in her voice.

Impossibly, my cock gets even harder. "Oh?"

"Besides, you belong with me."

"I'm with you right now."

"No, with me in my cave. You're my mate."

My jaw clenches. "I can't."

"Why not?"

"I couldn't be tied down to one place for too long."

She glowers at me. "What's wrong with my cave? I spent years collecting treasure and guarding my territory, which has prime hunting grounds. Any self-respecting male would be impressed and more than happy to move into my home."

That's enough to kill my erection. "Pyrah. I'm not a dragon."

"I know. Obviously."

My stomach lurches unpleasantly. What does she mean by that? Have I disappointed her as her mate? I can never be anything but a demon.

In the distance, thunder rumbles.

No.

Not thunder.

The sky remains blue and cloudless above, and dread clenches my gut when I recognize the sound. It's the rumbling growl of a dragon, the pitch deep and masculine and far too fucking familiar.

Pyrah tenses beneath me. "Scaldric," she whispers.

Deep in my gut, I know it has to be him, the golden dragon who claimed her as his mate and bit her without her consent. The fucker even tried to force her to marry him, before I interrupted their wedding. He shouldn't be breathing after that.

I yank on my trousers, buckle my belt, and lace my boots. "Hide."

She doesn't bother getting dressed. "Hell no."

"Pyrah, it's too dangerous."

Her eyes simmer with defiant fire. "You're sweet when you're protective, but I can take care of myself."

Naked, she strides to the window. God, she's going to jump.

At least we're high enough that she could probably shift before she ever hit the ground.

"Pyrah." I grab her wrist. I need to keep her safe.

"Let me go."

"Why do you want to go out there and confront Scaldric?" My heartbeat is pounding. "What good will come from it?"

"You want to let him fly through here unchallenged?"

I shake my head hard. "He's hunting for you. I don't want to let him find you."

She rolls her neck until it cracks, though she's still clenching her jaw. "Maybe I should have killed Scaldric."

My thoughts exactly. Out loud, I say, "But you didn't."

"I couldn't kill another dragon. We have already been hunted to the edge of extinction." She glances into my eyes as if seeking some reassurance from me. She's obviously troubled by the idea of murdering him.

Me? I'm less conflicted.

"What if Scaldric has come to make amends?" she wonders out loud. "What if he isn't allied with Queen Dulcamara any longer?"

My fingers tighten around her wrist. "That's a dangerous assumption." Especially since Queen Dulcamara is a cold-hearted bitch.

"I need to know."

"Then I'm coming with you."

My demand takes her by surprise. "You are?"

I dip my head in a curt nod. "Clearly, I can't stop you."

Another growl rumbles through the sky and echoes inside my chest. Louder this time. The golden dragon must be flying closer.

She glances at me. "Get your sword."

Since I can't stop her, I let her go. She jumps out of the window, falling two stories down, and lands on the ground in a crouch. I wince at the impact to her knees, though she heals fast since she's a shifter.

I grab my sword and twin daggers. Armed, I descend from the tower.

Pyrah doubles over, her body shuddering into a bigger shape. Her wings snap open from her shoulder blades and her tail slithers free from her spine. Red rushes over her skin as if she has been drenched in blood, and then it sharpens into shimmering, crimson scales. It's breathtaking, as always, though I don't have time to appreciate her transformation.

A roar rumbles through the air.

My head snaps up, but there's no sign of Scaldric yet. Not even a glint of gold.

"Get on," Pyrah commands.

I vault onto her back and settle between her wings. I bend over her neck and grip one of her spikes in my hand. With her muscles tensing beneath my thighs, she lunges into the sky. Her wings pump as she claws higher into the air.

We abandon Hexfall and fly over the Thornwood, a forest of cursed roses.

Scaldric plunges from the heavens. His wings snap open as he pulls out of a dive and rushes over the forest. Sunlight glitters on his golden scales. Spikes armor the length of his spine, all the way down his tail. My heartbeat thunders at his immense size and power.

He's a formidable male. It's impossible to deny his strength.

Scaldric circles around us like a vulture. An ugly scar cuts through the scales on his neck, courtesy of my sword the last time we fought. He could have bled to death, but clearly the healers saved him in time. I should have killed the fucker then and there.

He's wary of us now. Good.

Pyrah's wings churn the air as she hovers over the forest, waiting for Scaldric's next move. When he circles back, the heat of his breath rushes over us like a furnace.

His eyes lock with mine.

The darkness of his blown pupils consumes the yellow of his eyes. They could be dilated from either rage or desire. With Scaldric, it's impossible to tell. But I know he wants to fight me and fuck Pyrah, that much is clear. He flares his wings to kill his speed, then lands in the Thornwood.

We follow him down to the ground. Pyrah's claws dig deep into the earth, her muscles tensing, ready to lunge.

"Pyrah," Scaldric rumbles. "My mate."

Rage turns the blood in my veins to molten iron. How hard would I need to strike the motherfucker to behead him?

Pyrah bares her teeth. Smoke trickles between her fangs. "I'm not your mate."

I leap from her back and land on the ground. When I straighten to my full height, I draw my sword, the metal ringing as it leaves its sheath.

"She's mine."

The golden dragon towers over me, but I take an easy, relaxed stance. Nothing but a deception, since I'm ready to strike like lightning.

"The demon remains unworthy of you." Scaldric's forked

tongue flickers through the air, tasting her scent. "You aren't in heat any longer."

Pyrah snarls at him and flares her wings. "My body is not your concern."

"You still wear the bite of a dragon." Scaldric's gaze lingers upon her neck. "Mine."

He's not wrong. His fangs left scars upon her that will never heal. For a dragon, such a bite means more than a wedding vow, though he marked Pyrah after she refused him—a violation.

My muscles tremble from the effort of holding myself back. I want to slice open his throat and watch him bleed out. "Fuck off, Scaldric. Only the most pathetic of males would keep chasing after a female who didn't want him."

The golden dragon bristles, his spikes lifting. "You dare challenge me?"

I would relish the opportunity to kill him. "I defeated you once already, and I will do so again. Pyrah chose me, not you."

"You are no more than a cambion." His voice hisses like smoke. "A half-breed with corrupt blood, your seed useless and incapable of fathering a child."

His words hit me in the gut. I know I'm sterile, unable to get Pyrah pregnant, but sometimes I wish this was a secret. Everyone in the kingdom seems to know my weakness.

Pyrah arches her wing over me, a protective gesture. "Don't you dare insult my mate and expect to walk away from here unscathed."

Scaldric's deep voice rumbles with menace. "Because of him, you will bleed."

"Are you threatening me?"

"No." He tilts his massive head to one side. "You are a

woman. If your womb fails to grow the seed within it, you will bleed."

Surprise darts through me. Does he speak the truth? I keep my stare locked on my enemy. "Why are you here, Scaldric? To fight?"

"Not to fight but to warn you." Scaldric lashes his tail back and forth. "Queen Dulcamara is hunting for you."

I arch an eyebrow at his stupidity. "We know."

"The queen has placed a bounty on both of your heads, a fortune to whoever brings back the Gray Prince and his red dragon. She won't rest until you are hers."

"Why would you warn us?" Pyrah asks. "We have no reason to trust you."

Scaldric spreads his enormous wings. "Because no bounty can compare to you, my lovely Pyrah. Your fierce beauty outshines all the gold in the world. We belong together, my mate, and I will win you back."

What a piece of shit. His pretty words stink worse than a cesspit.

I glance back at Pyrah. "We could kill him." I say it with the bravado of a monster hunter who does this every day.

"No." She folds her wings against her spine. "Scaldric, I spared your life for a reason. Don't make me regret it."

Scaldric tilts his head, inspecting her with predatory curiosity. "I owe you a debt. Allow me to repay it by keeping you safe."

"Safe?" She spits out the word. "How?"

"I don't trust that demon to protect you. While you bleed, you won't be able to shift into a dragon. Let me fly over your territory during your time of weakness and watch over you."

"Like hell you will," I mutter.

Scaldric ignores me. "You will return to me, Pyrah. I will wait for however long it takes."

The golden dragon lunges into flight. His pounding wings create a wind that scatters fallen leaves and rose petals into the air. Bracing myself, I shield my eyes with my arm. He soars higher over the Thornwood before vanishing from sight behind the canopy of trees.

I return my sword to its scabbard. Today isn't, sadly, his day to die.

Pyrah relinquishes her dragon form, her body shuddering back into that of a woman. Her draconic ferocity fades away and betrays a deep vulnerability that she has often kept hidden. Her eyes look haunted with the fear of someone who has been prey before.

I touch her on the elbow. "Are you all right?" I ask.

"You were right," she murmurs. "We can't stay here."

The adrenaline begins to fade away from my blood, though I still can't shake the primal urge to fight. "Every time Scaldric looks at you, I want to carve his eyes from his skull."

"Don't. It's not worth it."

I'm unable to stop a growl from escaping my throat. "Pyrah, I admire your desire to protect your species, but Scaldric deserves to die. He has no respect for your independence."

"I know." She forces out the words as if they taste bitter. "But please don't become a dragonslayer. You're nothing like the man who killed my mother, or all the men who tried to kill me."

I grit my teeth. "I don't want you to look at me that way."

"Have you ever killed a dragon before?"

"Never. But Scaldric knows the boundaries of your territory. He won't wait for you to come to him, not when he can hunt you down and take you when you're at your most vulnerable."

"God, he's such a bastard."

I cock my head. "*I'm* a bastard," I say, mildly enough.

"I didn't mean it like that."

I shrug, not even insulted. "Everybody knows I'm the king's demon bastard. The word gets stale."

Her throat works as she swallows hard, clearly still bothered by what she said. "I'm sorry."

"No need to apologize." It's the truth, one that I have been aware of since I was no more than a boy. "I understand what you meant."

"Thank you, Rook," she says.

She stands on her toes and kisses me. I return the kiss, my fangs a sharp hint against her lips. My arms hook around her waist and hold her closer. She can never be close enough. The warmth of her body acts like a talisman that unravels some of the tension in my gut.

When we break apart, her fingers trace the scars on her neck, where Scaldric bit her without her consent. The haunted look in her eyes deepens, as if she's lost in a painful memory.

"I wish I could erase these," she says.

"Scars are reminders of our survival." I wait for her to meet my gaze. "And reminders of our strength."

"Sometimes, I don't feel strong."

Her words surprise me. "Pyrah, you are the strongest woman I have ever met. I'm in awe of how much you have overcome. I wish only that I was able to mark you as my mate."

By tomorrow, it seems likely that no trace of my fangs will linger upon her skin.

She smiles sadly. "Only a dragon can mark another dragon."

"I will find another way to mark you."

I never thought I would be blessed with such a fierce, beautiful woman as my mate. Whenever anyone looks at her, they should know these truths: she is mine and I will protect her with my life. Nothing in these worlds—not the Overworld nor the Underworld—will stop me.

# CHAPTER TWO

PYRAH

I can't stop shaking since Scaldric came for us. No, not us—*me*.

*Because of him, you will bleed.*

Was he telling the truth? My mother never told me anything about this, but she barely told me anything about my body. I knew only the vaguest of details about my first heat, which is a secret shame among dragon shifters. My mother and I lived alone, out in the wilderness, which meant I had no other female dragons to ask about my journey into womanhood.

Rook believes that I'm strong, but he doesn't understand how sheltered and alone I have been all my life. I wasn't quite sixteen when my mother was killed by dragonslayers. After she died, I had no friends or allies in this world until I met him.

"Was Scaldric telling the truth?" I ask, with a bitter taste on my tongue. "We all know I'm not in heat any longer. Will I start bleeding and lose the power to shift into a dragon?"

Rook tilts his head. "I don't know enough about female dragon shifters. But many females do have monthly bleeding."

"Monthly?" My mouth opens with horror. "How do they survive?"

"They manage."

I twist my face into a grimace. "That sounds awful."

Hot shame creeps through my face. Blood has never scared me before. Other women in this kingdom have been surviving their cycles every month, while I'm afraid of what might be a yearly occurrence.

*If* Scaldric is telling the truth.

Has he ever lied to me before? He was blunt about his intentions when he claimed me as his mate, though he never told me about our planned wedding, or that my wedding dress was embroidered with cursed aellurium to force my obedience to him.

Lies by omission, then.

How can I be strong, when I have such little control over my life? I have never been able to stop my enemies from hunting me down.

Not dragonslayers.

Not even Scaldric.

I'm lost in thought until Rook's voice grounds me again. "Pyrah, talk to me. I'm here for you."

I glance into his eyes, which glow even in the daylight. "Why would Scaldric lie about this?"

His jaw hardens as he ponders my question. "I suspect that he speaks the truth. I have heard of something akin to this before. Dragonslayers study the vulnerabilities of dragon shifters, and their lore claims that a female dragon loses the power to shift during pregnancy."

Shame creeps into my face, that old familiar feeling. "They do?"

"Your mother didn't tell you?"

"No, but it doesn't matter. We both know I can't be pregnant." My stomach twists into a knot the moment I say it, because his eyes sharpen with sorrow. "That would be impossible, wouldn't it?"

"It would," he says.

A tiny, secret part of me hopes that he's wrong. When I went into heat for the first time, it was always deeper than simply lust —for a female dragon, going into heat is a primal urge to breed.

*I want his baby.*

The secret thought whispers through my mind, unspoken. I can't even blame it on being in heat any longer. It's not something I can admit out loud, since it would only hurt him more than I already have.

"Forgive me for asking," Rook says, "but what about your father?"

His words catch my attention. "What do you mean?"

"You were alone in your cave when I found you."

*Alone*. That fails to capture how I endured years of solitude. "I never knew my father," I admit. "My parents were... unmated."

"I'm sorry," Rook says, though there's no judgment in his voice. "That must have been difficult."

I twist my mouth wryly. "More difficult than being the demonic, bastard son of the late king?"

He grunts. "My family was fucked up in its own unique way."

"At least you met your father. I don't even know my father's name. I don't know anything about him, just that he was a blue dragon."

"Was he a seadrake?"

"Yes, though I'm surprised you even know the word."

He lifts his shoulders in a shrug. "As a monster hunter, I make it my business to understand the monsters of these kingdoms."

"Not many in Chymeria do. They believe that all dragons are alike, and don't care what we call ourselves." I hesitate, my mind straying to darker thoughts. "My father could be dead or alive, and I wouldn't know either way. He might not even know that he has a daughter. My parents were never mates."

"That surprises me. You told me yourself that dragons can be traditional about mating."

"You're not wrong." I braid my hair to distract myself from the lump of emotion lodged in my throat. "My mother taught me that my virginity was a precious thing to be guarded and saved for my future mate. She must have been ashamed that I was born out of wedlock, and that we had no male to protect us or our territory."

Rook tilts his head. "Your mother must have been...lonely."

Heat scorches my cheeks before climbing into my ears. I'm sure that my face has turned scarlet. "What are you implying?" I ask, though I know damn well what he must mean.

"After entering their first heat, all female dragon shifters go into heat every year thereafter." He arches his eyebrows, keeping any emotion from his face. "Am I correct?"

I grimace. "Yes."

"How did your mother deal with such matters?"

*Deal with such matters.* That's such a polite way of phrasing it, but to be honest, I never thought of my mother's needs before. Perhaps I have grown up more sheltered and naïve than I ever imagined.

"I don't know. Even at sixteen, I was hopelessly innocent." Slowly, my eyes open wider as realization dawns on me. "I never questioned why my mother sometimes went on long hunting trips alone."

"Long, yearly hunting trips?"

"You're right." I rub my eyes with the heels of my hands. "She must have hidden everything from me." A bleak laugh escapes from me. "At least she never came back pregnant. I don't know what I would have done with a little brother or sister."

"Could she have been visiting your father?"

"No." I shake my head, refusing to believe such a thing. "I don't even know if my father is still alive. Why wouldn't she bring him back home? Why wouldn't she tell him about me?"

"We may never know. Not unless we find him."

Hope darts through me like a vivid bird in a dark forest—it's here and then gone again within seconds. "The Frostslayer clan dwells to the far north, several kingdoms away. I have never traveled there, nor to the ancestral homeland of the Darkdelver clan, my mother's family."

"Darkdelver," Rook repeats. "One of the firedraken clans?"

I touch my fiery hair, a shade closest to crimson. "Was it obvious? I'm a red dragon, after all."

"I wondered where you inherited such beauty." He gazes at

me with his lips slightly parted, as if in awe of me. "Dragon clans are matrilineal. When you claimed me as your mate, did I join the Darkdelver clan?"

"No, only our children would be born into it." The moment the words leave my lips, I regret them. I can't confess to imagining the impossible. "I'm sorry, I shouldn't have said that."

He gazes into my eyes for a long moment. "Is that what you want?"

Remembered words echo through my mind. *I would never believe you are unworthy for not being able to father a child.* I meant what I told him before, and it seems cruel to reveal my secret hopes.

I take one of his hands between mine. My fingertips trace one of his older scars, a twisting ribbon of silver that cuts across his wrist. "Rook, I want everything you can give me."

"I can't give you everything."

"I know." My eyes prickle with tears. "I know you can't."

"Pyrah." He speaks my name gruffly, and I can tell that he's burying his emotions deep. "We shouldn't linger much longer in Hexfall." He glances between the trees at the sky, his stance guarded.

"Where should we go?"

"Do you want me to fight Scaldric for you?"

"No." My stomach lurches. "Please, don't."

"Then you leave me with no choice." He exhales hard, his breath clouding the cold air. "While Scaldric still darkens the skies above your territory, I must find a place for you to hide."

# CHAPTER THREE

LARK

The Thornwood beckons me.

I hold a basket in the crook of my arm and abandon my cottage in the mist. My boots crunch lingering frost that clings under the trees. When I breathe in deeply, the rich, complex scent of earth and moss and leaves almost overwhelms me. God, I missed that smell. I wander deeper into the trees, hoping that the forest will swallow me up.

An ancient curse clings to this forest, cast by a sorceress whose name has been forgotten by most—Aetherlin of Myrkland. I will never forget her name. She was an unbelievably powerful woman. Her magic lingers in every bloodred rose that blooms everlasting.

Stranger still, Aetherlin's curse twisted the seasons themselves. Outside of the Thornwood, the kingdom of Chymeria has warmed into spring. Here, fragments of winter linger in the deepest, darkest parts of the forest. The curse is strongest here, the magic saturated. Frost glitters on roses in full bloom. A few snowflakes drift from the sky before they melt on the moss underfoot. I have often wondered if Aetherlin cast her curse during the winter, and I'm walking through an echo of her time.

Perhaps if I walk in her footsteps, I can gain some of her strength.

Right now, I feel anything but strong. I'm little better than a crystal vase that has been shattered and crudely glued back together. One wrong move and I will fall apart into pieces again.

Being outside still doesn't feel real to me. Memories of being trapped in the dungeon cling to my mind. I spent seven weeks locked away in the Forgotten Tower, that place my entire reality, never knowing if I would ever see the Thornwood again.

Tonight, I want to cook something to celebrate my newfound freedom. Besides, the pantry inside my cottage is all but empty. I don't have much left beyond mustard and a rare bottle of black wine from the Underworld that I have been saving for a special occasion.

I would rather not get drunk on an empty stomach. Once again, the wilderness will sustain me. I can forage for my dinner—moonlight chanterelles, if fortune favors me today. They have a lovely bioluminescence and taste even lovelier when cooked.

I lean against an ancient oak tree, the rough bark beneath my hands a comfort. The gnarled roots of the oak rummage in fallen leaves. Kneeling, I brush aside the leaves and hunt for hidden mushrooms.

A tiny clump of fungi sprouts from the rotten wood. They aren't moonlight chanterelles, but they have a beautiful purplish brown color. I don't recognize the species, so I let them grow. Perhaps later I can determine if they would be useful in any potions or spells.

For now, I just want my dinner tonight to taste like home.

I abandon the unusual mushrooms, for the time being, and wander deeper into the Thornwood. Red catches my eye, the crimson scattered across frost like drops of blood—winter strawberries. They often fruit during the bleakest of times, when nothing else survives. Down on my knees, I thank the forest and harvest the winter strawberries.

When the wind blows, my left horn aches from the cold.

*Broken.*

I shudder. How could I have forgotten what happened to me? What's *wrong* with me? When I entered the Forgotten Tower, I was still whole. Now, I can't deny that I have been irrevocably damaged by my imprisonment. A demon's horns can never grow back, not even with the help of magic. The best I could do is hide what has been broken.

My claws bite into a strawberry until crimson juice stains my skin like blood. I watch it trickle over my fingers, then devour the berry whole. Its flavor brings tears to my eyes. I believed, during the darkest of times, that I would never taste sweet things again.

The rustling of feathers catches my attention. A brown bird lands nearby, cocks its head, and chirps at me. *A skylark.* My namesake. Instinctively, a shiver crosses over my body.

The bird chirps again, its breath a puff of white in the cold air.

And then it speaks. "*Come back to me, Lark.*"

That voice. Zin's voice. I remember it echoing in my prison, taunting me, tempting me. *Gods, not that witch again.* I lunge at the bird, intending to cage it between my hands, but it bursts into flight and darts between the trees. The enchantment upon the skylark unravels with a scent like rosemary.

I'm left trembling on the ground.

The smell of rosemary always followed her like a cloud of perfume. I should have known it was her magic.

How did she find me? She's a dangerous sorceress, a dark-eyed witch whose talent rivals my own. After I escaped from the Forgotten Tower, I made sure to burn all my clothes to ashes, though sometimes magic clings to the skin like spider webs. She never stole any of my blood, so she shouldn't have enough of me to cast a tracking spell.

*My hair.* She could have plucked some of it while I slept.

It wouldn't be enough to divulge my location to her, though it would be enough for her to send me a message. The skylark can't fly back to her and tell her where I'm hiding. Without the enchantment, it has become a wild, innocent creature again. There's no point in hunting it down after the poor thing just regained control of its body.

*Come back to me, Lark.*

Why in hell's name would she expect me to come back to her, after everything that happened? For seven weeks, I was locked in the Forgotten Tower, and she never once tried to free me. She brought me food, every day, even though it was never enough. I became ravenous with hunger. A succubus can't survive without consuming lust.

She *knew* this.

I hated her for visiting me, hated her for pitying me. If she expected me to grovel, or beg for mercy, she was wrong. My defiance ran deeper than the very marrow of my bones. When the heat of our hatred blazed into passion, I kissed her like I wanted to hurt her. But by devouring her lust, I could taste how much she wanted this. Wanted *me*.

Without her, I would have starved to death.

The wind blows through the Thornwood again, though this time, I'm too numb to feel the cold. I wander deeper in the forest and discover more of the winter strawberries. I harvest them until my basket is full and I have no reason to linger outside any longer.

It's time to go home.

Back in my cottage, I stoke the fire in the hearth and bring out my cauldron. I will cook down the strawberries into jam. They will last much longer that way, rather than moldering and rotting. When I stare into the flames, I remember the skylark flying to me in the Thornwood. I haven't left the Forgotten Tower far enough behind.

I never should have touched that evil woman who put a spell on me.

No, not a spell—a curse.

# CHAPTER FOUR

ROOK

If you want to hide so well it's impossible to find you, you need magic. Luckily, my twin sister is a sorceress. Lark lives in a cottage on the outskirts of the Thornwood, not far from Hexfall.

Only fools wander through the Thornwood on foot. Monsters devour any travelers who stray from the Emperor's Road, which cuts through the cursed forest like a scar.

Nothing but rumors told by humans afraid of monsters like me.

Nevertheless, I would rather not walk the distance. I left my horse, Bolt, at a stable outside of Netherhaven, and I haven't returned for her yet. She's safer there for the time being, and deserves a warm stall and decent hay.

Besides, why ride a horse when you can ride a dragon?

Pyrah shifts into her draconic form and carries me high

over the Thornwood. I stretch out one of my hands, slicing the wind. My shoulder blades tense, my shadow wings still hidden, though I'm not incubus enough to be capable of flight.

Following my directions, Pyrah lands in a woodland glade. Her claws sink into a pelt of moss. Mist thickens the air, making it impossible to see through the swirling white vapor. I vault down to the ground.

"Lark?" I shout my sister's name. "It's me, Rook. I've come with Pyrah."

The mist ripples from some inner disturbance. It turns ragged and clears from the air. In its absence, a cottage is revealed.

Built from round stones taken from the river nearby, the cottage looks like part of the forest. Overgrown by moss, it shimmers with morning dew. A few ferns and a mushroom or two have taken root between cracks in the stones. Blue-white smoke uncurls from the chimney.

When I rap on the door, it swings open under my knuckles.

"Come in," Lark says, from somewhere inside.

There's no chance in hell a dragon would fit inside the cottage, so Pyrah shifts into a woman. She's naked, of course, and she shivers. I unbuckle my pack and toss her my cloak, a shirt, and a pair of trousers. I need to buy her clothes. She claims she never needed them before, living alone in the wilderness, since she rarely shifted into a woman.

I can't blame her, considering how many dragonslayers have hunted her down.

I hold open the door for Pyrah before following her into the cottage. It looks bigger on the inside and holds a surprising quantity of things. Books overflow from shelves alongside bottled potions and crystals. A fire crackles in the hearth. It smells damn good here, like drying lavender, woodsmoke, and baking bread.

Lark kneels by the hearth. She's half-demon, like me, courtesy of our succubus mother. Her silver skin glints in the firelight, and most of her bruises have healed. Black horns jut from her pale hair, one of them broken. My hands curl into fists. I'm a shit brother sometimes, since I haven't worked up the courage to ask her how it happened. Must have been during her time in the dungeon.

Lark prods the embers with a poker before she stands, dusting the ashes from her hands on her apron. "Back so soon?" It hasn't been long since we brought her home.

I lean against the wall with my arms crossed. "We need your help." My voice sounds calm. Emotionless, even.

"Why?" She glances between us.

"A golden dragon by the name of Scaldric. That fucker won't leave Pyrah alone. He thinks she belongs to him, and that he can force her to marry him and become his mate. He has the blessing of Queen Dulcamara."

Lark's shoulders stiffen. "The queen has a dragon?"

"Apparently."

"What do you want from me?"

"Magic. Can you hide Pyrah's cave with an enchantment?"

"Maybe."

Lark bends over the hearth again and, with the poker, lifts the lid from a cast-iron skillet. A delicious aroma rises from the bread baking inside. My mouth waters at the smell.

"Hungry?" she asks.

Yes, but I shake my head. "Lark. We aren't here for breakfast."

"Breakfast first. Never do magic on an empty stomach."

I peel away from the wall. "So, you will help us?"

"I can't let a dragon bite off your head." She glances at Pyrah. "No offense."

"None taken." Pyrah puts on an innocent face. "I never wanted to bite off Rook's head."

"That's a lie," I deadpan.

"Well, I'm glad you didn't." Lark looks into the embers of the fire, her gaze faraway. "While I was in the Forgotten Tower, I kept dreaming about hot bread from the oven, slathered with melting butter."

Her words hit me like a punch to the gut. It's such a simple luxury to have butter on bread, and yet she was denied it for so long.

I stand by my sister. My hand drops to her shoulder, a gentle reassurance. "Are you all right?"

"Well enough." But her smile looks brittle. "They fed me gruel cooked with rancid oats at the Forgotten Tower. Never want to see another bowl of that slop for the rest of my life."

"How long were you locked away?" Pyrah asks.

Lark's hand tightens around the poker, her knuckles whitening. "Too long."

"Seven weeks," I say, though it pains me to admit it.

"How awful," Pyrah mutters. "I can't even imagine. The thought of being locked in a dungeon for seven weeks, with no room to shift into a dragon, curdles my stomach. I'm sorry, I should have helped you get out of there sooner."

Lark shakes her head. "You don't have to apologize. You didn't know."

"I didn't," Pyrah admits. "Rook captured me and chained me in aellurium. He didn't free me or explain himself until later."

"Allow me to elaborate." I clear my throat. "I had no choice. She would have burned me to ashes like the dragonslayers before me. There was very little chance of me strolling into her cave and politely asking her for help."

Pyrah arches an eyebrow. "You're not wrong."

Fighting a smile, Lark turns her attention back to the bread. The skillet must be too hot to touch, but she grabs the handle without flinching. Pyrah stares at her, clearly surprised, while she carries it to a battle-scarred table.

Lark catches her staring. "It's a simple spell." When she lifts her hands, blue sparks fly from her fingertips. "Frost magic."

Pyrah whistles low under her breath. "I've been on the wrong end of frost magic before. It can be very powerful."

"Or extremely delicate."

The bread comes out of the skillet, its crust a rich, golden brown. Lark dusts off her hands, the magic disappearing from her fingers, and takes a knife. She cuts us each a thick slice. Delicious steam wafts into the air.

"Butter?" she asks. "Jam?"

"Yes, please," Pyrah says, begging with her eyes.

I sit backward on a chair and drape my arms over the furniture. It's rare for me to feel so relaxed, instead of always on edge and ready to fight. The warmth and safety of the cottage shields us from the outside world.

Lark butters the bread and slathers it with a generous amount of red jam. She slides our plates toward us. "Eat."

"Thank you," Pyrah says.

I take a bite of the soft bread. The jam tastes like strawberries. Sweet and tart, it reminds me of sunshine.

"Good?" Lark asks.

Pyrah nods vigorously, her mouth full. Her enthusiasm makes me smile.

We eat in silence, the fire crackling and popping in the hearth. It's a cheerful sound, unlike the destruction of dragonfire. That memory has been echoing in my head ever since we battled Scaldric in the temple at Netherhaven.

I shake my head to clear it. "Wild strawberries?" I ask about the jam.

"Yes," Lark says. "Winter strawberries from the Thornwood. I found them while looking for mushrooms."

The crumbs turn dry in my mouth. "Be careful."

"Rook, I know more about mushrooms than you do."

"I don't mean mushrooms. Are you sure you should be wandering around?"

Blithely, Lark licks the knife clean of jam. "The Thornwood isn't that dangerous."

I growl under my breath. "The whole kingdom of Chymeria is dangerous."

Pyrah tears off some bread with her teeth, chews for a moment, then swallows. "Scaldric. Queen Dulcamara. All her knights and sorceresses and any mercenaries who want the bounties on our heads. Am I forgetting anyone?"

I snort. "Anyone else needs to get in line."

"We're safe here," Lark says. "My magic will protect us. Not even dire wolves can sniff us out through the spell around my cottage."

Pyrah glances at me, an unmistakable gleam of hope in her eyes. This enchantment could transform her cave into a sanctuary. Undoubtedly, her home hasn't been this safe in years.

I reach under the table and give her hand a squeeze. *I'm here. I will protect you.*

"I never found those mushrooms," Lark muses. "Moonlight chanterelles."

"Are they rare?" Pyrah asks.

Lark's eyes always glow when she talks about fungi. My sister has a strange obsession with them. "They grow under only the most ancient oaks, deep within the Thornwood, which makes them almost impossible to find. But you can't make proper miranollen without them."

"Miranollen?"

"Mushroom dumplings," I say, since I remember them well. "Our mother brought the recipe with her from the Underworld. It was one of our favorite foods as children."

Lark laughs. "Remember how we always fought over the last dumpling?"

I smile. "Mum threatened to never make miranollen again."

"Will you cook them for me?" Pyrah gazes into my eyes with such innocent yearning, it's impossible to resist. "I've never eaten any demonic food before."

I frown. "We shouldn't gallivant deeper into the Thornwood just for mushroom dumplings."

"Please? I want to know more about you, Rook."

My defenses start crumbling. "I'm happy to enlighten you."

"And this would be the perfect opportunity for a lesson."

"God, woman." I let out a sigh before admitting defeat. "I surrender."

Lark smirks at me. "That was fast. I thought you had more fortitude than that, brother."

"I have found my undoing," I deadpan, and I speak the truth.

"Stand here for a second, Pyrah," Lark says.

While Lark judges her height with her hand, Pyrah looks somewhat amused by being measured. As a dragon shifter, she must spend most of her time towering over everyone else.

Lark rubs her chin pensively. "You aren't much smaller than me."

"I wouldn't fit in your cottage in my true form," Pyrah replies.

*True form.* Is that how she thinks of herself? More dragon than woman?

"Come with me," Lark says. "You can borrow some of my clothes instead of Rook's ragged old things."

"They aren't ragged," I protest, though both of them ignore me.

Admittedly, I haven't had time to fully wash and maintain my clothes and armor over the past few weeks.

I linger outside the cottage while they get ready. The cold morning air chills my skin and fills me with a deep sense of calm. It's a precious feeling, one that needs to be hidden and protected. I never want to leave this place. I never want to lose this feeling of family.

When Pyrah exits the cottage, she has swapped my

borrowed clothes for a blue dress and leather boots. The color of the dress turns her red hair into fire in the sunlight. Beautiful.

Lark locks the door behind us. The ornate iron key in her hand shimmers with magic. She has a basket tucked in the crook of her arm, one I recognize from previous quests for mushrooms. She has dragged me on several such expeditions in the past, dubbing me her bodyguard.

We follow Lark deeper into the forest. When I glance back, the enchanted mist swirls behind me, the cottage already gone. It has vanished into the ether. No one would ever know that a demonic sorceress calls this place home, which is exactly the point.

After Pyrah stumbles over a rock in the path, I catch her by the elbow. "All right?"

"I'm unaccustomed to boots." Her cheeks turn pink. "It's been years since I've worn them."

Lark's eyes sharpen with curiosity. "But you did before?"

"While I lived in Quickmire," Pyrah says. "I worked at a tavern and pretended to be nothing but a girl."

"What's it like, pretending to be human?"

Pyrah shrugs. "I wasn't very good at it."

"But you're a shifter. You can hide your dragon and walk among humans undetected." Lark studies her own black claws. "One glance at me, and they know that I'm monstrous."

Pyrah is silent for a moment as we walk. "I didn't even know how to *act* human."

"What do you mean?"

"They wanted me to be a girl who showed her teeth only when she smiled."

Lark twists her mouth with wry amusement. "Little did they know that your teeth could become fangs."

Pyrah's eyes gleam gold for a moment, on the edge of draconic. "Sometimes it's easier being a dragon than a woman."

I arch an eyebrow. "Even with the threat of dragonslayers?"

"Of course."

"Damn," I mutter. That's bleak.

Lark keeps her gaze focused on the path ahead. "Haven't you seen what it's like to be a woman in Chymeria? We shouldn't be ugly, or angry, or dangerous. We should be pretty, sweet, and obedient. We should be virgins or wives or mothers, because these are the roles most valuable to men. Otherwise, we have no worth."

"By that definition," Pyrah says, "I would be worthless."

I glance between them both. This conversation has entered dangerous territory, and it would be wise for me to tread cautiously. "You live in a different Chymeria than I do," I say, "but I will always stand by your side."

"We know," Lark says sweetly. "That's why we haven't murdered you in your sleep."

"Yet," Pyrah adds, her face the picture of innocence.

Lark laughs. "I think you like him too much for that."

"True." A smile tugs at Pyrah's lips. "There's a reason he's my mate."

We fall into a companionable silence for some time. We have strayed far from the Emperor's Road, though I trust that Lark and I can navigate the secret paths through the forest. Pyrah stays close to me, never letting me out of her sight.

Even during the day, little of the sun reaches the ground here. In the shadows, the light takes on an emerald hue from passing through so many leaves. Tiny gnats dart through a shard of sun like motes of dust. I breathe in deep. The air has a rich, earthy aroma.

We enter a grove of ancient oak trees, though I haven't seen any moonlight chanterelles yet. The cursed roses tangle thickly here, their red petals perfuming the air with a lush, dark scent that invites me to linger.

"What was the curse?" I ask, since I have often wondered. "What magic brought about the Thornwood?"

Lark glances back at me. "You lived every spare moment of your childhood in the library of the castle. Are you telling me you never found the story of Hexfall?"

"Correct."

"You never gossiped with anyone and heard the story told?"

I shrug. "I don't gossip."

"True." Lark circles the massive trunk of an oak tree. "To be fair, it's a long story best told by the fire."

"Wait." Pyrah can't stop staring at me. "Rook? Obsessed with libraries?"

I cock my head. "Is it so hard to imagine?"

"You don't look like a bookworm." She tucks her hair behind her ears. "I don't even know how to read."

That doesn't surprise me, since dragons often live in the wilderness, and I have never heard of a draconic written language. "I could teach you, if you wish. You could start adding books to your dragon's hoard."

She smiles. "You know how to tempt me."

She picks up her skirts, still somewhat unsure of clothing, and kneels under the oak. The roots of the tree rummage through the fallen leaves and moss like fingers. She brushes aside some of the leaves.

"What's this?" she asks. "Is this a moonlight chanterelle?"

Trumpet-shaped and white, the mushroom rises from the earth and glows with a hint of blue luminosity around the gills. By night, they stand out like a beacon, though of course, it's foolish to wander around in these woods after dark.

Not that it has ever stopped us before.

Lark drops down to the ground by the mushroom. "Yes!" She beams at Pyrah as if she has found her apprentice.

"Good work," I say. "Let's collect what we need and get out of here."

Watchful, I stand guard while they harvest a cluster of the chanterelles. Lark cuts them from the earth with a knife before tucking them into her basket. She handles the mushrooms as reverently as Pyrah touches her treasure.

"Rook," Lark says, "you don't need to cling to your sword."

My hand still rests on the pommel of my sword. "I'm keeping you safe. You're welcome."

I'm tall enough that Pyrah has to stand on her toes before kissing my cheek. "Thank you, Rook."

I resist the urge to kiss her back, and not nearly so politely. That would hinder my awareness.

Together, we return to Lark's cottage with a basket full of moonlight chanterelles. The sun has fallen lower in the sky, its light slicing through the afternoon forest and suffusing the mist with a golden glow.

"Come in." Lark unlocks the cottage door. "These dumplings won't cook themselves."

I hesitate on the threshold. We came here to ask my sister

for an enchantment, a fact I haven't forgotten, but it's so damn tempting to linger here just a little longer. This place grants me the room to breathe.

Pyrah's fingertips touch my wrist. "What's wrong?"

"Nothing." I shake my head, since that's not the truth. "Don't know if I remember how to relax."

"I know what you mean."

We look into each other's eyes for a heartbeat. Understanding strengthens the bond between us. We both want a space without the threat of danger, where we are allowed to simply be together.

*I'm in love with her.*

This inescapable truth lives in the marrow of my bones. She's a bright flash of fire in the otherwise dark gloom of my life. I would be lost without her, wandering through a world that couldn't care less if I lived or died.

She is precious.

She is mine.

I would do anything to keep her safe.

# CHAPTER FIVE

PYRAH

The way Rook looks at me, with such adoration in his demonic red eyes, turns my heart to molten gold. He sees me as something precious to be guarded and protected. If we were back in my cave, I would be tempted to kiss him until kisses stopped being enough.

We aren't alone, however, and his sister interrupts us.

"Put this on." Lark tosses an apron at Rook.

He catches it out of the air. "Am I making the dough?"

"We need your brute strength," she says, as if his question is obvious. "The dough needs to be kneaded half to death."

"Yes, ma'am." Rook all but rolls his eyes at his sister.

Lark glances at me. "Are you good with a knife?"

Her question takes me off guard. "Combat or the kitchen?"

"Kitchen," she says, with a laugh.

"I'm not much of a cook. I know how to stir a pot of stew."

"Stew?"

"Back when I worked at the tavern in Quickmire, I burned the bottom of the stew more than once."

Rook bites back a smile. "Dragons are good at burning things."

I fail to glare at him and end up laughing instead. "And do you claim to have the skill of a royal cook?"

"I may have picked up a thing or two."

"Really?"

"When we were children, we slept by the hearth in the castle kitchen."

"Like servants," Lark says. "We never even had beds."

"When I was a servant girl," I muse, "I liked sleeping by the fire."

"I'm not surprised," Rook says. "You seem fond of fire. I will admit, sleeping by the hearth has its benefits. Late at night, I would watch the embers smolder until I fell asleep. And whenever the cook made too many honey cakes, she let me eat the rest."

Lark snorts. "She made too many on purpose."

"Why?" I ask.

"Rook kept staring at her like a sweet little puppy."

It's impossible not to imagine a baby Rook begging for honey cakes. I flatten my hand above my heart and pretend to swoon over him. "How adorable he must have been."

Lark pretends to be disgusted. "My brother has always been a terrifying demonspawn, even as a newborn baby."

Both of us laugh. Rook frowns, trying to remain gruff, but a glint of amusement shines in his eyes.

"Why don't I watch you cook?" I ask.

He nods. "Excellent idea."

Lark starts dicing the moonlight chanterelles. Rook stirs wheat flour and water in a bowl. My gaze lingers on the muscles in his arms while he kneads the dough. He works with efficient confidence. I had no idea an apron would look this good on him, but there's just something attractive about a big, strong man who knows how to cook.

Lark fills a cauldron with water and hangs it over the fire to boil. Next, she chops an onion into pieces and adds it to an iron skillet heated by red-hot coals. She tosses a spoonful of butter into the skillet, almost as an afterthought. The smell of sizzling onions makes my mouth water. God, that smells delicious already. She adds the moonlight chanterelles next, which release an earthy scent similar to truffles.

"Rolling pin?" Rook asks his sister.

"The drawer behind you. On your left."

He divides the dough into lumps and rolls each into a small circle. Once the filling has been cooked, he spoons it into the circles and pinches them into crescent-shaped dumplings. By the time he's done, there must be a hundred of them. He drops the dumplings into the boiling cauldron, cooks them for a few minutes, and then ladles them onto a platter.

Wisps of savory steam rise from the dumplings. My fingers twitch with the temptation to steal a dumpling and stuff it in my mouth, but Rook catches me before I try any kind of thievery.

"Careful," he warns. "Don't scald yourself."

Lark clucks her tongue. "And wait for the mustard!"

"Mustard?" I arch my eyebrows in disbelief. "With mushrooms?"

"In my sister's defense," he says, "it's traditional."

Rook hoists the platter of dumplings and places it in the middle of the table, like a centerpiece. Lark brings out an earthen crock of mustard, then plates, goblets, and finally, a bottle of wine. Rook takes the wine from her and inspects the vintage. The glass has been stamped with strange markings that must be demonic writing of some sort.

I touch them with my fingertip. "Are those runes?"

"Yes," he says. "Umbric, the common language of demons."

"What does it say?"

*"Abyssal Estates."* Rook raises his eyebrows at his sister. "Black wine from the Underworld?"

"Of course," Lark says.

"Fuck, this must have cost a king's ransom."

She shrugs at how impressed he sounds. "The Demongate hasn't been closed forever. This bottle was languishing in some human princeling's estate for no more than a hundred years."

"You stole it?"

"No." She brushes away his comment. "He paid me."

"I'm not sure I want to ask."

Lark scoffs with disdain. "For my magic, Rook."

I'm not sure what else this human princeling could have paid her for, though I suspect it might have something to do with her selling her body. Their mother was the king's favorite concubine, and in this kingdom, many incubuses and succubuses work at brothels.

I clear my throat. "The Demongate isn't a legend?"

"It's not," Rook says. "It's how our mother traveled from the Underworld to the Overworld, before the Demongate was closed by order of Queen Dulcamara." His glowing red eyes burn brighter. "The queen didn't want any more demons in her kingdom."

"Too late." Lark sings out the words and drops into a chair. She flicks her hair over her shoulder. "Our dinner table is demonic as fuck. We have demon dumplings and demon wine."

"Don't forget the demon mustard," Rook adds.

Lark bares her fangs in a grin. "Let's eat."

Rook serves me first, loading my plate with a small mountain of dumplings and filling my goblet with black wine. I spoon a dollop of mustard on the side of my plate, not sure if I will like the taste. Bravely, I dip a dumpling into the mustard before nibbling a bite.

My eyes start watering as soon as it scorches my nose. *Damn, that's hot.*

"Spicy," I rasp.

"Sorry," Rook says. "I should have warned you."

I grin despite my stinging eyes. "I like spice."

Lark lifts her goblet in a toast. "Congratulations, Pyrah, you are now an honorary demon."

Her words choke my throat with emotion.

*I belong here.* Belonging isn't a common feeling for me, but she has welcomed me into her home and into her family. Not trusting my voice, I return her toast and bring my goblet to my lips. The rich, dark taste of the wine reminds me of cherries and woodsmoke. The flavor all but disguises the burn of alcohol.

Rook tilts his head. "Have you had much experience with wine?"

"Never wine," I admit. "Just some ale."

*Some* might be an understatement. I have the ability to drink most men under the table, a talent I discovered while I was working at the tavern and pretending to be a human like them.

"Take it slow," Rook says. "Black wine is much stronger than ale, particularly that weak piss brewed by humans."

I shrug. "It takes a lot for me to get drunk."

"Because you're a shifter?"

"Yes." Shifters do heal quickly, thanks to our faster metabolism.

Rook hums low in his throat, a thoughtful sound. "Still, you shouldn't underestimate demon wine."

"You're so sweet when you worry about me."

"Promise you won't get drunk and do anything foolish?"

I can't help smirking. "I can't make that kind of promise."

"You will be the death of me, woman."

He's joking, of course, but a cold shiver runs down my spine. He shouldn't joke about death while both of us have bounties on our heads.

Shuddering, I drink to disguise my fears.

# CHAPTER SIX

ROOK

Though our dinner is nothing but dumplings, mustard, and wine, I relish this humble food more than any royal feast at the castle. The taste of the dumplings brings me back to my childhood, a memory so powerful that I have to close my eyes for a moment.

*My mother, stroking the battle-scarred table in the castle kitchen, her fingers idly tracing the grooves. Laughing when I bite a raw mushroom and grimace. Her laughter always sounded like bells.*

She didn't often journey downstairs into the underbelly of the castle, since that was beneath her rank as the king's courtesan. He expected her to dress in silk gowns, even in the winter, and to always keep her wings folded demurely along her spine. Her tail's existence remained no more than a rumor in public. She obeyed, since she had little choice.

I swallow more wine to banish this memory back to oblivion.

Tonight, I want to forget.

Lark serves me more mushroom dumplings. "You're looking scrawny," she teases. She hasn't been taller than me since we were both thirteen. Not that she will ever let me forget it.

"Thank you," I say, for the distraction more than anything.

Outside, the evening sky deepens to the color of a plum as night falls upon the kingdom of Chymeria. An owl hoots from the forest. The hearth fire casts a golden glow inside the cottage.

Everyone I love in this world is safe here with me.

Pyrah's red hair glints with reflected flames. I'm lost for a moment in her beauty. She locks eyes with me as she drains her wine. Desire smolders inside me, still under my control. When she pushes her empty goblet over to me, I raise my eyebrows and pour her another drink.

"Have you ever been to the Underworld?" Pyrah asks me.

"No, never. The Demongate has been hidden ever since I was a baby." I frown at my sister. "Since *we* were babies. In truth, the birth of demonic twins may have been the reason why Dulcamara wanted it closed."

Lark hops up from the table. "That reminds me."

She washes any trace of dinner from her hands and hurries over to one of her bookshelves. She runs her finger along the gilded spines before stopping on one of them. It's a book I haven't seen before, one that looks ancient, bound in midnight blue leather. It thuds open on the table and releases a puff of dust from its yellowed pages.

"The Demongate is a portal," Lark says. "It's very old, very powerful. In the Underworld, many believe that the demon gods themselves created the Demongate."

I tilt my head, trying to read the page in front of me. The text was written in ornate, archaic Umbric runes, and it's hard to make out any of the words.

Lark flips through the book until she finds an illustration of a moon-shaped pool, a perfect circle, buried in the ground like a well. The water gleams blue with paint that must be crushed lapis lazuli, a color more valuable than gold. I wonder how my sister acquired this book.

Pyrah leans over the table. "Is that the Demongate?"

"A thousand years ago," Lark says. "Things have changed since then. This book claims that the Demongate in the Overworld was buried by frightened humans, though it was unearthed a hundred years later. The king of Chymeria built a gatehouse around the Demongate and demanded tolls from everyone who traveled between the worlds."

"Nine hundred years ago." I drink more wine, letting it linger on my tongue. "That must have been King Aurius the Great. He was famously rich."

"Infamously," Lark adds.

I narrow my eyes. "What happened in the past nine hundred years? We both know our mother traveled here through the Demongate not too long ago."

"The gatehouse of Aurius was destroyed in a rebellion, since the common folk believed their kings had been corrupted by wealth. The Demongate was buried under the rubble, though it can never be destroyed."

"Why does no one in the kingdom of Chymeria know where it might be hidden?"

"That's not true. The royal family has always known." She twists her mouth. "Present company excluded."

I grimace. "We never were a part of the royal family."

Our father made that clear.

Pyrah glances between us. "Where did King Aurius build his gatehouse? Wouldn't there be roads and inns around the place, for all the travelers?"

"Netherhaven." Lark's eyes gleam. "We all know the city has nine gates, but why not a tenth? The Demongate? Even the name of the city holds clues to its true history. *Nether* means 'under' and *haven* means 'harbor.' This city was once a safe harbor for Underworld travelers."

"That's a legend," I say, "nothing more."

Lark taps the illustration in the book. "There's always some truth to legends."

"The city would have prospered because of the Demongate," Pyrah says. "They would have been rich. Why would they ever close the gate between the worlds?"

I let out a sighing growl to indicate my displeasure. "Greed always has less power than hatred. There have never been many demons in Chymeria, but even that has been too many. Many humans want to keep the kingdom...pure."

"Fucking hypocrites," Lark mutters. "Their own king had bastard twins with a succubus." She replaces the book on its shelf before returning to the table.

I grunt. "Our mere existence infuriates many people."

Pyrah must be emboldened by the wine, because she says, "We all must have bounties on our heads. I wonder which one of us is worth the most?"

"Rook," Lark says, without hesitation.

I raise my eyebrows. "Really?"

"You're the Gray Prince."

"You're an escaped prisoner from the Forgotten Tower."

"You both helped me escape."

"True." That was why I had captured Pyrah in the first place. I down the rest of my wine to fortify my confidence. "Honestly, I'm curious. You never even told me why the queen locked you in her worst dungeon."

Lark leans back in her chair as if putting some distance between us. "God." She sighs out the word. "I was a fool."

I top off her wine, then pour myself another drink. "Fools run in the family," I deadpan.

Lark laughs, though it sounds a bit bleak. "Once upon a time, our father expected me to become a succubus courtesan in another kingdom. He never cared much for my potential as a sorceress. Queen Dulcamara stabbed him in the back and conquered the throne. And our lives changed irrevocably. Rook hid in Hexfall, but I lingered in the castle and studied magic."

I don't envy the choices my sister had to make. She survived the queen's rule by pretending to submit to her. She didn't escape, not like I did, and she had to endure small cruelties every day.

"I started traveling between villages, peddling spells," Lark says. "That's how I saved enough gold for this cottage in the Thornwood."

"What happened?" Pyrah asks, in a quiet murmur.

Lark's gaze falls to her goblet. She tilts it, watching the dark liquid ripple within. "I betrayed the queen."

My hands curl into fists on the table. "Betrayed?" I repeat. "Badly enough to be locked in a dungeon?"

"Queen Dulcamara asked me to be one of her royal sorceresses." Lark keeps staring into her wine, perhaps ashamed of her decisions. "And I said yes."

"Fuck. Lark…"

"I know. I said I was a fool. I did her bidding until she asked me to do something unforgivable."

"You expect me to believe she didn't ask you to do unforgivable things every day?" I ask, more than a little sarcastically.

"Believe it or not, she didn't." Lark glances into my eyes. "But this time, she went too far." She averts her gaze. "That's a story for another night."

"I understand." I sit rigidly in my chair. "Some things are too painful to be shared without hurting yourself again."

Pyrah rests her hand on the table, close enough to touch me, but she gives me the space to decide if I want contact. I place my hand on hers, craving this moment of small intimacy.

We eat without speaking for some time. The crackling of the hearth fire fills the silence.

"Lark," I say. "Tell us the legend of Hexfall."

My sister eats another dumpling and licks the mustard from her claws. "Once upon a time, there was a human king who scorned a sorceress and regretted it. The end."

Pyrah laughs, her eyes glittering in the firelight. "That can't be the whole story."

"Which king?" I ask.

"King Mallex the Wrong," Lark replies.

I nod, since this makes sense. "His statue stands in the courtyard at Hexfall. Who was the sorceress?"

"She wasn't just a sorceress but a princess." Lark's eyes glow a brighter red as she tells the story. "They were betrothed to marry, sight unseen."

"What happened to them?"

"Her name was Aetherlin of Myrkland. She traveled hundreds of miles from the north, all the way to Chymeria, and met King Mallex in Hexfall the evening before their wedding. When he saw her for the first time, Mallex couldn't hide his disappointment. He called her ugly before his whole court.

"In revenge, Aetherlin cursed Hexfall. Overnight, thorns sprouted from the ground and tore down the castle. By the time the roses bloomed, Aetherlin had abandoned Mallex, and the Thornwood has grown here ever since."

Pyrah toasts this ending before drinking her wine. "King Mallex was your grandfather, wasn't he?"

"Great-great-grandfather," I correct.

"He must have married another woman, since he had children."

"He did." I rub my thumb over my lips, trying to remember. "Queen Cerise. Don't remember much about her, other than her being our great-great-grandmother."

Lark taps her claws against her goblet. "Queen Cerise was obedient enough to avoid the history books."

Pyrah wrinkles her nose. "How boring." She reaches for the bottle of wine to pour herself a third cup, but I stop her before she can.

"How are you feeling?" I ask.

"Not drunk yet."

"Impressive." I surrender the bottle of black wine. The warmth of alcohol heats my blood.

Pyrah frowns into her goblet. "What happened to Aetherlin?"

Lark shakes her head. "No one ever told me her story. They cared more about the king."

I'm out of wine again, so I slide the bottle over and pour myself another cup. It's odd, sometimes, hearing legends about distant royal ancestors. Their bloodline will die out, since my sister and I can have no children.

Melancholy cloaks me like a shroud before I shake it away. "King Mallex was an idiot. Aetherlin would have been a powerful queen and ally, since she had the magic to summon the Thornwood overnight."

Lark rests her head back against her chair. "God, and to think I could have inherited her power."

I grunt. "That's a terrifying thought."

My sister scoffs at me. "You're just jealous. You're the twin without magic."

"I don't need magic."

"True. You have a different fate."

"Since when can you see into the future?"

"Rook." Lark looks me dead in the eye. "You can't deny that you are the Gray Prince. You will sit on the ruined throne and take back the kingdom."

I glower into my wine. This has been a well-worn argument between the two of us. "I don't believe in prophecies."

"You're the rightful heir to the throne."

"I don't need the deadweight of a crown on my head. Our father had no heir, only the two of us bastards."

"And you believe Queen Dulcamara should rule?"

My eyebrows descend. "No."

"You can't keep running away from your destiny."

"Fuck destiny. I don't have time for that."

Lark knocks back her wine. "Because you're so busy hunting monsters? You caught one. She's your mate." She smirks at her own joke, though I find it less amusing. "Are you going to drag her around the kingdom with you?"

"I'm not dragging her anywhere."

"I would rather drag him back to my cave," Pyrah confesses.

That's my chance to escape. "Right. Your cave. We should go." I push my chair from the table, ready to leave.

But the wine makes me clumsy. I grip the edge of the table as the room spins counterclockwise for a second. Fuck. I may have been overambitious.

Lark shakes her head. "You can't hide in a cave forever. I'm sorry, Pyrah, but your mate should be our king."

"Am I in the prophecy?" Pyrah asks.

"There's nothing about a red dragon. 'The Gray Prince will sit on the ruined throne.' That's it, that's the whole prophecy."

I scowl at my sister. "Haven't I already fulfilled the prophecy? I've been to Hexfall. I've sat upon the throne at least twice."

Lark stares into the fire. "If only it were that easy to satisfy destiny."

"The Gray Prince." Pyrah ogles me when she says it. "You would look good in a crown." She's slurring her words, just enough for me to notice it.

"Woman, you're drunk."

"Me?" She giggles. "No."

"You giggled. You never giggle."

When she tries to stand, she stumbles against me and nearly

knocks both of us over. I brace her with my arm around her waist.

"You were right," Pyrah says. "That's enough demon wine for me. Damn, it's powerful."

"I warned you."

She wrinkles her nose. "I'm too drunk to fly back."

Lark studies her with fascination. "What happens if you shift first? Wouldn't that be less wine in a bigger body?" She spreads out her arms to demonstrate size.

Pyrah's eyes flash gold. "Let's find out."

I catch her by the waist before she can escape. "Woman, that sounds like a very bad idea."

Pyrah leans against me, her hands traveling over my chest. "You aren't going to walk all the way home, are you?" For some strange reason, she's purring the words as if attempting to seduce me with them.

Lark sputters, laughing while drinking. "Rook looks so *confused*. Like he can't think with you so close."

"I'm not," I say gruffly.

"Not thinking?"

"Not confused."

But Lark laughs even harder, and Pyrah joins in, until it brings tears to their eyes and they gasp for breath. I had no idea I was so hilarious.

Pyrah clings to me to remain upright. She's helpless with giggles. "Stop," she protests. "I can't take any more. I'm dying."

I stare down at her, not sure what to do with her. "It's not my intention to amuse you."

They both surrender to mirth again. I finish the wine

myself, drinking it straight from the bottle. They don't need any more, but I might.

Finally, the women stop laughing, breathless.

"Stay here." Lark wipes the tears of laughter from her eyes. "You can sleep on the floor."

I nod. Finally, a sensible idea. "One night away from the cave won't hurt."

Lark tosses blankets and pillows on the floor. Pyrah crawls over and curls up like a dragon sleeping on gold. She yawns and burrows deeper under a blanket.

I stand with my hands on my hips. "When I'm back, there had better be room for me."

"Back?" Pyrah mumbles. "Where are you going?"

"To take a piss."

"Good idea." Groaning, she sits upright. "Take me with you. My bladder will thank me."

"Don't get lost," Lark warns.

I snort. "We won't."

Pyrah leans against me while we wander outside. Enchanted mist cloaks the cottage and hides the world around us. Fuck, no wonder Lark told us not to get lost.

"There's a privy by the river," I say, my speech careful enough to disguise just how drunk I am. "Somewhere deeper in the mist."

"What's wrong with pissing in the woods?"

I shrug. "It's a nice privy. Magic and all that."

"Where?" She squints. "I can't see a fucking thing."

We wander through the mist together, until it thins and we discover ourselves deeper in the woods. We're nowhere near the river, and the sound of rushing water in the distance sounds muffled. Which way should we go from here?

Pyrah hitches up her skirts and ducks behind a fern. Perhaps she couldn't wait any longer. I unbutton my fly and piss against a stump. Steam rises in the cold. With my head tilted back, I stare at the stars glittering in the sky. Pretty.

A dark shadow blots out the stars before flying onward and vanishing.

My heartbeat pounds in my ribs. Either I'm drunk enough to be imagining things, or that's a dragon on the prowl.

"Fuck," I whisper. "Did you see that?"

"See what?" Pyrah asks.

"That shadow in the sky."

She comes back to me. "What shadow?"

"Looked like a dragon."

We both stare at the sky together. Nothing, just the stars glittering high above. Though it's impossible to deny that Scaldric could be stalking Pyrah even now. That fucker still believes he can fly over this kingdom without consequences. He still believes she belongs to him.

Possessive instinct roars through me.

We should return to the safety of the mist, but blood rushes to my cock. I want to fuck her in the wilderness. I want to lay claim to her body where the whole world can see us.

I stroke myself in my fist and wait for her to catch me jerking myself off. When she does, her eyes fly open wide with shock. Her breath escapes as a puff of white in the cold air.

I speak calmly enough, but I can't keep the growl from my voice. "It could be a dragon. It could be anyone. But I don't fucking care."

"We shouldn't."

"You belong to me. Your pleasure belongs to me."

Her chest flutters as her breathing turns shallow. "Here?"

"Everywhere and anywhere." I run my tongue along my fangs, testing their sharpness, and my fist moves faster over my cock. "I want to fuck you where everyone can see you come."

"I dare you."

I pin her against a tree and hitch her skirts around her waist. She's not wearing anything under her dress. In the moonlight, her cunt looks divine.

I groan. "Wicked girl."

I hold my cock in my fist and stop just shy of penetrating her. She's already wet. Slippery. Her body is ready for more, but I need to hear her say it, especially after drinking so much wine.

"You want me to fuck you?" I ask, not even trying to be subtle.

Her breath escapes her in a shaky exhalation. "Yes."

That's the consent I needed. My shadow wings unfold from my shoulder blades. My cock thickens in my hand, armored by the ridges and spikes of an incubus. I'm unable to deny my fully demonic form.

I bend down and capture her mouth in mine. I kiss her, a devouring kiss, just enough to taste what she's feeling. When my cock enters her body, her pleasure intensifies. It's sweeter than nectar, richer than cream. Ambrosia. I can't get enough of her.

*More.*

My hips surge forward, my cock sliding all the way home. Pain tinges her pleasure. The taste of her desire turns bitter-sweet. I freeze, our bodies pressed together, her heart beating so hard I can feel it beneath my chest. I don't want to hurt her with the spikes on my cock—or the size of it.

"Don't stop," she demands. She hooks her legs behind my ass and lets me hold her off the ground.

"Easy," I murmur. "Breathe."

"I need you to fuck me."

"When I kissed you, I could taste a hint of your pain."

Her cheeks turn pink. "I didn't know you could." She looks into my eyes. "What do I taste like?"

"Bittersweet, but only because I hurt you. I'm sorry."

She kisses me again, her body melting against mine, until I can taste nothing but pure pleasure. She's so good at taking my cock.

"What do I taste like now?"

"Ambrosia," I confess. "The nectar of the gods."

She laughs, breathless. "I have no idea what that means."

"Do you trust me?" My voice turns velvety. "I don't want to be gentle with you. I want to fuck you until you scream with bliss."

She shivers, goose bumps on her arms. "I trust you."

I hammer into her without mercy. Rough. Ruthless. Her breasts bounce from the force of my thrusts. When I kiss her again, I'm surprised by her desire. She's already so close to the breaking point, the tension in her body barreling toward a climax.

My balls tense. I'm gripped by a primal urge to fill her up until she's dripping with my seed.

"Fuck." The word tears from my throat as a groan.

I'm too far gone.

I can't stop my own orgasm from obliterating all thought.

Grunting, shaking, I come deep inside her. My cock throbs hard with every pulse of my seed. Even my legs tremble from the strength of my climax.

She touches herself between her legs. She's filled to overflowing, my seed trickling down her thighs. She rubs herself, desperate for release. Her eyes close and her mouth turns into a circle of anguished ecstasy.

"Louder," I command. "Let me hear you come."

With her spine arched, she flings back her head. She screams out as she climaxes. The sound echoes in the forest before I devour her with my kiss. Her pleasure flows down my throat.

*Mine.*

Every last drop.

# CHAPTER SEVEN

PYRAH

Gasping, I struggle to catch my breath. "Sorry, Rook."

"What?" He still looks dazed from coming so hard.

"I got drunk and did something foolish."

He grunts. "You never promised otherwise."

"Am I in trouble?"

"You're already at my mercy, pinned against this tree by my cock." He slides his hand between us and touches his overflowing seed. He smears it across my cheek, marking me in a primal way.

"I want to be your *prey*." I whisper the last word just below his ear.

Groaning, he pumps his hips, his cock still harder than steel inside me. I shudder from the aftershocks of my orgasm. When he slides out of me, the loss of him makes me whimper in protest. He puts me down and I lock my knees to disguise the trembling in my legs.

"It's not safe," he says.

Even when he's clearly drunk, he's so damn *careful,* but my blood runs hot from lust and demon wine.

"Since when have I craved safety?" I ask. "Give me danger."

Rook frowns at me, his red eyes smoldering, and tilts his head as if warning me not to defy him. I slip out of his grasp, turn my back on him, and start walking deeper into the woods.

"Pyrah." He growls my name. "Where are you going?"

"Out for a stroll."

"Come back."

Judging by his voice, he's still standing by the tree. He must be expecting me to return to him. That's his mistake, since I don't have an ounce of obedience in my entire body. I keep walking without looking back and put a sway into my hips so he looks at my ass.

"You won't get far," he warns me.

If I'm such easy prey, why isn't he chasing me down?

When I glance over my shoulder, he has vanished into the darkness. I freeze on instinct. Cold wind flings my hair into my face, where it clings to his release smeared across my cheek.

Rather than stand here like a startled deer, I lunge into a run.

My knees haven't stopped shaking since he fucked me the first time. My panting sounds too loud, my breath clouding the air. More of his warm seed drips down my legs, a distraction. He must be able to smell himself on my skin. I can't wash myself until I find the river, and even then, the splashing would attract unwanted attention.

I stumble over a root, still clumsy wearing boots, and sprawl onto the ground. My mistake costs me valuable time. I scramble to my hands and knees, but it's already too late—he's coming for me.

Rook strides toward me with the grace of a predator. I crouch at his feet, still on all fours, and wait for his next move. He takes his hard cock out of his trousers, a strand of arousal shimmering in the moonlight as it falls down. My lips part, my surprised gasp clouding the air, as if I had a chance to catch his seed in my mouth but missed the opportunity to do it.

I curl my fingers into the dirt as my claws slide out of my nails. When he stops in front of me, he's so tall that his cock bobs above my face. I would have to get up onto my knees if he commanded me to lick him. Though if he wants me to suck his cock, he will have to defeat me first. I bare my teeth and dare him to touch me.

"Your pulse is racing," he says. "I can see it fluttering in your neck."

"I was running," I retort.

"Why did you stop running? You wanted me to catch you?"

The dark promise in his voice makes me shiver. Desire pounds between my legs with every heartbeat. Boldly, I brace myself with my claws in the dirt and straighten to my full height. He's still towering over me. His eyes smolder, their red color unmistakably demonic.

"I'm not afraid of you," I say.

"Liar." He strokes his cock in his fist as if this arouses him. "Let me taste you and find out for myself."

His shadow wings unfurl behind him—my only warning before he lunges and grabs me by the wrists. He drags me against his chest, imprisoning me in his arms, before bending down and kissing me. It's a rough, hard kiss, and his tongue invades my mouth as if he owns me. When he devours my lust, I can't stop myself from groaning.

My traitorous knees threaten to buckle. He keeps me trapped against him, barely even trying, the muscles in his body unyielding. I couldn't escape even if I tried, not without shifting into a dragon, but I don't know if I want to relinquish the shape of a woman.

He tears his mouth away from mine. "Your fear tastes...delicious." His voice rumbles through my chest, the pitch so deep and masculine it makes me shiver. "This arouses you."

It isn't a question. After all, he's an incubus—he *knows*.

I struggle against his iron grip. "Let me go."

He glances into my eyes. "Part of the game we are playing?"

"Yes."

"Good." He runs his tongue over his fangs as if testing their sharpness. "I'm not done with you yet."

He shoves me down to the ground. My back hits the dirt. He pins my wrists above my head with one of his hands, so much bigger than me that it's effortless for him to restrain me. With his other hand, he drags my dress above my hips and exposes me to the night.

When I shiver, he asks, "Cold?"

The back of his claws trace the inside of my thigh. Though he's a dangerous man, he knows how to be delicate. I arch my hips, trying to buck him off me, though he doesn't budge. The movement only brings me closer to his hard cock. He's so infuriatingly close to entering me. Groaning, he ruts between my thighs without penetration.

"You are mine," he says, his voice deep and velvety with desire. "Surrender to me."

I bare my teeth. "Never."

"I enjoy your defiance."

He bites down on my shoulder, not hard enough to break skin, just hard enough to sting. I gasp and arch into him more, seeking the release only he can give me. He slides his hand higher on my thigh, so close to touching me where he fucked me before. My legs are trembling now, both from need and fear of what might happen next.

"Look how filthy you are," he murmurs, toying between my thighs.

"That's your fault," I fire back.

"Though I remain unsatisfied. You could be much, much filthier. How many times can you come for me?"

"Once wasn't enough?"

"I want your cunt to be absolutely drenched."

*Fuck*. He has never said *cunt* before, and the word sounds like complete and utter sin in his deep, rough voice. I was already aroused before he said it, but now my body is begging for his cock.

"Please," I whisper, already tempted to submit to him.

He chuckles darkly. "Please what? Elaborate."

I grit my teeth, torn between my pride and my need for him inside me. "Please fuck me again."

"My pleasure."

He invades me, his cock sliding so deep that his balls nudge my ass. I cry out, my back arching from the ground, though I'm unable to escape the overwhelming feeling of being totally and utterly filled. The demonic spikes and ridges on his cock only heighten the sensation.

"You stopped running because you wanted me." He punctuates his words with another thrust, making my breath shaky. "You were begging to be fucked like an animal in the woods."

I glare at him. "You talk too much."

His growl rumbles through my body. "Your troublesome mouth would be better off taking my cock."

"Oh? Isn't your cock occupied?"

Somehow, I can't resist taunting him. I want him to fuck me like he's enacting revenge.

Rook's red eyes smolder, a dangerous sign. Without warning, he pulls out and flips me onto my stomach. I barely have time to catch my breath before he's lifting my hips and entering me from behind. His hand finds the nape of my neck before tangling in my hair. He tugs just hard enough to mingle pleasure with a hint of pain.

"Is this what you wanted?" he asks. "To be fucked like a beast in heat?"

I'm trembling beneath him, my fingers clawing at the dirt. "You know I'm not in heat any longer."

"And yet you can't get enough of me."

"Go fuck yourself."

He snorts at my response. "I'm busy fucking you."

He fucks me from behind, hard and slow and relentless. I bite back a moan, refusing to give him the satisfaction. But Rook knows my body too well. His shadow tail snakes between my thighs, and he starts rubbing circles around my clitoris, tormenting me with the promise of release. My body arches like a bowstring pulled taut.

"Beautiful," Rook murmurs, his voice a dark, velvet caress.

The hard point of his tail is driving me wild. I want to snarl back at him, to pretend I'm still in control, though all that escapes me is a moan. He's hitting that perfect spot inside me with each thrust, and my arousal spirals higher and higher without any relief.

It's too much and not enough all at once.

"More," I manage to beg. "Harder."

He tugs my head back so he can better see my face. "Look at you," he drawls, his words thick with lust. "Such a dangerous dragon, reduced to my trembling, whimpering prey."

A snarl rips from my throat, my draconic pride bristling at the taunt. But my body betrays me, clenching around his cock on the brink of climaxing. I'm close, so close to the edge.

"Surrender." Rook's voice drops an octave. "Come for me, Pyrah."

It's not a request but a command.

His words push me over the precipice. I climax with a scream, my whole body shuddering as ecstasy shatters me. He groans, his hips stuttering as he follows me over the edge. He comes so hard that I can feel his cock jerking inside me and the molten rush of his release.

We stay like that for a long moment, our bodies still joined together, as we struggle to catch our breath. Slowly, he withdraws, his seed flooding out of me. God, just how much can an incubus come? I'm impressed by the sheer quantity he poured inside me.

After he tugs me down to the forest floor, I rest my head on his chest. His heart pounds against my ear, matching the rapid rhythm of my own. The warmth of his body surrounds me.

"Was that dangerous enough for you?" he asks.

"It's a start," I joke.

"You're insatiable, woman," he grumbles.

I smile like a cat sated by cream.

"You got lost?" Lark asks.

"A little," Rook admits.

"And fell in the river?"

"Something like that."

Lark rolls her eyes. "You're a terrible liar."

We had the decency to wash up in the river, after we found it in the forest, though I'm still shivering from the cold. I have to clench my jaw to keep my teeth from chattering. Lark sighs, opens a linen closet, and tosses a towel at me. Wine dulls my reflexes, making me a little clumsy when I catch it out of the air. Rook guides me closer to the fire and dries me off with the towel. He always likes to take care of me.

"Good night." Lark wanders to her bedroom. "Going to bed."

"Night." I yawn, already sleepy.

We huddle in the nest of blankets on the floor. I ignore the pillows and rest my head on Rook instead, my ear pressed against his chest. The steady rhythm of his heartbeat comforts me.

"Tired?" he asks.

"Very."

He grunts. "After that much wine and fucking, I can't blame you."

"I'm a little sore," I admit.

"I'm sorry."

Back at the river, Rook washed me gently, soothing me with cold water, though my body still remembers exactly how hard he fucked me. Walking back to the cottage was a bit challenging.

"You're so warm," I murmur. "I want to steal your warmth."

"Take whatever you need." He kisses the top of my head. "I would give you everything I have and more."

My heart melts at his words. "You're so sweet for a big, bad demon."

He grunts, which seems very Rook of him, and holds me even closer. That's how I know he loves me.

# CHAPTER EIGHT

ROOK

My father wants to punish me.

I'm kneeling before his throne in Netherhaven Castle. I know deep in the pit of my stomach that I have failed him somehow. I have failed myself, at the very least, since I missed his anger before it was too late.

I should have seen the warnings: the way his eyes harden or how his nostrils suck in air to fuel what comes next. Somehow I didn't see them, and now I must endure his rage.

"Rook," my father booms.

I don't know what I did wrong, since so many things anger him, but it doesn't matter—the consequences will be the same.

*This isn't real.*

The thought whispers in the back of my mind, but I can't be distracted. My father reddens with rage, his human skin too pale to hide his emotions for very long.

"What have you done this time, boy?" he asks, his knuckles whitening as he grips his throne.

*You're dreaming.*

But in this dream, I'm a child, and children have little power over nightmares. It doesn't matter who I might be in the waking world. Here, I'm just a scared little boy who wishes his father would love him.

"Answer me," he demands.

"I'm sorry," I say, though I don't know what I might be apologizing for. "Forgive me, Your Majesty."

"Stop cowering like a dog."

When my father gets off his throne, I'm frozen on the floor in fear. His royal guards avert their eyes. We all know what happens next.

I lower my head and stare at my clenched hands. My father's boots click on the stones, the sound echoing under the high ceiling, and my heart beats faster and faster until I wonder if it might burst from my chest.

He grabs me by a horn and wrenches me to my feet. I'm smaller than him, weaker than him, and there's no point in fighting.

"That was a command," he says. "You want to keep cowering? I will give you a reason to cower."

*Wake up.*

He slaps me across the mouth, a humiliating blow, and my head jerks to one side. The *crack* sounds obscenely loud in the echoing throne room. One of the guards glances over at me before avoiding my shame again.

"Why did you do it?" my father demands. "How could you be so stupid? God, to think you're supposed to be my bastard son. Sometimes I wonder if your mother whored herself out to the village idiot to make you."

*Wake. Up.*

My father flings me to the floor as if I'm nothing more than a broken doll to be discarded. I sprawl across the stones. He's not done with me yet. I haven't been punished enough.

*Wake up wake up wake—*

I lurch into the waking world, my heartbeat still pounding as if I were sprinting. Worse, my head starts pounding when morning sunlight pierces my eyes. Fuck. I'm never drinking black wine again. Definitely not in such a generous amount.

Pyrah curls against me, her arm draped over me, snoring softly. I disentangle myself from her embrace without waking her.

Sleeping with my mate brought me some relief from the nightmares, but it didn't last forever. Bad memories have ruined my mind like bloodstains that can never be washed away.

No. Not ruined.

I refuse to believe that I'm too far gone. The fear and shame I felt as a child still clings to me, but I can't believe I'm powerless any longer.

My father is dead.

Sometimes, I have nightmares of the last day I saw him. These dreams are soaked in the color red.

When I found him, bleeding out in his bed, he told me to get the fuck out of his castle. I obeyed him without hesitation. I was always trying to be obedient back then, and I was too afraid to question him.

Could I have saved my father?

I'm not sure I could have convinced myself to try.

These thoughts aren't helping my headache. I need coffee. I go into the kitchen. Lark kneels by the embers of the hearth fire. She stirs them with a poker, then tosses in some kindling to feed the flames.

One glance at me and she grimaces. "Nightmare?"

"How could you tell?"

"I saw you sleeping."

My shoulders tense. "Oh?"

"You were gritting your teeth and clenching your fists. Like you were bracing yourself, even in your sleep."

"Pyrah hasn't noticed." I force myself to exhale. "Not yet."

"You ran out of the potion, didn't you?"

"I did," I admit.

My sister had been brewing me a potion to fight my plague of nightmares, but I drank the last of it while she was imprisoned in the Forgotten Tower for seven long weeks.

"Do you need more?" she asks.

I hesitate. "Dreams can't kill me, no matter how bad they get. And they haven't been that bad."

"Rook." She gives me a look, one that says she knows I'm full of shit. "You have told me about some fucked-up nightmares before. And we both remember Netherhaven."

I arch an eyebrow. "Why don't you have nightmares?"

"What happened there hurt me in different ways."

I touch her on the shoulder, trying to comfort her in one of the few ways I know how. "True."

She shakes her head. "I would brew you more of the potion, but I don't have most of the ingredients."

Time to change the subject. "Coffee?"

"Get the kettle."

Soon the bitter scent of brewing coffee fills the cottage. Pyrah shuffles over to the table. Blinking owlishly, she hides a yawn behind her hand. I'm not sure she's fully conscious yet.

Lark pours three cups of coffee for us. "I don't have any milk or honey. Let's say demons drink it black."

Pyrah watches steam rise from her cup before she takes a sip. "Rook, I think I might love Lark more than you."

"Why?" I ask.

"She brews coffee fit for a king."

I grunt, still too hungover to be amused. Besides, I have always had a poor opinion of a king's standards.

Under Lark's direction, I cook the three of us a simple breakfast of boiled eggs and bread toasted over the fire. Lark brings out the strawberry jam again, which started this whole quest to find mushrooms in the Thornwood. We have spent enough time here.

I drink my coffee until there's nothing but dregs. "We should go back to Pyrah's cave after breakfast."

Lark takes a scroll from her bookshelf and unrolls it on the table. It's a map of Chymeria. "Pyrah, where's your lair?"

Pyrah strokes the well-worn parchment. Her fingers glide over the Thornwood, the cursed roses inked in intricate detail, before lingering on a range of mountains near the far western edge of Chymeria. She must fly over this terrain often. I wonder if the map matches what she sees from the air. Dragons would make good cartographers.

"There." She taps the location. "By the lake with no name."

"Deep in the wilderness," Lark muses.

"Too far for a portal?" I ask.

"No such thing."

"Pyrah, have you been through a portal before?"

"Never. Why?"

"They can be...unpleasant. Especially the first time."

She puts on a brave face. "It can't be that bad."

After clearing the table from breakfast, we follow Lark outside. She summons a portal by cutting open the air with her hand. Sparks fly from the ragged edges of the portal. Beyond, water glimmers like iron beneath the sun—the lake with no name.

"Come on," Lark says. "I can't hold it open forever."

I take Pyrah's hand. I'm so much bigger than her human form that my hand surrounds hers. She clings to my calloused fingers.

We go through the portal together.

My stomach lurches and acid rises in my throat. I swallow hard, fighting the urge to cough, or worse, vomit. When Pyrah's knees buckle, I hold her against me. She's trembling, and her face has become a sickly white.

"Steady," I murmur.

"Unpleasant?" Pyrah spits the word out. "That was fucking awful."

"I know."

After Lark strides through the portal, it closes behind her with a crackle like burning wood. She twists her mouth, her throat working. Maybe she's also fighting a sudden rush of nausea. Even this sorceress isn't immune to portals, despite her fondness for them.

From the lake with no name, a path zigzags higher. It leads to a cliff at the mouth of a dragon's cave—Pyrah's cave. We begin the climb together. Halfway there, my boot scuffs something round and glimmering. Bending, I pick it up and bring it to my eye. My stomach plunges even farther than it did when I went through the portal.

"A coin," I say. "A silver one."

Pyrah yanks her hand free from mine and sprints the rest of the way. Her hair flies behind her in the wind. Gasping, her breath ragged, she runs to her home. I follow at her heels.

Empty.

Her cave is empty.

Every single piece of gold and gemstone has vanished. Gone.

Her treasure was stolen.

"We're too late," Pyrah murmurs, as if in a trance. "There's nothing left. They took it all from me."

I touch her elbow. "Thank God they didn't take you."

"What happened?" Lark enters the cave behind us.

"Thieves," I reply. "Could have been the queen's knights."

Pyrah meets my gaze, her eyes bright with tears. "I never should have left my cave unguarded."

"Pyrah." Her sorrow pains my heart in a raw ache. "You're worth more to me than any treasure."

"It's more than that. It's *mine*."

"Besides," I add, "you have no need for a dragon's hoard any longer."

"What?" She stares at me.

"You collected treasure and defended your territory, like all female dragons, to attract a mate. The size of your hoard means little to me. I need nothing from you but *you*."

Her eyes shift from blue to yellow. "As my mate, you should understand. Let me make this crystal fucking clear." She grinds out the words through gritted teeth. "Nobody fucking steals from me."

Clearly, I should not have opened my mouth. Is it too late for me to salvage this situation? Lark glances between us both before exiting the cave, no doubt to give us space and avoid joining the fray.

I frown. "Pyrah, why does this mean so much to you?"

"You don't understand."

"Enlighten me."

"You aren't a dragon." Her words shouldn't bite so much, and yet they do. "But not even Scaldric cared about the size of my hoard."

"Scaldric?" I bristle at his name. "Why would you give a fuck what that fool thinks about you?"

"I don't. God, that's the point."

I inhale hard through my nose, forcing myself to remain calm. "Scaldric never should have darkened the sky above your territory. Don't waste any of your breaths speaking his name, not unless you're asking me to slaughter him at last."

Her jaw drops. "Why are you being so possessive?"

"I'm always possessive of you." I'm unable to keep the growl from my voice. "You are my mate."

Her golden eyes burn with fire. "My life was not meaningless before I found my mate. I didn't guard my wealth for the sole purpose of being more attractive to a male."

"Then tell me why." I clench and unclench my jaw. "I'm listening. I'm trying to understand."

She stalks away from me and paces through her empty cave. "I don't have time to argue with you."

"I'm not trying to argue."

"I need to find those pieces of shit who stole from me. Now."

"Pyrah, I don't want you storming out of your lair in a fury and plunging into danger."

She glares at me. "Stop."

"Stop what?"

"Telling me what to do."

"I'm not. I'm worried about you. I want to keep you safe."

She pinches the bridge of her nose as if I'm giving her a headache. "For fuck's sake, Rook, I'm a dragon. Just get out of my way."

I match her glare with my own. "Are you going to hunt down the thieves without me?"

"You don't seem to care that they stole my treasure."

"That's not what I said."

Her glare intensifies until I wonder if she's on the brink of shifting into a dragon and breathing fire. "You told me it didn't matter."

"*You* matter to me." I force myself to retreat. "We're both too angry. This isn't helpful. I'm going outside for some air."

"You're leaving?"

"Yes."

I exit the cave and escape into the cold mountain sunshine. I stand by the edge of the cliff and gnash my teeth. Why does

Pyrah have such a hot temper? Her entire strategy can't be rage and rampant destruction. That's not a strategy at all.

Of course, if I told her this, she would think I'm being condescending. But why can't she just *listen* to me?

"Fuck!" My shout of frustration echoes off the slopes.

I should have known better than to argue with her about her treasure. It means more to her than I realized.

All that remains of her hoard fits in my pocket—a single silver coin.

I hold the coin in the palm of my hand. It's ancient, stamped with the face of a queen I don't recognize. Frowning, I read the words etched beneath her portrait: *Long live Queen Pallora*. This coin must be even older than I realized, since Pallora ruled over five hundred years ago.

Where did Pyrah find this coin? Dragon shifters don't live any longer than demons, so there's no chance she was alive when it was minted. It would have already been old when she found it. This coin belongs in a museum, or at the very least, the royal treasury.

An idea gnaws at my mind like a wolf on a bone.

The thieves must have dropped this coin while stealing from her hoard. That means they must have touched it, and if they touched it, magic could be used to track them down. I have seen Lark cast this spell before.

I glance back at the cave, knowing full well that an angry dragon lurks within. Has she had enough time to cool down? I'm not sure I have myself. God, I still can't believe she's thinking of Scaldric. If only I could erase him from existence.

Damn it, I need to talk to Pyrah. Bracing myself, I return to her cave.

At least she's still human and hasn't shifted into a dragon. Yet. She glares at me. "I heard you."

"Heard what?"

"Shouting profanity into the mountains."

"I won't make a habit of it."

"Hopefully the whole kingdom didn't hear you." Her mouth twitches as if she's fighting a smirk, but she keeps glaring at me. "Have you come back with another argument?"

"No." I glance down at my fist. The coin I'm holding digs into my skin. "I wanted to apologize."

She narrows her eyes at me. "I'm still angry at you."

"I know."

"You aren't wrong," she says. "Not entirely. Female dragons hoard treasure to impress their future mates. It's an ancient tradition. But it's more than that, too. Mothers pass on their treasure to their daughters. The women in my family had an unbroken chain of inheritance lasting three hundred years. I inherited my mother's gold and gems after she died. That's all I have left of my mother. *Had* left of her."

I swallow hard past the ache in my throat. "Pyrah, please forgive me. It was wrong of me to assume what this meant to you."

"It's as if they stole my memories of my mother from me." Her eyes glitter like broken glass, though her tears remain unshed.

When I flatten out my hand, the silver coin gleams in the gloom of the cave. "Let me help you retake what has been stolen from you."

"One coin. That's all I have left."

I grimace. "The thieves must have touched this coin. That means we can hunt them down."

"How?"

"Magic. My sister has cast this tracking spell before. I have seen her do it several times."

Her gaze drops to the ground. "They can't have gone far. The piss hasn't even dried yet."

I follow her gaze. In the corner of her cave, the stone floor still looks dark and wet. The foul scent hits my nose. A sickening mix of rage and disgust churns in my stomach.

"What kind of sick fucker would piss here after looting your treasure?" I ask, but it's not difficult to answer my own question. "They wanted to destroy and defile your home. Violate any sense of safety you had."

Pyrah hugs herself, looking more vulnerable than she usually does. "Sometimes I hate being a dragon in this kingdom."

"We will hunt them down together," I say, decisively. "Every single one of these fuckers needs to die a slow, painful death."

Restless, she paces through the emptiness of her cave. "I had thousands of coins, gemstones, and golden treasures. There must have been a small army of thieves."

"Fuck," I mutter. "It will take that much longer to kill them all."

Not that I won't enjoy every second of the slaughter. The demon blood in me calls for feral retribution.

# CHAPTER NINE

ROOK

We exit Pyrah's cave together and bring the coin to Lark. She takes it from me and pinches it between her fingers. When she summons her magic, a cold shiver rushes down my spine. The coin begins to glow an unearthly blue between her fingertips.

"They aren't far," Lark says.

My hand twitches to the pommel of my sword. "Lead the way."

It's been far too long since I've gone into battle with my sister beside me. I've missed her skill with magic.

Lark strides into the gloom of the forest. Pyrah rushes in next, her body tense, eager for revenge. I follow behind them, my senses keen and alert to any enemies. We aren't in the Thornwood any longer, though we're still in the wilderness of Chymeria.

The woods hold many dangers, even for a demon.

Or a dragon, though she might not believe it yet.

Lark leads us both through the forest. She holds the coin in her hand like a lantern to illuminate the way. Whenever the blue glow of magic dims, she stops and turns until it brightens again. While she watches the coin, I glance at the ground, though I have yet to find any footprints.

We walk deeper into the wilderness. Finally, after what feels like an eternity, something catches my eye: ferns, trampled underfoot, followed by hoofprints.

I kneel by the tracks and trace one with my fingers. The mud still feels wet and hasn't yet dried.

"We must be close," I mutter.

We're standing in a ravine, the ground sloping steeply before us. Ferns and trees choke the way and hide whatever lies ahead.

We don't need magic any longer. I follow the tracks across the ravine, the path as clear as day. They didn't even try to be stealthy. The thieves must be arrogant, dangerous, or both. Judging by the quantity of tracks, they definitely outnumber us.

Pyrah drags in a deep breath through her nose. "I smell them." She flexes her hands, her nails sharpening into wicked black claws.

"Wait," I whisper.

"Don't try to stop me." Her body shudders on the brink of the change, her pupils already draconic slits.

"We don't know how dangerous these thieves might be."

"Not as dangerous as a dragon." She speaks through a mouthful of fangs, her skin already shattering into crimson scales. She strips off her clothes and flings them away. Her transformation is inevitable.

I glance at my sister. "Lark?"

She clenches the coin in her fist, killing the spell, before pocketing the silver. "I'm ready to fight."

I look back to Pyrah. "Let's go."

With a shudder, she shifts fully into a dragon. Reckless, glorious, she charges from the ravine and unleashes a bone-shaking roar. Startled birds burst from the trees and cry out as they flee into the sky.

I sprint after her and enter a meadow.

We found the fuckers.

Knights in shining armor, more than a dozen of them, wearing the colors of Queen Dulcamara—black and purple. Ugly as a bruise, the livery was stolen from my murdered father.

The knights all ride horses and their saddlebags are bulging with stolen treasure—bursting at the seams. Their greed will slow them down. When Pyrah lunges for them, they shout and spur their horses into a gallop.

They think they can flee?

I snort at their arrogance.

The nearest knight thunders toward me on his horse. I grit my teeth. I hate killing horses and refuse to wound them, though it limits my combat. No matter. I'm deadly enough regardless.

The knight levels his sword at my neck, intending to behead me, but I duck and counterattack. Quick as lightning, I grab the reins of his horse, drag the beast sideways, and knock the rider from the saddle.

He crashes to the ground. His plate armor isn't invincible

and has weaknesses at his joints. Nothing but leather protects his groin. With a brutal stab, I leave him to bleed out.

Pyrah incinerates a knight foolish enough to attack her. His armor glows red-hot. He falls to the ground and sizzles in the wet grass. A disturbing thought darts through my mind that roasted human smells much like any other meat.

Lark strides into battle wielding magic, her long hair swirling around her like quicksilver. She casts a spell that locks the skeleton of a knight. Frozen, he stands helpless until I dispatch him with a cut to the throat.

Pyrah roars in pain.

A knight clings to her back. She tries to shake him off, but he grips her by the spikes and holds on. He jams a dagger between her scales, prying them out one by one, ruining her body's armor. Blood flows from her wounds.

He's hurting her.

He needs to die.

Rage bubbles inside me before boiling over. My shadow wings erupt from my shoulder blades. I shiver at the release.

With a snarl, I vault onto the dragon's back and tackle the knight from behind.

I have to save Pyrah.

He still clings to her like a leech. He's impossible to knock down. I hook my arm around his neck and yank him back, but the fucking asshole won't let go. I can't strangle him while he's protected by steel.

He sinks his dagger into my biceps.

*Fuck.*

A growl tears from my throat. Fury dulls my pain. I wrench the dagger out of my own flesh and stab him in the face.

My blade glances off his helmet until it pierces his visor and sinks through his eye. It's buried deep in his brain in an instant kill. He doesn't even have time to scream.

I shove the corpse to the ground.

I'm left with the wounds on Pyrah's neck. She's bleeding where he pried her scales from her flesh. Vulnerable to attack.

I vault to the ground. "Pyrah! Can you fly?"

"I'm not leaving you."

A knight runs at me on foot, trying to gut me, but I whirl behind him and slash his hamstrings with my sword. Screaming, he crawls across the dirt before I finish him.

"Go," I tell Pyrah. "You're safer in the air."

"No!"

I snarl. "Obey me."

Shaking with blood lust, I stand between her and the rest of our enemies.

We're outnumbered. Seven knights remain.

A frustrated growl tears from her throat. I dare her to defy me. Her wings thump the air as she launches herself into flight.

*Good.*

Like a goddess of destruction, Pyrah rains fire down upon her enemies. Lark parts the flames with a flick of her hands, shielding herself, then strides through the ashes.

The knights ride well-trained war-horses, but even these animals have started to panic. Whinnying, they shy from the fire, the whites of their eyes gleaming. The men struggle to control their mounts. One of the knights drops from the saddle and slaps his horse on the rump, urging it to flee into the forest.

I'm distracted by a flicker of conscience.

He wants to save his horse?

Fuck, it's dangerous to feel empathy for my enemy. I tell myself he only wants to save the treasure in his horse's saddlebags.

"Rook!" Lark shouts. "Behind you!"

I whip around.

Too late.

A knight's sword pierces me below my left shoulder, splitting my leather armor. The blade goes clean through my chest and juts out my back. I stare at it, shocked by how close it has come to destroying my heart.

My distraction could prove fatal. I won't survive another wound like that.

I wrench free from the blade.

Staggering back, I bare my teeth at my enemy. Rage hammers in my skull with every heartbeat. Pain has become a distant memory.

Pyrah dives from the air and catches the knight in her talons. She lifts him higher, her claws crushing his ribs, before she drops him. There's the sickening crunch of bones on impact. The fall alone should kill him.

Another knight attacks me.

I stab him again and again. I lose count. The only thing that matters is killing each one.

Violence sings through my veins. I lose myself to blood lust. Slashing, thrusting, and hacking, I whirl through a dance of death. Crimson flows beneath my sword and daggers.

In a frenzy, I fight until there's no one left.

Breathing hard, I can't get enough air. My lungs are on fire. Don't know why I feel like I'm drowning. A lung must have been pierced by the sword that went through me.

I drop onto my knees, drenched in blood.

Most of it isn't mine. Otherwise, I'd be dead.

"Rook!" Pyrah shifts from a dragon into a woman while she runs. Naked, reckless, she rushes over to me. "You're hurt."

I need to tend to her wounds. "Your back."

"I never left."

"No, your back...show me." It takes effort to speak without panting.

She shakes her head. "I'm fine."

But I know she must be lying to me, because pain sharpens her eyes. I brace myself on my sword before staggering to my feet.

"Show. Me."

Carefully, with my claws, I lift her hair from the nape of her neck. The skin between her shoulder blades looks red and tender, etched with the pattern of her missing scales. Dragon shifters heal fast, but they carry an echo of their wounds when they shift between forms. She's no exception.

"I'm healing already," she says. "But you—"

"You look like hell," Lark finishes, striding across the battlefield. My sister glares at me like I fucked up. "You aren't invincible, Rook. Can you dodge some of the blades next time?"

I bark out a laugh, which fucking hurts, and cough up a splattering of blood. "There might not be a next time."

"Shut up. Take off your armor. You need healing."

My sister is only angry with me because she cares. I unbuckle my leather cuirass and remove the armor. The shirt beneath clings to my skin, wet with blood, and I peel it from my body with a shudder.

"Lie down," Lark commands.

Already filthy, I drop back into the mud. She flattens her hand over the wound on my chest. I grit my teeth and brace myself for what comes next, since this isn't the first time she has healed me.

It doesn't hurt, not at first, not until magic rushes from her skin to mine.

Then every muscle in my body locks up, every nerve alive with agony. Magic crawls through flesh and bone, tearing me apart and remaking me from the inside out. I clench my jaws against a scream until it tears out of my throat.

I'm losing the battle to stay conscious.

Darkness consumes me.

# CHAPTER TEN

## PYRAH

When I cling to Rook's hand, trying to comfort him, he closes his eyes.

*Rook could have died.*

Lark places her hand over his wound before unleashing her magic. His skin starts glowing like red-hot iron. He chokes back a scream, though he can't hold it in forever. The raw anguish in his voice strangles my own throat until I can't remember how to breathe. He grips my hand, tighter and tighter, his claws digging into my skin. He's hurting me, though this pain must be nothing compared to what he's enduring.

I don't know how else to help him.

Blood drenches him, both from his enemies and himself, and it's impossible to tell the difference. One of the knights skewered him straight through his chest and out through his back. The knight's sword came far too close to piercing his heart and ending the fight. Does he fear death or welcome it with open arms?

Rook's grip slackens. Limp, he collapses back in the mud.

*Dead?* This question overshadows every other thought in my mind. My fingers shaking violently, I bring them to his neck and search for a pulse. *Please let me find a pulse.*

His heartbeat flutters beneath my fingertips, faint but undeniably there. I exhale a shaky breath. He's alive. The relief that washes over me is so intense it nearly brings me to tears.

"Rook," I say, almost pleading with him. "Rook, wake up."

"He won't," Lark says. "Not right away."

"Have you healed him before?"

"More times than I can remember."

I have never counted his scars, though they mark most of his body. It's obvious that he has survived a great number of wounds throughout his life. "What happened to him?"

Lark's eyes focus somewhere faraway. "Rook wasn't always like this. Wasn't always so willing to run straight into danger." She sighs. "God, I had hoped he would be less self-destructive after finding his mate."

"Self-destructive?" I echo. "Why?"

She grimaces, closing her eyes for a moment. "Our father, King Everhart, despised his children. Despised us. He ignored me, for the most part, but he treated Rook like the filth beneath his boots. Everhart called him bastard, demonspawn, monster. But Rook…" She flinches as if these memories are still too raw to remember. "Rook kept trying to prove himself worthy of love."

My throat tightens until I'm unable to speak. It's all too easy to imagine Rook as a little boy, desperate for scraps of affection, hoping his father would finally wake up one day and discover he was good.

Lark keeps talking, her eyes dark, her voice somber. "When the queen stabbed our father in the back, Rook found him bleeding out. I don't know if Rook tried to save his life. I've never had the courage to ask him."

I stroke Rook's battered knuckles, trying to comfort him even as he lies senseless. A memory stalks through the darkness of my mind—my own mother, dying in a pool of her blood—before I force it away.

"Rook started hunting monsters," Lark continues, "and flung himself into more and more perilous situations. Each hunt was a roll of the dice. He didn't care about the gold, didn't care if he lost the next fight."

"He wanted to destroy himself," I whisper, knowing this feeling all too well.

My fingers trace one of the countless scars on his chest, one that looks especially old and deep. How many times had he faced creatures that could have killed him? How many times had he hoped they would?

"The worst part was waiting for him to return from hunts," Lark says. "He would always come back soaked in blood. Sometimes he dragged himself back, half-dead, his body nearly broken. One winter, during the coldest time, he never returned at all. I tracked him down to a forest where he was alone and bleeding in the snow. He would have bled out or frozen to death if I hadn't found him."

Did he lie there, wondering if anyone would miss him?

Did he even care?

Rook has never hesitated to put himself between me and

danger, to pay the price of my safety in his own blood. I have always thought of this as protection, nothing more, though now I see the shadow of self-destruction in his actions. He has been like this ever since I first met him. To save his sister, he was willing to enter the lair of a dragon—*my* lair, back when we were still enemies.

"He captured me for my dragonfire," I say. "To save you."

"Thank God he did." Lark meets my gaze. "Something in him changed when he met you."

"What do you mean?"

"You are like a bright flame in the darkness, Pyrah. You guide his way through the shadows and give him hope."

The weight of her words should feel like a burden, but instead it makes my heart feel light enough to fly. She speaks the truth—I have seen the way Rook looks at me as if I'm something precious. He makes me feel like it's true.

I squeeze his hand tighter. *You are loved.*

"But he's still so reckless with his own life," Lark says. "Deep down, he still doesn't believe he's worth saving."

"How can we save him?"

"Someone lost in the darkness must find their own way out."

I'm silent for a long moment, contemplating what she said. "I remember what it's like to be lost in the darkness."

Lark waits for me to speak without pressing me for more. I'm grateful for her listening without judgment.

"Sometimes the darkness steals away your memories. I was sixteen when my mother was murdered by a dragonslayer." The words taste like ash in my mouth. "But I don't... I can't remember all of it."

"What do you mean?"

"There's nothing there. Just a blank space where the memory should be." My teeth itch, on the brink of becoming fangs, but I force myself to remain human. "I remember seeing the dragonslayer who killed her. His face, the gleam of his bastard sword. Then everything goes dark."

The next clear memory surfaces—the heat of flames against my skin, the scent of burning flesh. "The next thing I remember is building her funeral pyre. Watching her body burn."

"Your mind protected you from the pain," Lark says softly.

"But shouldn't I remember? She was my mother." My voice cracks. "I can't remember her final moments."

Lark reaches across Rook to touch my arm. "It's not your fault."

I stare down at my hands, remembering how they shook as I gathered wood for the pyre. "Sometimes I dream about it. Fragments, pieces that don't make sense. But I wake up before I can piece them together."

"Have you told Rook? About not remembering?"

I shake my head. "He knows I have nightmares. He knows my mother was killed by a dragonslayer."

"Why not tell him the rest?"

"I've never told anyone before." The confession slips out before I can stop it. "About the missing memories, the dreams that don't make sense. How sometimes I wake up screaming and can't remember why."

Lark's voice softens. "Rook would understand better than most."

"He doesn't know everything," I whisper. "I didn't tell him how I spent weeks afterward in my dragon form, unable to shift back, how I burned everything I could find until there was nothing left but ashes."

The memory of those dark days rises up, tangled with the scents of smoke and blood, ringing with the echoes of screaming villagers. I lost myself to rage and grief until there was very little of myself left. The taste of ash still coats my tongue when I remember, and sometimes I wake with my hands shaking, convinced they are still stained with soot.

"I'm not his bright flame in the darkness," I say, my words quiet. "I'm nothing but the destruction of dragonfire. I'm the thing mothers warn their children about, the monster in their stories."

Unblinking, Lark holds my gaze. "Sometimes we need dragonfire. Sometimes the world deserves to burn."

My mouth twists into a bitter smile. "Rook needed my dragonfire to break you out of the Forgotten Tower. That was an evil place, a dungeon we should have burned down to ashes and rubble."

"Yes," Lark says. "Destruction is often necessary for salvation."

"Salvation." The word feels strange on my tongue, since I have so rarely spoken it. Dragons care little for such things—we are creatures of blood and fire, of hoarded treasures and lonely caves. "To be honest with you, I'm not sure I believe in such a thing."

"Without belief, we have no guiding star." Lark speaks with the quiet certainty of someone who has seen too much darkness to doubt the importance of light. "And I believe in you both."

"Do you believe in the prophecy?"

*The Gray Prince will sit on the ruined throne.* Rook's words echo in my mind, making a shiver crawl down my spine.

Lark gazes at her brother for a long moment, her broken horn glinting where it has been destroyed. "Rook can't deny his identity as the Gray Prince, not for much longer." Her ember eyes simmer with conviction, reminding me so much of Rook's that it makes my throat ache. "The throne of Chymeria awaits him, whether he wants it or not."

# CHAPTER ELEVEN

ROOK

When I open my eyes, I'm lying on my back in the mud. Pyrah bends over me, her hand gripping mine. How long was I out?

"Pyrah."

God, my voice sounds unbelievably hoarse. Was I screaming? I don't recall screaming, though I must have been before I passed out. Nothing else would make my throat feel this raw.

Lark nudges my arm. "Drink."

She's holding out a bottle of red liquid. I recognize it as a healing potion. I take the bottle from her and push myself into a sitting position. When I swallow, I grimace at the bitter sludge.

"Did you brew this yourself?" I ask.

My sister scoffs at me. "You're welcome."

"Thank you." My response comes out gruffer than I intended.

Corpses litter the ground and the iron scent of blood is

heavy in the air. The stench clings to my nose and turns my stomach. Rather than lie among the dead, I stagger to my feet and pretend to be alive.

I'm weak with hunger.

Healing consumed most of the energy in my body. I need to eat—and food won't be enough. I can't deny my appetite as an incubus.

I must consume lust to survive.

"Rook?" Pyrah asks, and I wonder if she can tell what's wrong with me. I force myself to focus on the task at hand.

"We need to burn the bodies. Loot any treasure you find."

"This isn't even close to all the stolen treasure. Where's the rest of it?"

"Some of the horses escaped."

"Help me find them."

I jerk my head in a nod. "Lark?"

My sister cracks her knuckles. I can tell her fingers are stiff from summoning so much magic in battle. "Let me stay here and cast a spell. One that can help us return this treasure to Pyrah's cave."

"Good."

I crouch at the edge of the meadow. Horses scarred the mud with their hooves before they fled deeper into the trees. When I stand up, a wave of dizziness crashes over me. Hunger gnaws inside me, a persistent need. My hands tremble until I clench them into fists. I enter the forest, ducking beneath low-hanging branches that scrape my horns.

There's a pond near the meadow, choked by water lilies. I strip off my leather trousers and boots before I venture into the pond. Filthy with mud and blood, I want to scour the battlefield from my body.

When Pyrah wades in after me, she's too damn close to me. Still naked. Still tempting me. I take a deep breath to steel my nerves, but that only makes matters worse. Her scent, clovers and smoke, mingles with the perfume of lilies and invites me to do wicked things.

She smells...*delicious*.

I need to calm the fuck down. I have had years of practice denying my hunger, starving myself as an incubus. Ever since adulthood, my life has been one of painstaking discipline and restraint.

I would be a fool to lose control now.

I cup my hands in the pond and pour water over her shoulders. She shivers, her nipples hard from the cold. Gently, I wash the back of her neck, careful not to hurt her where she was wounded by the knights. I don't want to bring her any more pain than she has already endured.

Her long, wet hair clings to the curves of her body. My hand traces one of her collarbones before drifting between her breasts. I wash her without hesitation, my movements curt and efficient. I'm not trying to seduce her, I swear, but blood rushes to my cock. My erection nearly juts out of the water. I can't leave the pond without betraying my arousal.

*God, she's beautiful.*

My hand cradles her breast, my dark claws a stark contrast against her pale skin. I can't resist gliding my thumb over her nipple, just the slightest touch, and even that is enough to make her gasp.

My shadow wings unfurl from my shoulder blades. I fold them flat against my spine, but it's already too late.

"Your wings," she murmurs.

Her unspoken question lingers between us. Though I can hide my hard cock from her, I can't hide my wings. She already knows why they unfurled—it's an unmistakable sign of strong emotion or arousal.

There's a thin line between blood lust and lust.

The urge to fight has ebbed from my blood, replaced by the urge to fuck.

I stride out of the pond, trying to put some distance between us, but she follows me onto land. Water trickles over my body and guides her gaze downward. She can't stop staring at my cock. I close my eyes for a moment and recite a silent prayer for fortitude.

"Pyrah." I growl out her name.

"Why are you hard?" she asks, breathless, as if this surprises her.

I back her against a tree and trap her there, my arms bracketing her head. "I need...I need to request your consent."

"For what?"

My cock bobs, an involuntary movement, and aches to be touched by her.

"Let me devour you." I close my eyes and inhale against her neck, greedy for her scent. "Tell me you want it."

She nods.

"Use your words."

Her gasp betrays her desire. "Yes."

My claws bite into the bark of the tree with a crunch. I force myself not to lose control. She's willing and she wants me, but the kiss of an incubus could be dangerous.

Deadly, even.

I took too much from her once and vowed never to do it again.

"Are you hungry?" she asks.

"Ravenous."

I guide her hand to my cock. She strokes me in her fist, tormenting me, dragging out a pearl of arousal. I suck in my breath through my clenched teeth. I'm so hard that my erection has become almost painful.

"Are you always hard when you're hungry?"

"Not always." My fangs test her neck with no more than a hint of a bite, and her hand tightens around my cock. "But I know you like to be devoured by an incubus. Fucked by an incubus."

"I do," she confesses.

"I want to fuck you." My voice rasps on the words. It's both a request and a demand. "Tell me what you desire."

"You."

"Give me more detail than that."

She smirks, still teasing me. "Your cock."

I brace her against the tree, hooking her legs around my hips, and grab my cock in my fist. My ass clenches as my hips jerk forward. I'm trying to be slow, trying to be cautious, but I enter her fully with one savage thrust. That knocks the teasing smirk from her mouth.

"Fuck," she gasps.

She tenses, her body trembling, and I know she needs a moment to take the spikes on my cock. I don't want to hurt her, but I'm too far gone to hold back. I can't pretend to be more human than incubus any longer.

She was a virgin when she met me. Never had any other cock but mine. I need to be gentle with her, especially since I'm big.

I bend down and bring my mouth to the curve of her neck. When I lick her there, her heartbeat pounds beneath my lingering tongue. She melts under my touch. Her hips arch as she takes me even deeper.

"I need this," I murmur. "Need you."

I bring my mouth to hers and slide my tongue inside, just tasting her desire. The tiniest of whimpers escapes her throat.

I want to turn her whimpers into screams of bliss.

Her heels dig into my ass. She grabs me by the horns and clings to me while I fuck her harder and harder. I'm rutting into her like an animal, her back jolting against the tree. I curl my hand behind her neck to protect her skin.

"Oh fuck, oh fuck." She chants the words.

My shadow tail uncurls from my spine. It's hard at the end, the same as my horns, perfect for sliding between her soft thighs. I toy with her wet cunt. She gasps and rocks her hips, desperate for more sensation. When I kiss her on the mouth, I taste her desire.

She's close.

I want to break her just a little, just enough that she will never forget what it feels like to be fucked by me.

Feral, I pound into her until she opens her mouth in a silent scream.

I kiss her open mouth in a devouring kiss, the kiss of an incubus. Her lust flows down my throat like milk and honey.

I have fed a thousand times before, but none have ever tasted sweeter. I have fucked a thousand times before, but none have ever made me feel such bliss.

She comes hard, her cunt gripping me, milking my cock as if she wants to drain every drop of seed from my balls.

I lose control.

With a hoarse grunt, I slam my hips forward, my toes digging into the dirt. Pleasure roars through my mind and obliterates all thought. I unload my seed deep inside her. Pulse after pulse of my release fills her until it overflows down her legs.

I keep devouring her while I come, and it prolongs her own climax. She's whimpering, almost sobbing with bliss.

Enough.

I have to stop.

I wrench my mouth away from hers. Gasping, I close my eyes for a moment. I'm still hard, still deep inside her, because I'm an incubus and my body is designed to fuck without stopping.

I'm not a good man, because I don't want to stop. I want to keep drinking her lust until it slakes my thirst and pours down my parched throat.

Hell, I'm not just a bad man, but a monster.

"More," she begs. She's intoxicated by my kiss.

I force myself not to look at her mouth. "No." That sounds rougher than I intended, and I gentle my voice. "No, we should stop. I don't want to hurt you."

When I slide out, more of my release trickles down her thighs. I put her down, slowly, and she wobbles on unsteady legs. I hold her with an arm around her waist. She leans against me, borrowing my strength, and it does strange things to my heartbeat. A fierce urge to protect her rushes through me and aches in my chest.

"Dirty again," I say, stating the obvious.

She glances at me through her eyelashes. "I like it when you make me dirty."

A growl of a sigh escapes me. "Don't tempt me."

"Tempt you to what?" She smirks. "Fuck me again? Devour me again?"

I shake my head. For years, I have practiced burying my own needs deep. It will take more than that to tempt me. "Follow me."

Her eyes are wide and bright. "I would follow you anywhere."

I wish she wouldn't look at me like that, like I'm the Gray Prince, like I'm a hero. But I'm no hero. I'm nothing more than a demon haunted by memories and ghosts in the night.

I bring her back to the pond where we can bathe again. Careful of my claws, I wash between her legs. She shivers at the cold water, her nipples tight, and I resist the urge to lick them. I'm more than a demon of lust, and I need her to know that I'm capable of love.

"What's wrong?" she asks me.

"Nothing." I blink away the thoughts that cling to me like cobwebs.

She tilts her head, studying my face. "You look troubled by something."

I grunt, a neutral noise. "There's a lot to be troubled by. Even if we find all your treasure, we haven't defeated all the queen's knights, or the queen herself."

"Maybe Lark was right." She looks into my eyes. "Maybe this is your destiny."

Dread throttles my throat like an invisible hand. I don't want to think about returning to the castle at Netherhaven. I have been back to the city before, and it was hard enough. Once, when I was young and stupid, I called the place home. It will never be my home again.

"Rook?" she asks, and she looks at me as if she sees right through me.

"I don't want to go back. I haven't entered the castle since my father died. Since…"

"Queen Dulcamara murdered him." She finishes my sentence.

"Correct." I can feel myself turning cold, locking away my hurt. "There's nothing for me there but death."

"Why not the queen's death?"

My eyebrows arch. "You want to assassinate the ruler of Chymeria?"

Her eyes flash gold. "She's threatening my mate."

Damn, Pyrah might be even more possessive than me, which is admittedly quite a feat. I shake my head at her ferocity. "Not even a dragon, however fierce, can defeat the queen alone."

"You're right." The gold in her eyes intensifies. "We need an army."

I don't know what to say to that. We need to find her treasure before it's too late and it's lost to us forever.

I abandon the pond and crouch in the dirt, running my fingers over ground. There. A hoofprint dug into the mud. Together, we track down the missing treasure.

It's easier than expected, since gold coins glint among the

leaves and moss. They must have fallen from the saddlebags when the horses fled from the dragonfire. We find two horses, huddled in the trees, and they have calmed enough for me to take them by the reins.

We bring the horses back to the battlefield, where Lark waits for us.

"What took you so long?" she asks.

Of course, I would rather not tell my sister the indecent truth. But Pyrah can't hide her blush, not with her pale skin. It's unexpected from such a fierce dragon shifter. I had no idea she could look so...adorable.

My mouth twitches with a hidden smile. "We found most of the lost treasure."

Lark snorts as if skeptical. "Help me loot the rest of it from the dead."

We work together on our morbid task. Blood stains the stolen gold and jewels, a reminder of how many lives were spent to reclaim this treasure. We stack the dead knights like kindling for a bonfire. Finally, Pyrah shifts into a dragon and ignites the corpses with dragonfire.

Flames destroy our enemies. While they burn, the sight fills me with primitive satisfaction. Maybe it's wrong to enjoy death, and I'm too demonic at heart. Maybe I'm just too fucked-up to care.

Either way, nothing will stop me from protecting my mate.

# CHAPTER TWELVE

ROOK

What began as a sunny morning has descended into a gloomy evening. Thunderclouds cover the sky, the dark purple color of bruises. A storm is coming, more than just the weather. Pyrah's treasure glimmers on the battlefield, a small mountain of gold and jewels. Frowning, I stand by the treasure with my hands locked behind my back. One does not simply kill over a dozen of the queen's knights without consequences.

"We shouldn't linger here much longer," I say.

"We know," Lark snaps. She's still on edge after the battle. We all are. "While you were both gone, I finished my spell."

"Show me."

Lark rolls up the sleeve of her dress. A tiny, emerald green serpent clings to her wrist, basking in the warmth of her skin. Something about it looks unreal; there's a strange rippling around it like a mirage in the desert. The snake flicks out its tongue and tastes the air.

I frown. "A snake? Why?"

"Not just a snake. I summoned a verdant voidswallower," she says, which explains its aura of unreality. "It has a magical stomach that's much bigger on the inside, enough for all of this treasure."

Pyrah stares with fascination at the snake. "Is it real?"

"In this realm? Not entirely."

"Won't it digest my treasure?"

Lark shakes her head. "Voidswallowers can't digest anything in our realm beyond raw magic. It will spit out the treasure when I ask."

I arch an eyebrow. My sister has undeniable talent as a sorceress, and she can't resist an opportunity to demonstrate for an audience.

We feed all the treasure to the voidswallower. It gulps down every last gem and coin while retaining its small size. Impressive, I must admit.

I put my hand on Pyrah's shoulder. "Let's bring you home."

She nods and leans into my touch. I linger a moment longer, craving the warmth of her skin against mine.

"Lark," I say. "Are you all out of magic, or can you cast another portal?"

My sister rolls her eyes. "I can't run out of magic."

"I have seen you cast spells until you're stumbling, drunk with fatigue."

She shrugs. "I'm hungry, that's all."

Lark inherited demonic blood from our succubus mother, same as me, and she didn't escape the hunger for lust. If she spends too much energy on her magic, she will be forced to feed.

How has she been satisfying her hunger? I'm afraid to ask.

Sparks fly from her fingers as Lark sketches a portal with her hands. Through the portal, rugged mountains bite at the sky like teeth. Unmistakable, this place is Pyrah's home.

"Ready?" I ask.

In reply, Pyrah strides through the portal first, as if determined to prove her bravery. I follow in her footsteps, hoping she won't suffer too much from the magic. On the other side, Pyrah bends over a boulder, her face pale. She tries to speak, then turns away and vomits.

Damn, the portal hit her hard in the stomach this time. I hold her hair away from her face as she expels whatever remains in her stomach.

*Or she could be pregnant.*

The thought darts through my mind, unbidden and unwanted. But it's an impossible dream, and I have no choice but to let it slip away.

When she's done, she wipes her mouth on the back of her hand. "I'm sorry."

"Don't apologize." I rub her back. "Are you all right?"

"I will be."

After Lark travels through the portal, it crackles and closes behind her. The woodsmoke smell of magic lingers in the air. Pyrah takes a deep breath and stands up straight, trying to shake off the dizziness.

"The portal?" Lark asks.

I give her a grim nod.

Pyrah leans into me, her body trembling. I hook my arm

around her waist and help her back home. The journey isn't far, but she stumbles a few times, her steps unsteady. She's still recovering from the effects of the portal. I don't blame her. Lark's magic is powerful, and it's not easy to travel through it unscathed.

"Wait out here," I say. "Let me clean your cave first."

"Rook, you don't have to do that."

"Those assholes pissed in your home. I won't tolerate it."

I hike down to the lake with no name, fill my canteen with water, and soak a coarse rag. Thank fuck I carry a bar of soap in my pack, made of good, strong pine tar. I scour her cave until only the spice of pines fills the air, then jog back to the lake to wash the sweat and dirt from myself.

Pyrah meets me at the lake. She cups water in her hands and rinses out her mouth.

"Feeling better?" I ask.

"Yes." She shakes her head. "I have a strong stomach, I swear."

*She's not pregnant. Don't even mention it.*

"I believe you," I say, since it's the safest thing to admit.

"Thanks. And thank you for cleaning my cave."

Standing on her tiptoes, she kisses my cheek. Pride turns my spine to steel and makes me want to conquer the world for her.

Instead, I sweep her off her feet. She gasps and clings to my neck. "Rook!"

"Let me carry you, woman."

"I can walk."

"I know you can."

Without waiting for her next protest, I hike higher on the zigzagging trail. Was the path always this fucking steep? My arms and thighs start aching, just a little, but I would be damned if I dropped my mate.

At last, I conquer the cliff.

"Didn't even break a sweat," I say with a straight face.

She laughs. "Liar."

I put her back on her own two feet and can't resist squeezing her ass. I was trying to be subtle, but she dances away from me and swats at my hand. The way she's looking at me, I know she wants to retaliate tenfold.

Her stomach growls. "God, why am I so hungry?"

"You haven't eaten all day."

"I'm ravenous," she murmurs. "I blame you for devouring me."

Guilt sits like lead in my stomach, though I keep my face blank. I can't deny that my demonic hunger has been leeching her energy. The kiss of an incubus offers nothing but physical pleasure in return. She deserves more from me, at the very least, sustenance.

We return to Pyrah's cave, once more laden with treasure. She falls to her knees and cradles handfuls of gold with reverence. Her treasure means more to her than I expected. It's valuable, certainly, though a dragon would never sell a single penny of their hoard.

I rest my fingers on the nape of her neck. "Pyrah."

While she stays kneeling, I bend over her and capture her in a kiss. Not a devouring kiss but a claiming one to prove she's mine. She clings to me by my horns, pulling me closer, using me to hold herself upright.

Lark clears her throat, reminding us she's still here.

Pyrah's cheeks turn pink. It's fascinating to watch her blush, but I resist the temptation to kiss her again and embarrass her further.

Lark gazes outside. "It's evening. Good time to hunt."

Pyrah jumps to her feet, unable to disguise her excitement. "Let me take you hunting. I could find every deer trail in my territory with my eyes closed."

Lark tilts her head, her face unreadable. "I'm uninterested in deer."

"Have you been hunting for different prey?" I ask.

"Humans offer more of a challenge."

"Lark." Just that one word, her name, echoes with a quiet warning.

She smirks at me. "Don't worry, they always say yes."

I glower at my sister. "You better make damn sure they do. It's never worth feeding without willing consent."

"But you must admit, scaring them tastes that much sweeter."

I hate to admit she's right.

"What's the nearest town?" Lark asks.

"Havenwold," Pyrah answers. "There's an inn there, called The Raven's Head." She grimaces. "There *was* an inn there, at least, before I turned into a dragon and smashed through the roof."

Lark cocks an eyebrow.

"Long story," I say. "The queen's knights came looking for us."

"The queen's knights make good prey." Lark licks her lips as if remembering the taste of their desire.

I stare at her, aghast. "Have you been fucking Dulcamara's men?"

"And a few of her women."

"*Lark*." Grimacing, I pronounce her name like profanity. "What the fuck are you thinking?"

She snorts. "I'm pretty sure you would say I'm not thinking."

I shake my head in disbelief. Lark has always been reckless, but this is risky, even for her. One of these days, she's going to get herself killed. "Why don't you just fuck the God of Chaos while you're at it?"

"I absolutely would. Have you seen the statues of him?"

Pyrah arches her eyebrows. "Not yet."

"I'm sure you would appreciate him," Lark says with a smirk.

These women are insane. I shake my head at them both. "This isn't the time to be lusting after demon gods. Or the queen's knights, for that matter. We just broke you out of the Forgotten Tower. Your face must be on wanted posters across half the kingdom."

Lark rolls her eyes. "God, Rook, I know how to lurk in the shadows."

I pinch the bridge of my nose. "Don't get thrown into another dungeon. And don't disappear for too long."

"I promise."

"Meet us back at the cave by midnight."

"Of course," she says, though she sounds irritated by me.

Lark combs her hair with her fingers and flicks it over her shoulder. With a sweep of her arm, she slices the air open into a portal. That means she's been to Havenwold before. Otherwise, she would need a map to know where the hell she's going. That's one of the requirements of portal magic. After she strides through, the portal crackles shut behind her.

"Are you worried about her?" Pyrah asks.

"My sister isn't stupid. Usually." I glower at her lingering footprints. "But fuck, the queen's knights?"

"If Lark drains the life out of a knight or two, you won't see me crying at any funerals." Pyrah glances sideways at me with a wicked glint in her eyes. "Is the God of Chaos real?"

"Some believe he is."

"Is he handsome?"

I don't dignify that with a reply.

Pyrah grins. She must enjoy teasing me, particularly with my sister's help.

"Let's hunt," I say.

"With pleasure."

"Where are the best deer trails in your territory?"

"Follow me. There's one not far away."

We start walking deeper into the forest. After a few moments, she says, "Do you worship the demon gods?"

I grunt. "My mother raised us to believe in them. Secretly, of course, since my father would not have approved of heathen practices from the Underworld. He taught us to worship one god, the human one."

She's quiet for a moment, her gaze downcast. Her boots pad over the moss. "Whenever you talk about your father, you sound…"

"Angry?"

"No. Sad."

"You weren't supposed to notice." It sounds joking enough when I say it, but I can't deny the ache lodged deep in my ribs like an old wound. "I bury my emotions deep for good reason."

"What reason?"

"Survival."

She lets out her breath in a sigh. "I understand."

I believe her in the marrow of my bones. Life isn't easy for a dragon shifter, especially not one hunted by the crown. She lost her mother to dragonslayers when she was only sixteen.

"Wait," she says. "Look."

She drops into a crouch and traces her fingers over the ground where the cloven hoof of a deer has pocked the dirt.

I rub the dirt, noting how it's still wet, and my fingertips glance against hers. It's nothing more than a slight touch, but it's enough to bring my skin to life. When she meets my gaze, I'm lost in the blue of her eyes.

I'm obsessed with her.

"Who wants to take down this prey?" she asks.

I want to indulge myself by watching her. "Show me how you hunt."

Her eyes flicker from blue to gold. She walks away from me, putting some distance between us, before she transforms into a dragon. Her shift takes my breath away. It does every damn time.

Stretching, she arches her spine like a cat, then lunges into the air and flies over the forest. Dragons hunt by sight. I follow on the ground, slipping between the shadows, careful not to spook her prey.

There.

A buck stands between the trees. He still hasn't shed his antlers this spring. He nibbles at the new growth of leaves, unaware that he's being hunted.

I drop to my knees and keep my breathing quiet. I have a crossbow on my back, part of my regular gear, but I'm not going to steal Pyrah's kill. She's nowhere to be seen, not even as a hint of crimson in the sky.

Where did she go? Maybe she's hiding behind the clouds.

Wind rushes through the forest. The buck lifts his head, his ears alert, but the noise of rustling leaves disguises any other sounds.

Death plummets from above.

The red dragon dives from the heavens. Like a bird of prey, she leads with her talons. Startled, the buck bursts into motion. He springs high into the air and twists away from the dragon.

Too late.

Her talons strike his back and knock him to the ground. Biting his neck, she severs his spine with brutal efficiency. A successful hunt. She flares her wings and shadows her kill from the sky. Perhaps she has an instinct to hide it from other dragons.

The last of the dying sunlight glows behind her outstretched wings. Magnificent.

Pyrah licks the blood from her teeth. "Are you hungry?"

"I am."

That's not the whole truth. Food is never enough to sustain me. The demon in me battles with my humanity, urging me to devour her lust again.

"Time to cook the venison," I say to distract myself from my primitive urges.

"I'm not much of a cook."

"Allow me."

We work together in companionable silence, needing no words to communicate. Pyrah brings me wood while I build the campfire. I place a flat stone near the edge. I take out my fire steel on habit, then smile to myself when I remember dragonfire is faster.

"Pyrah, I want you to light the fire."

She brings her mouth close to the stacked wood and breathes out a jet of flame. The wood ignites at once. It will burn down to coals while I prepare the meat for cooking.

Pyrah relinquishes her kill to me, then watches with fascination as I harvest the best cuts of venison. I'm no butcher, but I have hunted enough over the years. Once the meat is ready, I sprinkle water onto the flat stone. It hisses into steam. That's the right temperature.

"Cooking on a rock?" she asks.

"Yes."

"I'm impressed."

I arch an eyebrow. "Don't be impressed until you eat it."

I sear the venison on the stone, flipping it with my knife, until it's tender. The smell makes my mouth water. I nudge it away from the heat with my blade. I want to give it enough time to rest in its juices.

"Let me feed you," I tell her.

She shifts back into a woman. Kneeling, she glances at me through her tumbling red hair. Firelight flickers over her naked skin. She could be down on her knees for a much better reason.

Her mouth could be tasting my cock.

I drag my mind out of the gutter. She needs to eat. I can't devour her while she's starving. That would be dangerous. But fuck, I wish my cock could understand that. It's already getting hard. She licks her pretty lips, which makes this so much worse.

I slice the venison with my blade and offer it to her. She takes it from me with her teeth. My thumb lingers against her bottom lip. Fuck, her mouth is soft. It's impossible not to imagine it sucking me. When she lets out a moan of satisfaction, my cock strains against the leather of my trousers.

Her eyes close as she savors the taste of the venison. "This is delicious. I want you to cook for me every night."

Devouring her once today wasn't enough.

I'm nowhere near satisfied.

# CHAPTER THIRTEEN

LARK

I lied to my brother.

The queen's knights make good prey—that part is true—but they aren't who I'm hunting for tonight. I can't stop remembering who satisfied my hunger in the Forgotten Tower, the forbidden trysts that still linger in my mind, forever tied to the scent of rosemary perfume.

Unseen, I prowl the crooked streets of Havenwold. Moonlight gleams on the cobblestones and turns the city into something pretty. Even the gutter water looks like quicksilver, hiding its filth.

When the wind changes, it carries a hint of desire to my nose.

*Of course.* I'm near a brothel. The flimsy windows do little to muffle the moans inside. Closing my eyes, I breathe in the primal scent of lovers tangled in sheets, of quick fucks in darkened corners.

None of it appeals to me. Not like *her*.

Zin still haunts my mind—I can't stop craving her rosemary scent, good enough to eat. I need to banish her from my memories. Pausing in an alley, I press my forehead against the cold stone of the wall.

*You need this,* she would whisper to me. *Need me.*

How I hated that she spoke the truth. I have never been able to deny my nature as a succubus. Refusing to feed upon lust would lead only to starvation. She knew that when she touched me, when she—

*No.*

I bite the inside of my cheek until my fangs draw blood. The sharp pain cuts through my emotions and brings clarity.

What I had with Zin wasn't love. It was nothing more than survival.

I turn my back on the brothel. They would welcome my services as a succubus, maybe even pay me in gold, but I'm not interested in feeding there tonight. Many in the kingdom of Chymeria think demons like me are whores. We often have no other way of survival.

Zin never treated me like a whore.

Even after we became enemies, even after she hated me, she always acted as if I had value. My traitorous body remembers her touch, the way she would pet my hair and tell me how much it looked like moonlight. I let her stroke my head, drunk on her spells and my own desperate hunger.

Every shadow holds echoes of dark eyes and darker magic.

I push away from the wall, forcing myself deeper into the city's maze of streets. There must be someone else who can satisfy me. I refuse to let Zin have this much power over me, even now, while I'm meant to be free.

The Raven's Head stands as a charred skeleton against the night sky. Smoke still curls from the blackened beams of the once prosperous inn, though it must be days since its destruction. One of my favorite hunting grounds has been reduced to ash. I had found good prey here—lonely travelers seeking pleasure, merchants whose pockets jingled with gold.

The scorched stone bears telltale signs of dragonfire, too hot for a mundane blaze. This must be Pyrah's doing. I vaguely recall her and my brother mentioning this inn's destruction over dinner.

Movement catches my eye—a city guard nailing fresh parchment to a post near the ruins. Not just any parchment but wanted posters. After he leaves, I creep closer to examine them in the torchlight.

There we are, the three traitors to the crown.

Pyrah's likeness shows her as a dragon, soaring over a village, her jaws raining down flames. The artist captured her fearsome beauty, I will give them that. Five thousand gold pieces for her capture.

My own portrait is less flattering. They drew me with wild hair and glowing eyes, like some nightwitch from a fairy tale. Seven thousand gold pieces. The price has gone up since I escaped the Forgotten Tower.

But Rook...

A mirthless laugh escapes me. "Damn," I whisper.

For the Gray Prince, dead or alive, the reward is ten thousand gold pieces. The sketch shows Rook as a looming shadow with a tail and demon wings, which isn't entirely wrong. Queen

Dulcamara must be truly desperate to offer such a fortune. Desperate, or furious at his freedom.

"Well, brother," I murmur, "looks like the queen hates you most of all."

Pyrah had asked about bounties over dinner, curious about her own worth to the crown. The answer hangs here in stark black-and-white, though I doubt she will take much comfort in being the cheapest outlaw.

Distracted by the wanted posters, I almost miss the sound of guards on night watch. Their boots scuff the cobblestones as they patrol the city. I slink deeper in the shadows, my heart pounding, ready to fight or flee.

Their voices sour the night air, thick with ale and derision.

"Did you see what that red dragon did to The Raven's Head?" The shorter guard speaks first, his words loud and sloppy. Careless. "Took out half the city by breathing fire down on our heads."

"Aye. Best ale in Havenwold, gone up in smoke." The taller guard kicks a chunk of charred wood. "Thanks to that scaly bitch."

"Fucking hate dragons."

I resist the urge to laugh. If I had to guess, Pyrah would be amused by her reputation. The Raven's Head was hardly half the city—just one inn and maybe a few nearby buildings that caught fire from drifting embers.

"Captain wants us to check every shadow twice." The shorter guard's hand rests on his sword hilt as they inspect the wanted posters. "The Gray Prince, his dragon, and that witch who escaped the Tower."

"Sorceress," his companion corrects, tapping my portrait. "This one is supposed to be right dangerous with magic."

"I hear she's worth at least a quick fuck," the other guard muses.

"Who, the dragon?"

"God, no." He snorts. "I'm talking about the succubus. Haven't you ever wanted your cock sucked by a succubus?"

"Those bitches have fangs. I won't let her anywhere near my cock."

My claws bite into my palms as their disgusting laughter echoes down the street. Rage burns through my blood and sharpens the gnawing ache of hunger in my gut. How many times had I heard similar words in the Forgotten Tower, spoken by guards who wanted me to hear them?

"They get desperate without it," the first guard continues, loosening his belt. "Feed on lust like we feed on bread."

"That's how the king's whore got him, wasn't it? Sucked him dry till he couldn't think straight."

*My mother*. They still gossip after her even years after she vanished.

The first guard braces himself by the wall and starts to piss. Steam rises and drifts over to where I'm hiding, though he doesn't look in my direction. "Wonder if the daughter's got the same talents."

Blood wets my palms where my claws break skin. The iron scent mingles with the foul stench of the guards, making my head swim, and yet the hunger still claws inside me, demanding to be satisfied. I could drain them both dry until nothing remained but husks.

Do they know what a man looks like after a succubus destroys him?

Their corpses would turn ashen gray and wither. Their remains would crumble apart into dirt for the worms.

But I can't—*shouldn't*. I would be a fool to attack the guards tonight, even if it wasn't unprovoked. I can't afford to be captured again. While their boots scrape against cobblestones and their vulgar jokes fade into the night, I remember their faces. Perhaps another time I can drain them in some forgotten alleyway and discard them like garbage.

Gods, I'm still hungry. I continue my hunt through the streets of Havenwold.

A young man stumbles from a tavern, his cheeks flushed pink. Perfect prey. I follow him into the shadows between buildings. His lust trails behind him—bittersweet, tinged with unrequited desire.

"Are you lost?" I step into his path.

His jaw drops and hangs open. "No, milady… I was going out to..." He sways, caught between fear and longing. Prey often recognizes predator, an instinct deep inside most humans, but ale dulls his senses.

I move closer, letting moonlight pour down upon me, turning my silver skin and pale hair luminous. "Do you want me?" The words drip from my mouth like honey, though my muscles coil with predatory intent.

His drunken mind struggles to process the question, but his body knows the answer. "Fuck, yes." His glassy stare travels over me, seeing nothing more than a pretty face and willing flesh.

He stumbles forward, his hand groping for me, though he's drunk enough that he catches himself against the alley wall instead. The reek of piss-water ale mingles with his thickening lust. Such a simple creature, driven by nothing more than primitive urges. Undoubtedly, he cares nothing for matters of consent.

He reaches for me. "You're the most beautiful—"

"Shh." My smile lets him see just a hint of my fangs. My fingers trace his neck. His pulse jumps beneath my touch, fear and desire warring in his blood. "No need for pretty words."

When I touch him, his lust drowns my senses—raw, animal want without complexity or care. He sees me as nothing more than a vessel for his pleasure. Little better than a free whore.

*Good.* That makes this easier.

My fingertips press harder into his neck, feeling his rapid heartbeat. His hands paw at my waist, clumsy with drink, before squeezing one of my breasts. No finesse, no tenderness. This isn't about care or emotion. In the shadows, neither one of us has time for pretending.

"Close your eyes," I whisper against his ear. He obeys without hesitation, swaying slightly on his feet.

*What a fool.*

I press him against the alley wall. His resistance crumbles as I kiss him, just beginning to devour him. The taste of him floods my senses—young, potent, flavored with heartache. He wanted the tavern wench tonight, I can taste it in his kiss. She rejected his clumsy advances, leaving him drunk and desperate, aching to find someone to release his tension.

"Let me help you forget her," I promise him.

"Her?" Fear ripples across his face. "How did you—?"

I press a finger to his lips. "You know what I am."

His throat bobs as he swallows hard. "A succubus."

"Do you know my name?"

He shakes his head, his eyes glazed with ale, either too stupid or too drunk to connect me to the wanted posters in Havenwold. Maybe he hasn't seen them yet. Maybe he doesn't know how to read. It's not uncommon for the peasants of Chymeria to be unfamiliar with books.

This is dangerous but not *too* dangerous. Not for me.

My kiss devours him, drawing out his essence with each heartbeat. His fear adds a sharp edge to the sweetness of his desire, like bitter herbs in honey wine. His erection juts against my belly, trapped between our bodies, and he starts rocking his hips while I feed from him.

He can't resist the kiss of a succubus, the overwhelming pleasure it brings.

His hands fumble at my skirts, pushing me back against the rough stone wall. Irritation prickles my skin.

"No, not like that." I catch his wrists, but he mistakes my iron grip for passion.

"Come on, beautiful." His drunken breath washes over my face as he presses closer. "We both want this."

But I don't want to grant such intimacy to a stranger. Not tonight.

"You don't understand what's happening here." My voice sharpens with anger, but he's too far gone to hear the warning.

He traps me with his weight, assuming his larger size gives him control over me. His fingers tangle in my hair as he tries to force a deeper kiss. How arrogant of him to believe he's the hunter here.

He knows I'm a succubus, and yet he still believes he's stronger than me.

"Let me feel you." His words slur together. "Let me make you scream."

I almost laugh at his pathetic bravado. If only he knew what truly lurked in these shadows. His crude pawing is nothing compared to the sophisticated torments I have already known.

"Such bravery." My voice drips with scorn as I trail my fingers down his chest. "But haven't you forgotten something?"

He frowns at me. "What's that?"

"I'm not your prey." I grip his chin, forcing him to meet my gaze. Let him see what I truly am—the glowing red eyes, the broken horn, the cruel smile full of sharp teeth. "You are mine."

Fear finally shatters his ale-soaked haze. "Please."

He might be begging for me to spare his life. But it's far too late for second thoughts. Far too late to run.

His terror tastes like frost on my tongue, crystallizing the sweetness of his lust into something sharper. His essence floods my veins like liquid fire. Such potent desire made even richer by his fear.

He struggles weakly against my grip, but I pin him down with inhuman strength. His protests die in his throat as I feed, replacing them with helpless moans of pleasure. Even as his mind screams danger, his body betrays him, responding to my touch. His hips jerk as he chases mindless pleasure.

He spills in his trousers, unable to resist.

It would be so easy to take everything. To drain him until nothing remains but a withered husk, another nameless victim found in an alley. The temptation, an urge down in the marrow of my bones, shudders through me. I could feast on more than just his lust—I could consume his very soul.

My brother refuses to kill with the devouring kiss. Unlike me.

But I'm trying not to be a monster tonight.

Instead, I summon my magic and find specific memories, unraveling the threads of tonight like picking apart a tangled skein of wool. The taste of ale on his tongue grows fainter. The tavern wench's rejection blurs at the edges. My silver skin and red eyes fade into shadow.

By morning, he will remember nothing but drinking too much, perhaps a hazy dream of pleasure in the dark. No face to describe to the guards, no horns or glowing eyes to match against wanted posters.

When I finally release him, he slumps against the wall. His eyes flutter closed as he slides down to the dirt. He will wake with a crushing hangover and confused fragments of memory, nothing more.

I step back into the shadows.

My power thrums beneath my skin, the stranger's essence still burning hot in my veins. I flex my fingers, watching silver sparks dance between them. Such delicious energy begs to be used.

Havenwold isn't big enough for the prey I seek.

The portal tears open with barely a thought, midnight blue shadows swirling into a doorway. Beyond it lies the cobblestone streets of Netherhaven, the biggest and most dangerous city in Chymeria.

I step through the portal, letting it close behind me with a whisper. The shadows welcome me, wrapping around my silver skin like a lover's embrace. Here, in the heart of Netherhaven, surrounded by the queen's guards and spies, I should feel afraid. Instead, I feel powerful.

Hungry.

The mediocre taste of the stranger's lust only whet my appetite for something more refined. Something darker.

Morel & Sons looms before me, a familiar apothecary, its windows dark except for a single candle flickering in the upstairs apartment. *Her* apartment. My skin tingles with awareness.

I press my back against the rough stones of the alley, watching that lonely light dance behind the curtains. The rosemary scent of her magic drifts down, mingling with dried herbs from the shop below. My fingers trace the broken horn on my head, remembering how she used to touch it in the Tower, how she made even my imprisonment bearable.

"Zin," I whisper, tasting her name on my tongue.

Is she thinking of me, too, up there in her sanctuary? Does she remember how I begged for her during those long nights?

Her silhouette blocks the candlelight behind the curtains. My breath catches as I watch her undress near the window, each movement precise and graceful. Even her shadow stokes the embers of my hunger.

My claws bite into the stone, nearly gouging it, as she strips off her robes and tosses them away. I imagine her dark eyes, the way they sparked with cruel amusement whenever I pleaded for more.

Tonight, I'm not her prisoner. Tonight, I'm powerful with stolen desire.

I could climb those stairs to her apartment. Knock on her

door. Let her see what her torture has made of me. The thought sends shivers down my spine—fear or arousal, I can't tell anymore.

The night air smothers me with anticipation. I need her hands on me, need her magic burning through my veins. Need her to hurt me, heal me, break me apart, and put me back together.

But I stay in the shadows, watching her candle burn low.

Some hungers are too dangerous to satisfy.

# CHAPTER FOURTEEN

ROOK

What's wrong with me? I'm behaving like a virgin who just discovered fucking, even though I have all the experience of a successful incubus in his prime. Hell, Pyrah was truly a virgin when we first met, though she knew what she wanted and she wasn't afraid to demand it from me.

"You're hard again," Pyrah says.

"With you, I'm often aroused." The words rasp out of me, betraying my desire.

"How often?"

Her question lingers in the air between us. "Far more than I want to admit."

Her eyes darken, her pupils blown. "I'm still hungry."

Somehow, I don't think she's talking about just food, though it's unlikely she wants me as much as I want her.

I'm an incubus. A sex demon. No one has ever been able to

match my appetite. During her heat, I feasted on her lust, gorging myself by bringing her orgasm after orgasm, but now…

Now I'm hungry again. And she won't be in heat again until next year.

Despite my obvious arousal, I turn my face to stone. "Eat."

I offer her another slice of venison. Thank God she obeys me, biting it from my hand. I contemplate my next move. It would be safest to bury my needs deep, where no one—not even myself—can find them.

"You must be rock hard." She reaches for my erection.

I capture her by the wrist before she can touch me. "Don't."

She sucks in her breath, her eyes flying open wide, betraying a hint of fear. This shouldn't arouse me, and yet it does. As an incubus, I love it when my prey wants to run away from me.

"Don't touch me there," I clarify, "unless you want me to hunt you down in the forest and fuck you like my prey."

She shudders, unable to hide her reaction. "That *is* what I want."

I release her wrist as if her skin scalded me. It's dangerous to touch her for too long, dangerous to succumb to my primal desires. "Are you certain? You would be the prey of an incubus."

"Would you devour me?"

"Correct."

"Yes, please." She shivers. "Hunt me down."

Filthy thoughts flood my imagination. I want her begging me to fuck her harder, so slick with my seed and her own arousal that she's dripping between her thighs. A shaky breath escapes me.

"You consent to it all?" I ask.

"I do."

I'm the luckiest demon alive.

My shadow wings erupt from my shoulders, menacing. "Run."

She leaps into a sprint and flees deeper in the forest.

The muscles in my thighs tense. I'm tempted to lunge after her, but tonight, I'm feeling indulgent. I need to give her a head start. Otherwise, this hunt will be over far too soon. My tail snakes from my spine and whips with impatience. I wait until my erection subsides.

Evening shadows gather beneath the forest. I prowl into the gloom. I can see in the dark, but so can she. It makes her more challenging to hunt down. I stop and hold my breath to listen for any sign of movement. A dead leaf crunches underfoot. It's surprisingly close. I cock my head, listening for movement. She must be taunting me, circling me.

Of course. She's a dragon shifter. Always the predator, never the prey.

Until tonight.

I breathe in deep until I detect her scent drifting in the air. She's sweating. Her heart must be pounding. Does she fear me? Does she fear what I will do to her? I would be lying if I said this didn't thrill me.

Pyrah flees from me. I glimpse a flash of her red hair before she disappears again. Leaves rustle in her wake, the forest closing behind her again.

I veer to the left, faster than her, and overtake her.

When she runs past me, she doesn't even see me crouching behind a tree.

I'm ready for her. My body is a weapon.

I lunge. We hit the ground hard, my arms caging her. She

struggles to break free, but I flip her onto her back and pin her wrists down to the dirt.

"Mine." I grit out the word.

She braces her legs on the ground and tries to push me off her, but she succeeds only in lifting her hips against mine. I grind against her, my cock still trapped behind leather, and a sweet little whimper escapes her throat.

"Your cunt belongs to me," I say.

She gasps, her eyes even wider, and keeps fighting me. The intoxicating scent of her arousal thickens the air. She likes the word *cunt*. Good.

My shadow wings arch high above us both.

She's my prey, and I don't want anyone else to see her.

When I release one of her wrists, her hand fists in my long hair. She holds me there, her teeth bared at me, before grabbing me by one of my horns. She's still battling for control.

"Fuck you." She's daring me to do something, her eyes challenging me.

"Fight me as much as you want, but you won't break free." I slide my hand between her thighs. My voice has plummeted an octave. "Not while your cunt is drenched for me."

I dip the hard point of my demonic tail into her wet heat. She shudders, her eyelids flickering shut, her mouth rounding with momentary bliss.

"You want me inside you." It's not a question, but I pause long enough that she can refuse me or revoke her consent.

"I do," she confesses.

When I claim her mouth in a fierce kiss, she gasps against my lips. I swallow the sound along with a hint of her desire. I'm not devouring her, not yet. Her hand slides down the armor on my chest before finding my cock, still trapped beneath my leather trousers.

She breaks the kiss. Breathless, she speaks. "Get off me. Let me go or I can't suck your cock."

Fuck. My mind blanks.

She's never sucked my cock before. How did she know the fantasies in my head? Perhaps I was staring for too long at her mouth while she was kneeling. This wasn't part of our game. It wasn't one of the rules of our hunt, though I would be a fool to refuse her curiosity.

"You haven't done this before, have you?"

"Never."

Cautiously, I release her and let her crawl away from me. She gets onto her knees. Her cheeks look pink, betraying her innocence at this kind of fucking. There's so much we have yet to explore together.

"Close your eyes," she says.

Suspicion jolts through me, but I obey, knowing damn well what she's about to do next. My eyes fly open the instant she flees from me. She laughs with delighted fear. It's a dare for me to catch her.

I chase her down and tackle her from behind. I pin her against a tree, her breasts pressed against the bark. She's struggling beneath me, trying to escape. I admire her beautiful ass from behind.

"Wicked girl." A low growl rumbles from my throat. "Don't you dare trick me."

I want to punish her with bliss.

When I unbutton my fly, my cock springs free. I stroke myself in my fist. The spikes on my cock glide with my foreskin, sensitive to the slightest touch, and ache to be buried inside her. She fights to break free, but I part her thighs with my knee and bare her cunt to me.

The blunt head of my cock demands entrance. She tenses up beneath me.

"Easy." I murmur the word as if speaking to a wild animal.

"Rook," she gasps.

"I don't want to hurt you." It sounds like a gentle threat when I say it, which wasn't my intention. "Tell me when to stop."

"Don't stop."

She's shivering beneath me, her whole body alive with unspent tension. I stroke into her slowly. The ridges on my cock grind into her, harder than flesh, until she's forced to take all of me.

My breath hisses out through my gritted teeth. "Your cunt feels like heaven."

She shudders, her inner muscles clenching around me like a prelude to climax.

I fuck her from behind. Slow at first, then faster and harder. She arches her hips, seeking more pleasure with shameless little whimpers. Her legs start trembling beneath her so I hold her against me.

"Please," she whispers, breathless.

I close my shadow wings around us both, hiding us in a dark cocoon. My wings have spikes on them, one for each digit, much like the claws on my fingers. I'm careful not to hurt her with them.

My tail wraps around one of her thighs with a mind of its own. I slide it higher between her legs and play with her cunt until her whole body tenses. She flings her head back against my shoulder. My claws twist in her hair and hold her exactly where I want her, a willing victim for an incubus.

When I devour her mouth, it's enough to push her over the edge.

She cries out, coming hard, and I drink down the sound along with every drop of her ecstasy. Her knees buckle and I let her fall down to her hands and knees. At this angle, I can fuck her deeper. I slide my claws along her throat, no more than a sharp caress on her skin, and tilt her head skyward so I can keep kissing her from above. Ruthlessly, I hammer into her until she's writhing beneath me and trying to ride my cock from below.

She's close again, I can taste it, but she needs more.

"Come inside me," she begs. "Fill me until I'm overflowing."

Fuck. My balls tense up. Her request evokes a primal urge in me, and I'm forced to obey. Groaning, I chase my own climax. An intense wave of pleasure roars through me. I slam my hips forward with a hoarse grunt and unload my seed in her. She follows me a second later, screaming through her climax until I silence her with another devouring kiss.

Lost to bliss, she collapses beneath me. I roll us over, protecting her from the hard ground, and let my body be her bed. We lie there together, staring at the sky, while the first stars blink into life. Finally, the gnawing empty feeling inside me is gone, and my incubus hunger is satisfied for one night.

One night has to be enough.

"My cunt feels like heaven?" she asks, echoing my words from before.

I grunt. "I'm not lying."

"Says the man with a cock from hell."

I freeze. Was she disappointed by me? "Would you like me to be less demonic?"

She shakes her head. "Wouldn't you need to be less aroused?"

"Yes."

"Then I wouldn't ask for anything else. Although I won't lie, your cock scares me sometimes. It's so big and it has spikes."

"They aren't sharp," I say, in my defense.

"I know."

She gives my cock a squeeze, even though it's soft right now and my spikes are hidden, much like my shadow wings and tail. I'm not sure anyone has ever touched me there in a gentle way before.

"What are you doing?" I ask, puzzled.

"Sorry. I can't keep my hands off you."

"Even when I'm not hard?"

"You're still Rook. Still mine."

I'm silent for a moment, pondering her words. She loves my body even when I'm not aroused. It's an unusual feeling for an incubus, a sex demon.

"We should go back," I say.

She laughs softly. "Sorry, I can't walk. My legs have become boneless."

I grunt. That's easy enough to solve. With minimal effort, I lift her into my arms. She leans her head against my chest as if she wants to hear my heartbeat. We aren't far from her cave, so I carry her all the way back home. Beneath the darkening sky, the lake looks a deep purple, the color reminiscent of plums.

"Let me take care of you," I say.

I bring her down to the water. It's cold enough that she sucks in her breath when I wash her. The lake must be fed from snowmelt higher in the mountains.

"Sorry this isn't a hot bath," I say.

"The inn in Havenwold had a nice one."

My mouth twitches with a smile. "Shame you destroyed the place."

"I blame the queen's knights."

I would rather forget the queen right now. "How many times have I needed to wash you, woman? You're always dirty."

"I blame you."

"It's a price I'm willing to pay."

Pyrah rolls her eyes at my joke. She walks back to her cave by herself, even though I'm more than capable of carrying her there. I can't help admiring her ass while she walks ahead of me. We enter the shadows of her cave together.

"You're shivering." I hold her close against me, trying to lend her my warmth.

She yawns. "I'm so tired."

"Sleep."

She glances down at her naked body. "Not like this. I always shift into a dragon when I sleep in my cave. It's more comfortable that way. Safer."

"I can't hold you in my arms while you're a dragon."

"You could try." A corner of her mouth bends into a smile.

I fold my arms across my chest. "Don't tease me. It won't work."

"But I like teasing you," she purrs.

That's a decent attempt to distract me, but I have work to do. "Save your seduction for later. I'm heading out."

She hugs herself as if she's cold without me. "You're leaving?"

"Can't forget the rest of the venison. And we left the campfire burning."

"Don't start any wildfires in my territory."

"Not tonight." I twist my mouth into something that resembles a smile, just to show her I'm joking.

Alone, I return to the campfire, which has died down to embers. I scatter them with my boot and kick dirt over the remnants.

When I turn around, my blood turns cold. Like ice in my veins.

The deer carcass is gone, nothing left of the venison but bloodstains. Not even bones or antlers. I crouch by the trampled grass. Judging by the tracks, the deer wasn't dragged away, so a predator must have consumed it here.

Dire wolves? I'm not aware of a pack this far outside of the Thornwood. Even dire wolves would have left bones behind.

Only a dragon could have swallowed a deer whole.

"Fuck."

Dragon shifters are rare. Too rare to leave me with much doubt about our intruder.

# CHAPTER FIFTEEN

PYRAH

Inside the gloom of my lair, a mountain of treasure glimmers in the shadows. Kneeling, I scoop up handfuls of gold coins and gems before letting them trickle through my fingers. With a shuddering sigh, I close my eyes and savor this moment. It takes me a minute to name this feeling, which I haven't felt in far too long. The sensation glows inside my chest.

*I'm happy.*

Though I should be shifting into a dragon and sleeping on a bed of gold, I linger in the body of a woman. If Rook wants to hold me in his arms tonight, I can wait for him to come back and keep me warm.

Besides, I enjoy being smaller than him. When I'm with him, I don't need to worry about protecting myself, and I'm comfortable removing the armor of my dragon scales. He has given me the safety to be vulnerable and surrender to him in ways no other man ever could.

I touch my mouth, finding my lips swollen from his kisses. My breasts are also unusually tender. I cradle them in my hands, wondering why they feel so full and heavy. He didn't pay special attention to them this time. My nipples have become sensitive to the slightest of touches.

Even stranger, a cramp twinges through my belly.

*Am I pregnant?*

The old legends about dragon eggs aren't true—we dragon shifters birth our babies and nurse them with milk, just like human women. My breasts have never felt this way before. Could this be why?

I place my hand flat against my belly, imagining a flicker of life inside me. Rook told me himself that he's a cambion and he's incapable of fathering a child. But what if, against all odds, he's wrong?

My mother never told me about such things. She died before she could explain what pregnancy means for our kind. I can only piece together what I have heard gossiped among human women. More than a few maidens in Quickmire whispered their secrets in the tavern—a tumble in the hayloft with their lover, followed by a hasty wedding.

Hope flutters inside my chest like a caged bird. When I close my eyes, I can't help imagining what our baby might look like. Would they have his silver skin? My blue eyes? Would our child inherit my ability to shift into a dragon, or his power to walk through dreams?

My eyes sting with unspent tears. Rook might see this as a miracle.

I imagine the look on his face when I tell him. His ember eyes would glow brighter, stoked by a breath of hope. That determined, often grim set of his jaw would soften into wonder.

I never wanted children before. The thought of being a mother terrified me, after dragonslayers murdered my own mother and left me desolate. For years, I could think only of my own survival, living alone in my cave, guarding my hoard. Wanting a baby was far too vulnerable.

But now, sitting among my treasure, all I can think about is how empty this cave feels. Gold and jewels glitter around me, but they're just *things*. Cold metal that offers no warmth, no love in return. They hold memories of my mother, but memories stopped being enough.

Rook has changed everything.

The truth of it strikes my heart. *I want his baby*. Someone to love and nurture, someone who would never know the loneliness I have endured. I would protect our baby with all the ferocity of a dragon mother.

Am I hurting myself by allowing myself to hope?

The next cramp doubles me over. Intense pain slices through my abdomen like a dagger. Shuddering, I collapse onto the gold coins and curl into a ball. Something warm trickles down my thighs.

My heart pounds as I look down. Blood. Bright and red against my pale skin.

The sight hits me like a fist to the gut. Not a baby. Just my body betraying me in a new, cruel way. The pain twists deeper, as if punishing me for daring to want something I can never have. Tears blur my vision, and I hate myself for crying. Dragons don't cry. Dragons don't bleed like this.

But they do.

Scaldric's voice slithers through my mind, dripping with cruel satisfaction: *Because of him, you will bleed.*

Moonlight streams through the entrance of the cave, casting long shadows across my treasure hoard. I press my hands against my cramping belly, each wave of pain a reminder of my empty womb.

Rook will never give me a baby.

The truth buries me like an avalanche. I had known this, of course—cambions can't father children. But it never felt like reality until this moment, watching my blood stain the gold beneath me.

My throat aches, a hot coal of pain lodged inside. I don't even know if Rook longs to be a father. He has never confessed such a thing to me. I could be dreaming of a future he doesn't even want.

More tears spill down my cheeks before I swipe them away. Even alone, I despise this display of weakness. My mother taught me better than this. Emotions make you vulnerable. Tears make you prey. But I can't stop crying. The pain, the humiliation, the utter helplessness of this situation—it's too much to endure. I'm no longer the fearsome dragon who guarded this cave. I'm just a woman, crying on the floor, bleeding and afraid.

I close my eyes and reach for that familiar power inside me, the dragonfire that burns in my blood. My bones should be lengthening, scales armoring my skin, wings unfurling from my back.

Nothing happens.

I try again, desperate now. The transformation has always come as easily as breathing. But the dragon within me has become distant, unreachable, like trying to grasp smoke with my bare hands.

"No," I whisper. "Please, no."

My shift is locked away, leaving me small and vulnerable in this echoing cave. The treasure around me mocks me. What use is a dragon's hoard to a woman who can no longer be a dragon?

I pick up a sapphire from my hoard, turning it over in my trembling hands. The gem's familiar weight anchors me as another cramp tears through my belly. Bigger than a goose egg, the blue stone catches moonlight from the cave's entrance, glowing with an inner fire.

I focus on the gem's perfect facets rather than the bleeding staining my skin. My reflection fragments across the cut surfaces—a hundred tiny versions of my pale face, each one distorted. I trace the largest facet with my fingertip, watching the moonlight dance through the crystal's heart. The deep blue reminds me of mountain lakes, of summer skies I once soared through on dragon wings. When I'm a dragon, I'm more like this gemstone.

The sapphire doesn't feel pain. It doesn't dream of the impossible.

The gem's coolness seeps into my hand as I cling to it as if it might save me. Each glint distracts me from the cramps, if only for moments at a time. I count the faces, name each angle, catalog every flaw and inclusion—anything to distract myself from my body's betrayal.

I hear footsteps at the cave entrance. Rook.

My time hiding has run out.

I clutch the sapphire tighter, willing my hands to stop shaking. The gem's cold weight grounds me as I hear his boots scuff against stone. I keep my back to him, pretending to examine the jewel's facets in the shadows. In truth, I'm holding my breath, waiting for him to speak.

"Pyrah, we have a problem." I brace myself, certain he has already noticed the iron scent of blood, but his next words aren't what I expected. "The deer is gone. Completely vanished."

"What?"

His footsteps draw closer. "Are there dire wolves in your territory?"

When another cramp hits me, I bite my lip to keep from crying out. I shake my head and focus on breathing through the pain. "No wolves would dare hunt here. Not in my territory."

"My thoughts exactly. Which means—"

"Another dragon." My voice sounds hoarse. "Scaldric?"

"Has to be." He stops in his tracks. "Pyrah? What's wrong?"

I have doubled over, the sapphire slipping from my grasp. It hits the pile of gold with a musical chime. The pain has become too intense for me to hide my weakness from him any longer.

"I'm bleeding," I whisper. "Scaldric was right."

# CHAPTER SIXTEEN

ROOK

My throat throttles at her words, stealing my breath away. Blood stains the gold where she must have been resting, waiting for me to return. It was foolish of me to imagine this ending any other way.

Foolish of me to hope.

“Shift into a dragon,” I say, already fearing the worst.

Shivering, she hugs herself, looking more vulnerable than ever. “I can’t.”

"You tried?"

"Of course I tried." Her eyes gleam with sorrow. “It’s as if that part of me is locked away without a key.”

Scaldric was right again, despite being a useless idiot. I would bet gold on that fucker lurking around here, lying in wait for Pyrah. She's all but defenseless without the ability to become a dragon.

"We wasted time," I say, glowering. "We should have been ready."

"This has never happened to me before." She glances at her red fingertips as if still disbelieving her own body's weaknesses. "What do I do? Find some rags? I don't even have my own clothes."

"I should have bought you some sooner." Instead of lusting over her while she was naked. I succumbed to my own worst tendencies instead of taking care of her like a decent man. "I can still help."

"How?"

"Bleeding is bleeding. I have bandages."

"Bandages? Rook, I'm not wounded."

I give her a long look. "Are you in pain?"

"Yes, but—"

"Don't argue with me, woman. You aren't even standing up straight."

Wincing, she rubs her belly again. "You win. I surrender."

"Good."

My pack waits at the edge of the cave. I crouch down and rummage through it. Besides the bandages, my supplies are limited. I find a clump of dried bog moss, useful for treating injuries, though I remember that human women also use it to stanch their monthly bleeding.

I left most of my things with my horse, Bolt, locked away in the stable outside Netherhaven. I need to go back and ride Bolt here, but it's a long way to the city without taking a portal.

"What if Scaldric comes back?" Pyrah asks.

"I will kill him." Despite the anger simmering inside me, my voice sounds deadly calm, and I speak nothing but the truth. "Don't try to convince me to spare his life twice."

I bring her the bandages, moss, and some of my spare clothes. She slips on one of my shirts, which falls to her knees.

"You have no undergarments, do you?" she asks.

"Unfortunately not."

"That was never a problem until now." She stares at the bandages and bog moss, then laughs, a broken kind of sound. "What should I do with these? I have never had to do this before."

"We may need to get creative."

"Sometimes I hate being female. This couldn't get any more mortifying."

Keeping my face blank, I tilt my head. "Would you prefer some privacy?"

"It doesn't matter. I don't care." The glittering in her eyes spills over into tears. "I can't turn into a dragon."

"I'm sorry." My words make her cry harder, though I don't understand why. Her pain echoes inside me. I touch her cheek with my thumb and rub away one of her tears. "Pyrah, *lirithel*."

"*Lirithel?*" She stumbles over the word. "Is that demonic?"

"Umbric, the common language of the Underworld."

"What does it mean?"

"Roughly translated, it's an endearment that means 'my dream.'"

She stares at me as if spellbound. "Rook." Tears keep rolling down her cheeks. "I don't deserve you."

"That's not true."

The words rasp out of me. She couldn't be more wrong. Of all the beings in the Overworld and the Underworld, she's the one who deserves every scrap of care I can offer, though I'm still learning how to give it. I drag her into an embrace, her cheek pressed against my chest.

"I don't want to get blood on you," she protests.

I shake my head at her concern, which is sweet but misguided. "I have been far bloodier during battle."

"True." She laughs through her tears. "Will you help me?"

"Without question."

Together, we fashion the bandages and moss into a makeshift undergarment. It's enough to keep her comfortable for tonight.

I glance at the piles of gleaming treasure in her cave. "Where do you sleep?"

"Curled up on the gold." Her cheeks flush pink as if she's embarrassed by this confession. "I don't need a bed when I'm a dragon."

How did she survive without me? A little comfort won't hurt her.

I sigh. "I will be your pillow tonight."

After unbuckling my armor, I unbutton my shirt and tug it over my head. She can't resist glancing at my bare chest, though temptation wasn't my intent. I have nothing but a blanket to spread on the cold, hard stone, since I left my bedroll in the stable with Bolt. This will have to do. I lie down, wait for Pyrah to follow me, and tuck her into the crook of my arm.

"Why have you never spoken Umbric to me before?" she asks.

"It's a crime in Chymeria."

"Was that Queen Dulcamara's command?"

"For this, she can't be blamed." I frown. "It has been a crime since the time of my great-grandfather, King Thorin the Great, son of King Mallex the Wrong. He didn't want demons in his kingdom."

She's silent for a moment. "Sometimes I forget you have royal blood. You're the descendant of kings. The Gray Prince."

"I'm not royalty."

"Rook, there's no other heir to the throne. Just you and your sister, and there's a prophecy with your name on it."

I hum low in my throat, a neutral noise, before falling silent. It's dark outside the cave, and it has started to rain. Its whispering fills the night. The rich, sweet smell of wet earth drifts inside.

I never thought I would find such peace.

Pyrah shivers. "I'm cold." She burrows deeper under the blanket.

"Let me keep you warm."

She huddles against me as if she wants to steal my heat. "Do demons dream?"

"Of course." I tuck the blanket closer around her body. "An incubus hunts for prey in the dreams of others, but we also have dreams of our own."

"What do you dream about?"

I pause, pondering her question. I don't wish to tell her about my nightmares. "On good or bad nights?"

"Good."

"You," I confess. "*Lirithel* is more than simply an endearment."

"Are these dreams filthy?"

"On occasion. Though not always, despite my incubus nature."

She's silent for a long moment. "And on bad nights?"

I hesitate, not wanting to burden her with my darkest thoughts. But her question hangs in the air, demanding an answer.

"On bad nights," I say, "I dream of my father."

"Nightmares?"

My words roughen with remembered pain. "He hurt me. Often."

"Why?"

I don't often delve into this darkness, for the fear that it might swallow me whole. My shadow wings unfurl, an involuntary reaction that betrays my distress. I'm unable to will them away.

"Sometimes he had a reason," I admit. "Sometimes he had none at all."

Pyrah embraces me tighter, as if she can shield me from my own memories, from the shadows within myself. The protective love in her touch means more than words ever could.

"You never deserved what he did to you," she whispers.

Relief floods through me. I had expected her to question me, but she's giving me the space to heal and the gift of silence.

"Thank you." My voice comes out rough.

My shadow wings fade away as the tension ebbs from my muscles. Here in the darkness of her cave, with the hush of rain and her warmth pressed against me, I feel something unfamiliar.

It takes me a moment to name it as *safety*.

We're silent for some time, while neither one of us is asleep yet. The rain falls harder outside, drumming against the ground. The steady rhythm isn't enough to lull me into slumber. I'm still distracted by what lies ahead of us. My mind gnaws at the future like a dog with a bone.

"Lark will return by midnight," I say.

"What if she doesn't?"

"Then I will find her in Netherhaven." I don't mention my fears out loud, as if that will prevent them from coming true. Lark could be captured or hurt.

"Don't go."

"Pyrah." My arms tighten around her. "If I do go, I will return. I promise."

It's not a promise I intend to break, but an undercurrent of dread flows through my veins.

Scaldric won't stop until he has captured her.

Queen Dulcamara won't stop until she has defeated us both.

Snow drifts down upon Hexfall in the night, the castle returned to its former glory. Despite the winter chill, the cursed roses in the Thornwood still bloom everlasting. Their red petals splash the white like blood.

The statue of King Mallex the Wrong wears a mantle of icicles. I walk across the snow-blanketed courtyard of the castle and enter the throne room. The ruined throne gleams in black marble, still cracked down the middle, but the unraveling tapestries and shattered windows have been replaced.

This does not surprise me, though I don't know why. I wander through the castle and climb upstairs to a bedchamber, the room furnished with royal luxury. In the fireplace, cheerful flames crackle.

Pyrah sits in a chair by the window and watches the falling snow. When she sees me, she smiles. She's holding a baby to her breast.

A baby with pale skin, a soft wisp of white hair, and the nubs of horns.

*Our* baby.

I know that the baby is a girl. I have a daughter.

I drop to my knees and reach out to the baby. With the back of my knuckle, I stroke one of her pudgy little fists. When she opens her eyes, they glint a strange yet beautiful violet, unlike the blue eyes of her mother or the red of her father.

What is her name? How old is she?

Why have I forgotten?

The perfection of this winter night shatters beneath my skepticism.

I jolt awake. My chest aches as if it has been carved out and left hollow. A profound sense of loss fills the void inside me.

I glance down at Pyrah, who's still asleep in my arms. She's snoring, quietly, the sound reminiscent of a bumblebee. I spoke the truth when I said I dreamed of her, but I can't confess this dream of having a baby with her.

It's an impossible future. Glimpsing it brings me nothing but pain.

I hold Pyrah a little tighter, praying that she won't wake and ask me why I'm hurting. I'm not silver-tongued at the best of times, and words would fail me now. It's a cruel thing to want what remains forever out of reach.

I never asked to be born a cambion. Sometimes I hate myself.

I stare into the darkness until I can numb myself to my feelings. They mean nothing when they are irrelevant to survival. I learned this truth through years and years of hard experience.

At the brink of the cave, Lark whispers my name, "Rook."

She's back. Thank hell and heavens. I employ stealth and escape without waking Pyrah, then follow my sister outside.

The moon shines white like a fat slice of cheese. Lark perches on the edge of the cliff and swings her legs in the air. Unlike me, she can fly. Our shadow wings aren't enough, but she was also born with magic. With more caution, I sit near the edge. Far below, the lake with no name glistens black in the darkness.

"What time is it?" I ask.

"The bells rang once in town."

"One o'clock. You're late."

Lark flashes her fangs in a grin. Her silver skin looks lustrous in the moonlight, the mark of a well-fed succubus.

"Kill any knights?" I ask, without any judgment in my voice.

"Not this time." She runs her tongue over one of her fangs, as if she can still taste some lingering desire. "Do you miss it?"

"Miss what?"

"Hunting your prey in taverns, bathhouses, and back alleys."

I snort. "Not in the slightest."

Her gaze intense, Lark searches my eyes. "You're in love with her, aren't you?"

My eyebrows jump skyward. "How could you tell?"

"You try to hide it beneath that grim face of yours, but you do have a heart."

I scratch behind one of my horns. "This is how I am."

She elbows me in the ribs, not hard enough to hurt. "I've never seen you act so devoted. You follow Pyrah around like a lost wolf pup."

"I'm no pup."

Lark smirks at me. "I'm surprised you haven't started wagging your tail."

"Now you're just fucking with me."

"I'm not. Mum would agree."

My stomach drops like a stone. "Mum's gone."

"I refuse to believe that."

Queen Dulcamara loathed our mother, who was the king's favorite courtesan. Our father never gave Dulcamara a baby, a proper heir to the throne, though he had the audacity to grant our mother bastard twins. And so the court whispered behind Dulcamara's back, calling her the barren queen.

Lark clings to the misguided hope that our mother fled from the castle at Netherhaven and escaped the queen's wrath alive. It's a fool's dream, though I don't want to break my sister's heart into even smaller pieces.

"Look." Lark gazes at the sky. "The Underworld."

Far above, it's nothing more than a blue gemstone in the sky. Stare hard enough, and you can discern its twin moons. I have never set foot upon the Underworld myself, though I have seen paintings of its moonrises. Years ago, the queen ordered the Demongate between the worlds to be sealed.

Lark keeps staring at the sky. "What if she's waiting for us in the Underworld?"

I don't need to ask who she means. "Mum died."

"We don't know that. We never buried her." My sister speaks fiercely, as if my disbelief is tantamount to blasphemy.

"I don't want you to foolishly hope."

"Hope is one of the few things we have left."

Her words should inspire me, and yet they bring more despair. I have learned to hold on to nothing but small fistfuls of hope. Anything larger would slow me down too much when I need to run away.

"I need to take care of Pyrah. She's vulnerable right now."

"Vulnerable?" Lark frowns. "How?"

"She can't shift into a dragon."

Her breath catches in her throat. "Why not? What happened?"

"She started her bleeding."

"Oh. *Oh.*" Lark grimaces with a knowing nod. "Dragon women can't shift during their flow? That sounds awful."

I square my shoulders. "We may need your help."

"I can brew a tea that will help Pyrah with any pain."

"Thank you. I'm in your debt."

Her smile fades, her eyes turning sober. "You saved me. My debt to you can never be repaid."

"Lark." I glance at her broken horn. "What happened to you in the Forgotten Tower? I understand if you don't wish to tell me, though it may help to unburden yourself from these memories."

She turns her gaze onto the black waters of the nameless lake. "First, I should tell you how I betrayed the queen."

"I'm listening."

"When I became Queen Dulcamara's royal sorceress, I quickly won her favor. She praised me for my magic in front of the whole court. But I never should have trusted her intentions. Her words were nothing but poisoned honey."

She swallows hard, her throat working, and I wait for her in silence.

"Dulcamara brought me a baby boy, a pitiful little thing from some orphanage, and a finger bone dug from our father's grave. She commanded me to work dark magic, a wicked alchemy to turn the baby's blood royal."

My teeth start aching until I force myself to unclench my jaw. "She wanted an heir." It's not a question.

"And I refused to give her one."

I let out a harsh breath. "What happened to the baby?"

"I couldn't return him to the orphanage, since I knew he wouldn't be safe there any longer. I cast a portal to a distant temple where priestesses care for foundlings. They took the baby from me."

"Dulcamara must have been furious."

Lark laughs bleakly. "I thought she might try to strangle me herself. Gods, she was so angry. She said I must be the one who cast the spell, and when I refused her demands, she banished me to the Forgotten Tower."

"Why you? Why couldn't another royal sorceress do it?"

"She said it had to be me, since I have the king's blood in me. Robbing his grave wasn't enough."

"Fuck." I shake my head and repeat, with emphasis, "*Fuck*."

"I know."

My hatred for the queen burns like an unquenchable fire, but I'm unable to deny my twisted sympathy for her. She wanted a baby when she couldn't have one. I understand what that means.

We're silent for a moment, until I think to ask, "Who broke your horn?"

"One of the guards," Lark says, with a nearly imperceptible shudder. "He did it after I tried to escape from the Forgotten Tower. He was a blacksmith before he worked for the queen, and he knew how to wield a hammer. He stopped me from bleeding out by holding a red-hot poker to the wound."

The horns of a demon have blood vessels within the bone. Breaking one could be fatal without treatment, but breaking one just to maim seems especially cruel. I swallow hard. The queen's men have no souls.

"Do I need to kill him?" Though I speak softly, rage roughens my voice.

"I don't want to go back to the Forgotten Tower."

My mind wrestles with a dark question. How did Lark survive in that tower?

Demons like us need to feed on lust to survive. Without it, we waste away until death, our silver skin turning gray as ash.

"Someone helped you." The words tumble from my lips.

Lark's shoulders stiffen as she hunches over. "What do you mean?"

"Whatever happened in that dungeon, whatever you had to do to survive… I won't judge you for it."

She shakes her head. The movement catches moonlight on

her broken horn. Her silence tells me she doesn't want to share. But if someone helped keep her alive, I need to know if they are a threat.

When I speak again, I tread carefully. "Was it another prisoner?"

"No." Her voice comes out small.

"A guard, then?"

When she hesitates, my stomach sours. The queen's guards would never show her mercy, not without demanding payment in return. And without her magic, Lark's only currency would be her body.

"Not a guard," she says.

I frown into the darkness. "When you worked as a royal sorceress, was anyone in the queen's court an ally?"

Lark's eyes meet mine, her breath escaping in a cloud of white. *She's ready to tell me,* I think.

But then she jolts to her feet. "Is that him?" she whispers, her face tilted skyward.

I'm surprised by her reaction until I follow her gaze. Far in the distance, a glint of gold flashes in the moonlight.

The golden dragon is on the hunt.

I lunge to my feet with my hand on my sword, though I'm still bruised from the last battle. That won't stop me from defending my mate.

"Rook, no." Lark grabs my arm. "Don't."

"Scaldric." I spit his name like a curse. "Go back to the cave. Hide."

"And leave you alone? Like hell I will."

"He hasn't seen us yet."

"He will if you keep standing on the edge of the cliff like some moronic hero."

*Fuck*. She's right. "Let's go."

# CHAPTER SEVENTEEN

ROOK

Pyrah tosses and turns under my blanket, her sleep restless. Perhaps she dreams of nightmares without me.

She has no idea that she's being stalked.

Crouching, I touch her arm. "Pyrah. Wake up."

"Come back." She mumbles the words. "I'm cold without you."

"We can't. Scaldric is outside."

That catches her attention. She jolts upright before grimacing and holding her stomach. "He's here?"

"He's flying over the forest. He must be looking for us." I shake my head and correct myself. "Looking for *you*."

Pyrah's hand darts to the scars on her neck, no doubt remembering when Scaldric bit her without her consent.

Lark misses nothing. "That dragon bit you, didn't he?"

"He did," Pyrah admits, "even after I refused him."

My sister's eyes burn like hellfire itself. "And you haven't killed him yet, Rook?"

Beneath my ice-cold calm, simmering rage flows through my veins. "That can be arranged." My hand drops to the hilt of my sword. I'm resisting the urge to charge into battle. "Though it may be a wiser choice to hide at this moment. Lark, how long will it take you to cast the spell?"

Lark glances at the mouth of the cave. "Not long."

"I will stand guard outside."

Pyrah pushes herself to her feet. "I'm coming with you."

"Absolutely not."

"I won't cower in my cave while an enemy dragon flies over my territory." She locks eyes with me, as if daring me to stop her from doing something reckless. "I will show no weakness to Scaldric."

"No." I glower down at her. "You can't shift."

"He doesn't know that."

I'm more than capable of keeping her safe, even if I'm not her expected mate. I'm no dragon, but demons are fiercely loyal and dangerous to anyone who threatens their loved ones.

"Pyrah." I don't blink. "I must protect you."

"I can protect myself."

"As your mate, I consider it my responsibility and privilege."

Some of the fight leaves her eyes, betraying the emotion she buried deeper—fear. "What if he attacks?"

"That's my excuse to destroy him."

Before she can protest, I stride into the night and guard the mouth of her cave.

Both women follow me. Lark begins to cast the spell while Pyrah watches her. There's no sign of the golden dragon, but I know he's out there, lurking, ready to pounce on any opportunity.

I don't intend to give him one.

Lark moves with the fluid grace of an accomplished sorceress. Magic flies from her fingertips in indigo sparks. She strokes the air as if painting it with light, tossing fistfuls of magic against the rocks around the cave. It has a strange scent, one that reminds me of a library full of musty old books. Not that I've spent much time in a library since I left the castle.

I liked to read, once, when I was a boy, but that Rook died a long time ago.

Turning my back on the magic, I stare out into the darkness, grateful that my demonic blood gives me excellent night vision. Every muscle in my body remains tense and ready for a fight.

Pyrah takes her place by my side. Her hair streams behind her in the wind, and her face looks even paler in the moonlight. She must still be in pain. Maybe she's weakened from blood loss.

"Sleep," I say, knowing she won't obey me.

She exhales in a cloud of white. "I can't."

"If he tries to touch you, I will kill him."

"Murder isn't always the answer."

"It solves the majority of problems."

Pyrah glances sideways at me, perhaps bemused by my reaction. "Or it increases the bounty on your head."

Emotionless, I shrug. "It would be worth it."

Luminous blue mist creeps into the air between us. It pours over the cliff like a waterfall and spreads over the nameless lake, where it fogs the dark water. The moon hides her face behind wisps of mist. We behold a world of surreal beauty. I turn around, slowly, as if lost in a dream.

Lark shapes the air with her hands. Mist trails from her fingers and swirls through her silver hair. Undoubtedly, it's the same spell that hides her cottage in the Thornwood.

Soon the magic cools off, and the mist fades from blue to white.

"My cave," Pyrah says. We can't even see it from where we stand. "How do I find my way back?"

Lark flicks the lingering magic from her hands. "Don't believe whatever you feel, but trust that you will make it through."

Dewdrops of mist cling to Pyrah's hair. She journeys deeper into the pale void, feeling the space ahead of her with her hands, before she vanishes from my sight. She must be safe, but my heartbeat quickens.

I frown at my sister. I know there are always rules with magic, so I ask her, "What are the rules of this spell?"

"Only the three of us can find the way through. If anyone else tries, they will be lost in the mist until they leave this place behind. Not even dragonfire can burn through the mist."

"Good. That was one of my concerns. How long will the spell last?"

Lark tilts her head. "Seven months or so. That's how often I strengthen the spell around my cottage."

I take both of her hands in mine. "Thank you."

"Of course." She glances into my eyes. "I'm still in your debt."

"Not forever."

A smile shadows her mouth. "You had better follow Pyrah."

I do as I'm told.

The mist swirls around me, disorienting me. My heartbeat pounds inside my chest. One wrong step, and I might plummet over the edge of the cliff, wishing I could fly.

Lark's words echo in my mind. *Don't believe whatever you feel, but trust that you will make it through.*

The endless mist all around me erases any sign of a path. My eyes convince me that I can't go onward. That's nothing but a lie, since my senses can't be trusted. I exhale hard and imagine myself sinking like a stone to the bottom of a lake.

I stumble into the darkness of the cave.

Pyrah catches me in her arms. I drag her into a tighter embrace. Instinct urges me to never let her out of my sight again, though that would be impossible.

"Rook." She sounds breathless. "You're squeezing me too hard."

I loosen my grip. "Sorry."

It's gloomy inside the cave, more than I had expected. Even I'm struggling to see in the dark. Only the slightest hint of moonlight passes through the enchanted mist.

Lark joins us in the shadows. She cradles an egg of pale green light between her hands. After she tosses it high into the air, it shatters against the stone. Glowing green mushrooms sprout from the walls and illuminate the cave. Treasure gleams under the luminous fungi.

Pyrah escapes from my embrace. When she touches one of the mushrooms with her fingertip, it quivers on its stem and glows a little brighter.

"Beautiful," she breathes. "Thank you."

Lark smiles a tired smile. "I'm glad you like it. Rook doesn't appreciate my prettier spells."

It *is* a pretty cave, even I can admit that, though it's a pity we can't see who lurks outside the mist.

*Pyrah is safe.* I have to tell myself that.

Lark hides a yawn behind her hand. "Good night."

"See you in the morning," I say.

Lark vanishes into the enchanted mist. I'm sure she's taking a portal home, and the crackle of magic confirms my suspicions. The sorceress has gone.

Pyrah gazes at her cave, admiring the glow on her treasure. "Your sister loves mushrooms, doesn't she?"

"Tell me something I don't know." That sounded too gruff, so I soften my voice. "We should go back to bed."

"Bed," she repeats. "I wish we had one."

"I can try to put something together in the morning. Until then, I can protect you from the ground."

"You always want to protect me from something," she says wryly.

I lay down on the blanket and drag her down with me. She rests her head against my chest and closes her eyes. The mist outside cloaks us in silence.

"I can hear your heartbeat," she whispers.

Can she tell how it's pounding with unspent adrenaline? I stroke her hair under my hand, though I'm not sure if I'm comforting her or myself. "I can't sleep," I admit. "Not yet."

"Why not?"

"I won't be able to watch over you."

"You're my mate, Rook, not my bodyguard. We might be in the darkest part of the fairy tale right now, but we still deserve our own happily-ever-after."

My heart aches at her words. "This isn't the darkest part."

"True." She's silent for a moment. "There's too much left undone and unsaid. But I still think we deserve our happiness together."

"What would it look like for you? Happily ever after?"

"This doesn't look too bad."

We lie together in the darkness. The rhythm of my breathing slows to match hers. Unable to resist, I kiss the top of her head.

I never thought I could have such intimacy without lust.

"Damn it," Pyrah whispers. "I can't sleep, either."

I tighten my arm around her. "I'm sorry."

"It's not your fault." She presses closer against me. "I like listening to you talk."

"Why?"

"You have such a deep voice. Gravelly."

"Do I?"

"I love it. I could listen to you speaking for hours."

I grunt. "I never talk that much."

"What's your favorite color?"

Bemused, I frown into the shadows. "My what?"

"Everyone has a favorite color. I want to know more about you."

I ponder this question. "Red." I'm looking at her hair when I say it. "Even before I met you."

"I find that hard to believe." There's laughter in her voice.

"I swear it's the truth. I have always liked wild roses, even the cursed ones at Hexfall." I pause. "And you?"

"Purple."

"Why?"

"Amethysts are my favorite gemstone. They aren't rare, but the color reminds me of twilight on the lake with no name."

"We should name that lake."

"Probably." She plays with my long hair, twisting a lock around her finger. "What's your favorite scent?"

I answer without hesitation: "You."

"You're making me blush. What do you think I smell like?"

"Clovers and incense smoke." My voice drops an octave. "You're also my favorite taste."

"Rook!" She laughs. "You can't be serious."

"I love to devour your desire. And I love to lick your cunt."

She shivers in my arms. "Don't say such dirty things while I'm meant to be resting and not fucking."

"You like it when I say that word, don't you?"

"I do," she confesses.

I have mercy on her and don't continue my seduction. "And you? What scent do you love the most?"

"After your answer, I should change mine." She laughs again. "You do smell good, though, like pine sap. But my favorite smell is the sky after thunder and rain."

"How poetic."

"What's your favorite food?"

"Midnight plums. I stole them from the royal orchard. I loved their sour skin and sweet flesh."

She murmurs her approval at my choice. "I remember these almond cakes in Quickmire, baked for the spring festival. The villagers danced around a maypole and disappeared into the forest for trysts. They thought fucking would bring a good harvest later, not just babies." She snorts. "You weren't my first kiss, you know."

"Oh? Who was it?"

"A pretty boy at the festival. He had green eyes."

My lips twitch with a smile. "Should I be jealous?"

She clicks her tongue. "How many women have you kissed before?"

"I haven't been keeping count."

"Wait, women *and* men." She sounds triumphant. "I remember you telling me that before. That's twice as bad."

I reply without emotion. "I have little choice. A devouring kiss is more than just a kiss. I'm an incubus, and I must feed."

"Would you starve if you didn't?"

"Eventually."

She lets out her breath. "I shouldn't have teased you. I didn't mean to say anything hurtful."

"I'm not offended. I would tell you otherwise."

"Will I be enough for you?"

I mull over her question for a moment. "Once an incubus or succubus finds their mate, they promise to feed from no other. It's an ancient tradition, and demons have survived this way for thousands of years." My arm tightens around her. "My devouring kiss will belong to you and you alone."

"You haven't answered my question," she murmurs.

My chest aches with emotions I don't know how to put into words. They dart through me like birds, too wild to catch. "You are more than enough. It was my fault, not yours, when I took too much from you before. We do need to find our equilibrium, though."

"Our what?"

"Equilibrium. The word makes more sense in Umbric. *Kelrial.* The balance between two partners. In the Underworld, an incubus usually marries a succubus. Each of them must consume lust to survive. To help them find their equilibrium, they undergo a ritual together after their wedding."

"What kind of ritual?" Curiosity sharpens her voice.

"That, I don't know. It's a secret, intimate ritual." I swallow hard. "I know that it requires a soulstone."

"What's a soulstone?"

"A gemstone from the Underworld. My mother inherited one that had been in our family for hundreds of years. Her soulstone looked like the dark twin of a diamond, the color of deepest purple, glittering with trapped fire."

"Oh." Pyrah breathes out the word. "I have nothing like that in my dragon's hoard. Is it valuable?"

"Very." I smile at her obvious desire to covet this gem. "Lark heard rumors of it in the castle at Netherhaven. She thinks our mother hid the soulstone in the royal library, though I have never been back to look for it myself."

"Since you are a dragon's mate, my gold and gems belong to both of us. They have become our family wealth. Would one of them work instead of a soulstone?"

"Unfortunately, they would not. Rare magic from the Underworld imbues a soulstone."

She lifts her head to look at me, her eyes gleaming in the dark. "Why don't we steal the soulstone back from the castle?"

Incredulous, I arch my eyebrows. "We aren't going on any quests together to loot the castle."

She rests her head on my shoulder. "Why not have a dragon wedding instead?" Sleep thickens her words.

I hold my breath for a moment. "Are you asking me to marry you?"

"That was a suggestion. If we followed the rules of dragon courtship, you would be the one asking me."

Some of the tension eases from my muscles. "Understood."

"Can you put your hand on me?"

"Where?"

She takes me by the wrist and brings my hand to her belly. "It helps with the cramps."

This surprises me, though I suppose it must be the weight and the warmth of my touch that comforts her pain. Her breathing deepens. When I glance down, she's already asleep. She found some peace in my arms.

Behind my closed eyes, the lost soulstone glitters with dark fire.

Would it be foolhardy of me to return to the castle?

# CHAPTER EIGHTEEN

ROOK

Pyrah's absence wakes me. I have slept alone for years, but without her beside me, I feel cold and empty-handed.

I go outside. It's dawn, and sunrise paints the sky pale gold. She's standing by the cliff, watching the day begin. The mist thins at the cliff's edge, just enough to give us a view of the blue sky above and the nameless lake below. The air has the icy, crisp scent of possibility.

"How are you this morning?" I ask.

"Better." She exhales in a cloud of white. "It doesn't hurt so much."

"I'm glad." It was difficult for me to watch her in pain, though I tried to keep my worry from my face.

She stares far, far down at the lake below. "It's strange, not being able to shift into a dragon. I miss flying."

I hold her by the wrist as a precaution. "Be careful, woman. I can't save you if you plummet over the cliff."

"I'm not that close to the edge." But perhaps heeding my warning, she moves away. "What's for breakfast?"

"There must be fish in that lake."

We take the path that zigzags down the cliff and leads us to the lake below. Pyrah sits by the shore and hugs her knees against her chest. Wind tosses her hair into her eyes, and I brush it from her face.

"Cold?" I ask.

"Yes," she admits.

"I can build a fire to keep you warm."

"It won't be as fast as dragonfire," she jokes.

I bite back a smile. "I know."

I gather up pieces of driftwood by the lake and arrange them for a campfire in a circle of stones. There's an art to starting a fire, particularly in challenging conditions such as these. Damp clings to the rocky shore of the lake. With my dagger, I carve a stick for tinder, shaving it into thin curls of wood. When I take out my fire steel, Pyrah watches me, her eyes bright in anticipation of flames.

I hit the fire steel with a piece of flint. Sparks leap onto the tinder, though they fade away within seconds. I strike the steel again, harder, and this time the sparks survive. I cradle them in my hands, protecting them from the wind, and blow gently until they glow brighter. Smoke wisps from the tinder as it starts to burn.

*Not bad. Only took two tries.*

I feed the fire more wood, until it grows big enough that the wind does not defeat it but only makes it stronger.

"That was fast for a fire steel," she says. "Even for a dragon, I'm impressed."

"Thank you."

"I like watching you work. There's nothing so attractive as a man doing his job well."

"You flatter me," I deadpan. I gaze out over the lake. "What kind of fish swim in these waters? Have you ever gone fishing?"

"No, never." She tilts her head, her eyes lovely in the morning light. "My mother was a red dragon, like me, and she taught me how to hunt the creatures of the land. Though my father must have known how to fish, as a blue seadrake. They have a fondness for water." She stares out over the lake. "Perhaps that was why I was drawn to this place." She shrugs. "Honestly, I don't feel much like a seadrake. When people look at me, all they see is a red dragon, and I was raised in the ways of the firedraken."

She's not wrong. It's impossible to ignore her crimson scales or her flame-colored hair. Both of her forms, dragon or woman, scream *firedrake* to me. But I understand why she feels conflicted about her identity.

"Sometimes," I admit, "I don't feel human at all."

"But your father raised you in the castle. King Everhart must have shown you what it meant to be a human man."

My teeth gritted, I keep the memories of my childhood at bay. "You presume that King Everhart had what they call humanity."

She looks into my eyes as if searching for an answer. "What happened to you when you were a child? What did the king do to you?"

I shake my head. "Let's not speak of such things before breakfast."

*Let's never speak of such things,* I think, though I don't say that out loud. It remains, at best, uncomfortable for me to remember what it was like growing up in the castle as a demon, and as the bastard son of the king. It hurts to remember my father's cold disdain for me, as if I were too difficult for him to love.

Even now, I doubt that I'm worthy of love. I know it must not be true, but it *feels* true in the marrow of my bones.

"Rook…" she trails off, clearly not sure what to say to me.

If I told her more about my childhood, it would do nothing but darken the morning sunshine. I might not be able to articulate what happened to me, or worse, she might not understand me. Not even my sister knows everything.

Time to change the subject. I turn my attention back to the lake. "It should be interesting to find what's lurking below the surface."

"You have a fishing rod?" she asks.

"I don't need one. Wait here."

I hike back up to the cave, where I left my belongings. I'm fond of fishing with a crossbow, so I already have the right gear —a spool of silk line and barbed bolts. They cost more gold than I care to admit out loud, but I consider them essential to surviving out in the wilderness for weeks at a time.

Only a fool would wade into a lake wearing leather trousers, so I unbuckle my belt and strip them off. In their place, I wear a kilt, the traditional fashion for men in Chymeria. Of course, a true prince would wear the royal colors—black and purple— but since I'm a bastard prince, a commoner's gray will have to suffice. I buckle my belt, holster my crossbow on my back, and return to the lake.

When Pyrah sees me, her jaw drops. "You aren't wearing those tight leather trousers any longer." Her gaze travels over my body. "Damn."

"Damn?" I repeat.

"I can't decide if I like the trousers or the kilt better."

I shrug. "This was a practical decision."

I take my crossbow from my back, load one of the barbed bolts, and tie the silk fishing line just above the fletching. The other end of the line leads to a spool hooked to my belt.

I will get only one shot. If I fail, I will have to return to shore and reload.

I unlace my boots. Barefoot, I wade into the icy waters of the lake. It must be fed by glacial melt. I don't go in too deep, since I don't want to freeze my balls off. They have already made a tactical retreat closer to my body heat.

By the shore, the water looks crystal clear, all the way down to the silt at the bottom. Insects hover around the surface, a good omen for fish. I wade slowly through the water and keep the ripples to a minimum.

There.

A trout swims beneath the shadows of a tree. I bring my crossbow to my shoulder. Taking into account the distortion of light underwater, I aim just below the fish. A breath escapes my lungs. My finger squeezes the trigger.

The bolt strikes true. The trout thrashes in the water, but it can't escape.

I let the line go slack, allowing it to unwind from the spool, before the trout begins to tire itself. I drag the fish out of the water and haul it onto the shore. Unsheathing one of my daggers, I deliver a mercy killing and close my eyes in silent thanks. This animal died so that we may eat.

Prey should always be respected.

Nothing tastes better than fish cooked over the fire in the wilderness. While Pyrah savors every bite, pride swells inside my chest. I have no greater purpose in my life than making her happy.

Finished with her food, she licks her fingers clean. That's distracting, though it's worse how she keeps inspecting my kilt.

"You're staring," I say, unable to hide my amusement.

"I can't help it," she murmurs. "You decided to put on a kilt."

I arch one eyebrow. "The kilt is traditional Chymerian clothing."

"I know." She wipes her thumb across her lower lip. "Tell me, do you follow all the traditions? Do you wear nothing underneath?"

"Why not find out for yourself?"

Her quick intake of breath betrays her desire. "Here? By the lake?"

"That's exactly what I mean."

Pyrah kneels before me and places her hand on my thigh, just below the hem of my kilt. Blood rushes to my cock. My shadow wings unfurl, betraying my arousal. Damn these incubus instincts.

She smiles, clearly pleased by my undeniable reaction. Her fingers trace the edge of my kilt. My cock stiffens and strains toward her touch, tenting the cloth in a way that's impossible to ignore.

She kisses the inside of my thigh, right where my pulse

pounds in the artery there. Her eyes darken with desire. "I have a confession."

"Tell me." I speak in a rough, hoarse voice, little better than an animalistic growl. *I want to bend her over and fuck her like an animal.*

She hesitates, her cheeks a pink color. Pretty. "I have been wanting to ask you something."

"Ask me anything."

"I want… I want to…" she trails off, her eyelashes fluttering.

"To what?" I ask, intrigued.

She takes a deep breath. "I want to take you in my mouth." Her voice is husky. "I want to taste you."

My heart pounds against my ribs. We have been intimate in a variety of ways, explored each other's bodies with a passion that never seems to fade. But this…this is new territory. Uncharted waters.

"We've never…"

"I know." Her gaze finally meets mine, vulnerability flickering in her eyes. "Would you like that?"

I swallow hard, my throat working. Lust spikes my blood and threatens to drown out all logic and reason. The thought of her lips on me, the heat of her mouth around my cock… It brings me closer to spilling my seed right here and now.

But I must confess the truth to her first. "I've never let anyone do this to me before."

Pyrah blinks, her eyes round with shock. "Never? Not once?"

I shake my head. "I'm an incubus. Trust doesn't come easily to demons like me. We're the ones who take, who dominate."

"But..." She struggles for words. "But you've been with so many lovers."

I shrug, looking away. "My past lovers... They were meaningless."

"Really?"

I hunt for the right words. "They wanted what an incubus could give them. The pleasure, the escape, the thrill of bedding a demon. And I took what I needed in return—their desire, their lust."

Pyrah stays kneeling before me. Her eyes shine as she peers up at me. "That sounds lonely."

"It was transactional." The admission burns in my throat. "They didn't care about my pleasure. I was a means to an end, nothing more. And I accepted that. There were never any consequences. They never wanted anything real."

Her fingers stroke my thigh. "But this is different?"

"Everything about you is different." I cup her face, my thumb brushing her cheek. "You see me. Not just the demon, not just the bastard prince. You see *me*."

"Rook..." She leans into my touch.

"No one has ever wanted to please me the way you do. No one has ever cared enough to try." My voice roughens. "What we have... It's not a transaction. It's not about taking or consuming."

Her eyes gleam. "You know, I love it when you devour me." She leans closer, her voice a sultry whisper. "I would love to devour you. Would you let me try?"

There's no way in hell I would refuse her request. "Yes."

"I might need some help," she admits. "Tell me what to do."

"We can figure this out together."

She slides her hand beneath my kilt, finally, her fingers curling around my hard cock. I hiss in a breath, the muscles in my abdomen tensing at the contact. With her other hand, she tugs aside my kilt and exposes my erection. She kisses the crown of my cock, then laps at it with her tongue, just the slightest lick.

"Like this?" she whispers, pausing to glance up at me.

I grunt. "Just like that."

She bends down again, her silky hair brushing against my thighs. Her hot, wet breath caresses me. I'm trembling with anticipation, ready to feel her mouth on me.

"Pyrah," I growl, a warning and a plea all at once.

She looks up at me, her eyes filled with a heady mix of desire and curiosity. "Tell me if I do something wrong," she says, her voice barely above a whisper.

"Just...go slow."

She nods, her eyes never leaving mine. Her lips slide around my cock as she takes me into her mouth.

"Fuck." The word escapes me, a cross between a groan and a sigh.

Her mouth is a revelation, a hot, wet haven that turns my blood to molten iron. My knees threaten to buckle, and I lock them in place, fighting to stay upright as she takes me deeper. The sight of her, on her knees, her blue eyes looking up at me with a mix of innocence and desire, is almost too much to bear.

I'm not in control here. Not like I usually am. It's a strange feeling, giving up the reins, letting her set the pace. But there's a thrill in it, too. A sense of discovery, of vulnerability that I've never allowed myself to feel before.

"Pyrah," I groan, my voice barely recognizable. My hands

find their way into her hair, not to guide her but to anchor myself. Her name becomes a chant on my lips, a prayer to whatever gods might be listening. "Pyrah, fuck..."

She hums around me, the vibration sending a jolt of pleasure through my body. My hips jerk involuntarily, and I force myself to still, to let her explore at her own pace. It's torture, the sweetest kind, and I'm drowning in it.

Her tongue swirls around the crown of my cock, teasing, tasting. She's tentative at first but grows bolder with each stroke. I can feel her confidence building, her enthusiasm growing. It's intoxicating, this shared journey of discovery.

My shadow wings stretch out behind me. But for once they are not a sign of my dominance, my control. They are a sign of my surrender.

I'm at her mercy, completely and utterly. And it's terrifying. And exhilarating. And I wouldn't have it any other way.

"Pyrah," I groan, my voice pure gravel. "You're killing me, woman."

She pulls back just enough to look up at me. "Is that a bad thing?"

My cock throbs, begging for her touch again, still glistening from her spit. "Not at all," I manage to say. "But if you keep doing that, I might come inside your mouth."

"Good."

She takes me deeper, her eyes meeting mine with fierce determination. The sight of her like this—my dragon shifter on her knees for me—brings me even closer to the brink.

# CHAPTER NINETEEN

PYRAH

When I pull back, his cock slides from my mouth with a wet pop, the sound wonderfully obscene. A drop of his seed pearls at the tip. Without thinking, I dart forward and lick him clean.

My eyes fly open with surprise. The taste of him explodes on my tongue—dark, rich, and bittersweet.

"You taste…delicious." I murmur. "Why didn't you tell me sooner?"

Rook chuckles, a low rumble in his chest. His thumb strokes my cheek. "Some believe an incubus's seed is an aphrodisiac."

"Is it?"

His eyes, embers in the firelight, search mine. "You tell me."

"Yes." My own heartbeat pounds between my legs. I want him to fill my mouth. To drown me in that rich bittersweet taste.

Before he can speak, I pull him closer. My hand wraps

around him, guiding him to my lips. Greedily, I suck. Like I'm parched and only this, only *he,* can quench my thirst.

I lavish attention on him with my tongue, exploring every ridge of his demonic cock. His blunt spikes seem especially sensitive. Whenever I lick them, his hips jerk and he struggles to remain quiet. I'm amazed by how close this strong demon has come to whimpering.

He closes his eyes, his face tight with exquisite agony. His hips buck, his hand twisting in my hair, pulling me closer, deeper. His taste intensifies, darker, richer. A wave of heat washes over me, pooling between my legs. My own body trembles, mirroring his.

His shadow wings snap open wide, twitching in time with his cock, and his tail lashes behind him.

"Pyrah," he gasps. "I can't—"

He comes with a shuddering cry. It's a raw, vulnerable sound.

His seed floods my mouth, hot and thick and so, so rich. I swallow, the taste exploding on my tongue. He keeps pulsing, spasms racking his body, each one sending another surge of his essence into me. I drink him down, every last drop, savoring him, until the final tremor fades and he's utterly spent.

He falls to his knees, his eyes closed, his mouth slack. His chest heaves as he struggles to catch his breath. He looks... undone. There's a raw vulnerability in his expression that pulls at something deep inside me. I have never seen him like this. So open. So exposed.

I reach out to him, my fingers tracing his jaw. He flinches at my touch, his eyes fluttering open. He says nothing and makes no sound. He just stares into my eyes. Understanding drifts down inside me.

He's not just undone by pleasure. He's undone by *me*.

I stroke his cheek again, marveling at how he leans into my touch. His silver skin glistens with sweat, his chest rising and falling with each ragged breath. Those fierce red eyes that once frightened me now hold such raw emotion.

"Rook?" My voice comes out as a whisper.

His shadow wings and tail have vanished. Gone is the predatory tension that usually coils through his muscles. He's let his guard down completely.

"No one has ever..." He swallows hard, his words trailing off. His hand finds mine, fingers intertwining. "I don't let anyone..."

I know what he means. The Gray Prince, the fearsome monster hunter, never allows himself to be vulnerable. He's always the one in control, the one doing the taking. But here, now, he's given that control to me.

My heart aches for him. I lean forward, pressing my forehead to his. His breath mingles with mine, warm and unsteady.

"Thank you," I whisper. "For trusting me."

A shudder runs through him. His arms wrap around me, pulling me close against his body. He buries his face in my neck. I hold him tighter, understanding the magnitude of what he's given me.

This isn't just pleasure—it's surrender. Complete and absolute.

"Never felt like this before." Rook's voice cracks, rough and raw. His chest rises and falls against mine, heart thundering beneath his ribs. "Not with anyone."

The admission strikes deep in my chest. His vulnerability,

freely given, makes my heart ache. I stroke the nape of his neck, my fingers threading through his hair.

He draws back, those ember eyes searching my face. "Do you need—" His hand slides down to my waist. "Let me take care of you."

"Rook," I say softly. "Wait."

I can't help thinking about his comment before. *It was transactional.* I don't want to remind him of that, to make him feel obligated to repay me somehow. I want him to know that he's worth all this and more.

His eyes search my face, brows drawing together in confusion. The vulnerability from moments ago shifts into something more uncertain. I recognize that look—he doesn't understand why I'm refusing his touch.

"Pyrah." His voice is rough, hesitant. "I'm not asking to feed. I want to please you."

"You don't owe me anything."

"This isn't about owing or repaying," he continues, voice dropping lower. "This is about wanting. And gods, do I want you."

My breath catches. The raw honesty in his voice makes my heart skip. The intensity of his gaze pins me in place.

"I'm still bleeding," I protest.

He laughs, a wonderfully dark sound. "I'm an incubus. It takes far more than a bit of blood to frighten me away from what I want."

I frown, pondering his earlier words. "Are you sure?" I swallow hard. "You don't need to feed?"

His eyes darken. "Not yet."

The pause before his answer makes my chest tighten. His

jaw clenches, a tendon jumping, a subtle tell I have learned to read. The predator in him stirs beneath the surface.

"How often?" I ask. "How often must an incubus feed to survive?"

Rook's grip on my wrist tightens, then loosens. His thumb strokes across my pulse point. "It varies."

"Tell me the truth." I wait for him to meet my eyes. "How often do you need the devouring kiss?"

His jaw clenches. The shadows around us seem to deepen, perhaps responding to his tension. His silence speaks volumes.

"You fed from me that night in the forest," I say.

"Two days ago," he admits.

"Are you hungry now?"

When he speaks, it's so quiet I almost don't hear him. "No."

I'm not sure he's telling the truth. He would lie to me if he thought it would save me. "When will you need to devour me again?"

"I can survive for days without feeding." Something in his tone catches my attention. A slight hesitation, perhaps.

"Is it longer because you're only half-incubus?"

He shakes his head, hiding behind his long hair. "I don't know. There's no guidebook for cambions."

"How long have you gone without feeding before?"

His whole body stiffens. The silence stretches between us, heavy with unspoken pain. Whatever memory I have stirred, it left deep scars.

"Rook?" I touch his shoulder.

His muscles bunch beneath my fingers. When he finally meets my gaze again, the vulnerability in his eyes makes my chest ache.

"You don't have to tell me," I whisper, though curiosity nibbles inside me. What happened to him? What forced him to go without feeding for so long it left this raw wound in his soul?

He inspects my face as if looking for judgment or disgust. Finding neither, he lets out a shaky breath.

"I was eighteen." Rook's voice sounds hoarse. "Father discovered what I was. What I had inherited from my mother."

A tremor runs through his body—not of pleasure but of pain.

"He said he would make a man of me." Rook's jaw clenches. "Locked me in one of his favorite brothels. Told the whores to tempt me but ordered me not to touch them."

My stomach turns. How cruel, forcing a young incubus to resist his very nature. "How long?"

"Days." His voice cracks. "He paid them to dance for me. To touch themselves. To beg me to take them." His shoulders hunch, as if he's trying to make himself smaller. "I never... I didn't want any of it. Didn't agree to it."

The vulnerability in his eyes breaks my heart. King Everhart may be dead, but his cruelty lives on in the scars he left on his son. I want nothing more than to burn his corpse to ash.

"The hunger..." Rook shudders. "By the fifth day, I couldn't think straight. Could barely remember my own name. My hands wouldn't stop shaking. My whole body felt numb."

"Rook," I whisper, wanting to comfort him, not sure what he needs at this moment.

"Father said it would toughen me up." He grimaces. "Make me resist the demon blood in my veins."

I can't stop the horror creeping through me as Rook continues his story, his voice hollow and distant.

"I broke on the seventh day," he says. "The hunger... It consumed everything I was. I wasn't myself anymore. Just a monster."

"What happened?" I whisper.

"I fed from all of them." He speaks without a trace of emotion in his voice. "Every last woman in that brothel. I couldn't stop myself. The hunger was too strong."

"Did you hurt them?"

He shakes his head. "I left them weak, drained. But alive. And then..." His jaw clenches. "Father found me there, surrounded by unconscious women. He *laughed*. Clapped me on the shoulder as if I'd done something to make him proud. Said I was finally a real man now."

I fight back the rage building in my chest. "He was wrong."

"I never want to be that monster again," Rook says. "Never want to lose control like that."

"It wasn't your fault."

He bows his head. "Sometimes my hunger takes over. Even when I don't want to feed, even when I would rather starve..." His voice cracks. "My body betrays me."

"What happened at the brothel was your father's cruelty, not yours. You tried not to hurt them."

"That's why consent matters so much to me now. Why I need to hear the words. Need to know it's freely given." He lifts his head and meets my gaze. "But even then, even when they say yes...sometimes I wonder if I truly have a choice myself."

I stare at him as the weight of his words hits me. The hunger that drives him isn't just about pleasure or sustenance. It's a chain that binds him, forcing him to act even when he doesn't want to.

"Like my father's punishments," he continues, voice rough. "The beatings. The humiliation. I never had a choice then, either." He pushes his hair from his eyes, his hands trembling. "Sometimes I wonder if I will ever be free."

"You will," I say. "You *are*."

"No." His hands cradle my face, his claws so gentle. "I need you to understand something, Pyrah. I must have my own choice in this."

My heart clenches. "What do you mean?"

"I have to leave." His thumb strokes my cheek. "Not forever. Just long enough to find the soulstone in the castle. It will bring us equilibrium. *Kelrial.* I won't put you in danger any longer. I won't be such a slave to my hunger."

*Kelrial.* The ancient Umbric word for balance strikes deep in my chest. I think I understand what he means—the soulstone might give him true freedom of choice.

He pulls me into his arms, the warmth of him surrounding me. "I'm sorry," he murmurs into my hair. "I don't want to leave you."

Fear claws at my heart at the thought of him invading the castle alone. I breathe in his scent of woodsmoke and pine sap, trying to calm myself down.

"Please be careful," I say. "Come back to me safely."

"I will."

"When will you leave?"

He strokes the back of my head with his hand. "Not yet." His voice falls to a whisper. "Tonight."

# CHAPTER TWENTY

ROOK

I swing my ax into another pine branch, watching it fall with a satisfying thud. Physical exertion helps quiet my mind but worry keeps gnawing at my gut. Lark should have returned hours ago. My sister promised she would return in the morning, bringing tea for Pyrah, and I haven't forgotten.

The sun climbs higher in the sky, marking time's relentless march. Sweat drips down my back as I gather the fragrant boughs. My muscles burn from the repetitive motion, but I welcome the distraction. Each strike of the ax drowns out visions of Lark back in that cursed dungeon, trapped behind those cold stone walls.

My body freezes as memories of the Forgotten Tower bubble up—the guards, the chains, the isolation that nearly broke my sister's spirit.

If Dulcamara's men found my sister...

The ax bites deeper into the next branch as rage builds in my chest. If they have touched a single hair on her head, I will tear apart every knight in Chymeria.

The familiar crackle of magic pierces the air. I spin around, ax raised, only to see Lark striding through a shimmering portal.

"Where the hell have you been?" My voice comes out rougher than intended, masking the wave of relief that crashes through me.

"Nice to see you, too, brother." Lark narrows her eyes. "Brewing the tea took longer than expected."

I bury my ax in a log and force down the urge to embrace her. "Could have sent word."

"With what? A carrier pigeon?" She rolls her eyes as if I'm joking.

I shake my head. "Magic."

Remembered dread creeps through me.

*I'm riding along the Emperor's Road. A raven lands in the road, hops across the stones, and croaks at me:* Lark is locked away and forgotten. *The spell unravels, the raven bursting into flight and disappearing.*

I spent a few days in grimy taverns, spying on the queen's guards and bribing tavern wenches, before I understood that *forgotten* meant *the Forgotten Tower,* and that the queen had taken Lark here.

"Just don't disappear like that again." I turn back to my work and yank the ax free, hiding the tremor in my hands.

"Rook." Her voice softens. "I know what you were thinking. But I'm not going back to that tower. Ever."

I grunt, refusing to acknowledge how close she hit to the

truth. Losing my sister has spawned far too many of my nightmares.

"Why are you butchering that tree?" Lark asks.

I yank down another bough. "I'm building a rough bed for Pyrah. It's hardly a mattress with featherdown pillows, but it's better than nothing. I want her to be comfortable."

*With or without me,* I think, though I don't say that part out loud.

"I went to Havenwold," Lark says. "Saw the ruined temple. Dragonfire?"

I grunt, continuing to strip branches. The memory of that night flashes through my mind. I'm haunted by the gleam of Pyrah's wedding dress, embroidered with cursed aellurium, when Scaldric tried to force her to marry him.

"The whole city's still talking about it." Lark kneels beside me, picking up fallen pine needles. "A dragon and the Gray Prince, wreaking havoc on holy ground. The priests are beside themselves."

Another grunt escapes me as I swing the ax. "Blame Scaldric. We had to fight him to free Pyrah."

"You could have been more subtle." Lark's tone carries a hint of reproach. "Drew quite a bit of attention to yourselves."

I pause midswing. "Subtlety wasn't exactly the point."

"Clearly." Lark picks up another branch, examining the cut. "Though I doubt the queen will take kindly to you burning down her temples."

I bare my teeth in what might pass for a smile. "I don't care."

"Your face is plastered all over Havenwold with the biggest bounty I've ever seen." Lark shoots me a pointed look. "Ten thousand gold pieces. Queen Dulcamara must really want your head."

I grunt, returning to my task. Bounties are nothing new—I have had a price on my head since I first escaped into the Thornwood. The amount doesn't matter. They will have to catch me first.

"You could at least pretend to be concerned," Lark mutters.

"Why start now?" I swing the ax, letting the sharp crack of wood split the air. "Besides, you're worth almost as much these days. Five thousand, wasn't it?"

"Seven," she corrects with a hint of pride. "Though Pyrah's bounty is only five thousand. The queen must not consider her as much of a threat."

"Yet." The word slips out before I can stop it. "I'm worried her bounty will grow because she's with us."

Lark grimaces. "I hate that you're probably right."

We work together to fashion the pine boughs into a bed. It looks more like a nest, in the end, which seems oddly suitable for a dragon shifter. I test the bed myself. It's definitely better than lying on the stone floor of the cave or curling around heaps of treasure—though of course I'm a demon, not a dragon.

There's nothing more satisfying than spending the day on hard work, then admiring your rewards at the end of it. I should be happy, but I'm tormented by a hollow feeling in the pit of my stomach.

Something is missing.

Something I must find.

*This isn't enough.*

The branches crackle beneath my weight as I lie on them. My throat burns with thirst, a constant reminder of my incubus needs. This morning by the lake, when Pyrah took me in her mouth, I held back. Kept my incubus nature locked away, refusing to feed on her lust.

I couldn't risk draining her further, not when she needs her strength.

But the hunger claws at my insides now, a ravenous beast demanding satisfaction. Without the soulstone to balance us, to let me feed without harm, I'm trapped between starvation and the fear of hurting her.

I cross my arms and dig my claws into my skin, welcoming the sharp sting of pain. It's better than this constant thirst, this maddening balance between desire and restraint. Without the soulstone, every touch, every kiss, every moment of passion becomes a dangerous game.

Later that night, we linger around the campfire by the lake. Lark cooks mushroom soup in a cauldron she brought from home. Bits of wild onion and foraged sage float in the broth. The savory aroma of dinner should make my mouth water, but I'm distracted by the hollow ache in my stomach, the weakness spreading through my limbs.

Reflected flames glitter in the black waters of the lake. Out there in the darkness, there are quests I have not yet begun. I can't stay here any longer, not while I'm haunted by everything left unsaid and undone.

Firelight dances across Pyrah's face as she laughs at something Lark said. I missed whatever it was.

"Rook." Lark stirs the soup like a witch brewing a potion. "Remember when we found those giant puffballs outside the castle? Mum cooked them with butter and garlic."

I grunt. "That was a long time ago."

"Puffballs?" Pyrah leans forward, eager to hear more stories of our childhood. "What do they taste like?"

"Earthy," Lark says, "with a hint of a nutty taste. Sometimes they grow bigger than your head."

"You have me convinced. Would you cook them for me someday?"

"Of course."

They both imagine a future with good food and good company. I'm afraid the truth looks far bleaker.

Lark ladles the soup into bowls before Pyrah brings me mine. Her fingertips brush against mine, and even this instant of contact makes my heartbeat pound. Hunger gnaws deeper in my stomach, a primal need that has nothing to do with food.

I swallow hard before muttering, "Thanks."

I should have fed this morning by the lake. But I lied to Pyrah, told her I only needed to feed every few days. The truth is far worse—as a cambion, my incubus nature demands that I feed nearly every day.

My fingers clench around the wooden bowl. Even now, Pyrah tempts me like a delicious fruit. My mouth waters at the memory of her sweet desire. But I can't devour her again. Not so soon.

"Rook?" Pyrah says. "You haven't eaten a bite of your soup."

I force a smile that feels more like a grimace. "Just tired."

Lark's keen gaze pins me to the spot. As a succubus herself, she understands the hunger that plagues demons like us.

But Pyrah remains innocent. She doesn't know how much I need her. Doesn't know how dangerous I could become. Each time I feed, I risk taking too much, draining her life until nothing remains.

"Here." Pyrah sits right beside me, her thigh pressing against mine. "At least try the mushrooms. They taste delicious."

Her scent drifts over to my nose and tugs at me like a fish-hook. The muscles between my shoulders twitch as my shadow wings threaten to escape. I edge away, putting space between us.

"I need some air." The words sound gruffer than I intended. I stand, avoiding the hurt on Pyrah's face.

I stride away from the firelight, into the darkness where the hunger can't betray me. Where I can't hurt her. The unspoken truth burns in my throat. I'm terrified of what I might do if I let myself feed from her again. Terrified of becoming the monster my father always said I was.

Footsteps crunch in the gravel behind me. I don't need to turn around to know who it is—Pyrah's scent wraps around me like an embrace.

"What's wrong?" she asks, quietly. "You're acting strange."

"It's nothing." I keep my back to her, my fists clenched at my sides.

Gravel pops underfoot as she comes even closer to me. "You're hungry, aren't you? I can tell."

"Not very." The lie tastes bitter on my tongue.

"You haven't fed at all today." Her fingertips brush the back of my hand.

I jerk away from her touch. "I said I'm fine."

"Kiss me, then. A devouring kiss."

I slice my hand through the air, dismissing her at once. "No."

"Why not?"

Something clicks into place, a truth I had never considered before. "Because I don't want to."

She steps in front of me and meets my gaze. "What?"

"My consent matters, too." The realization strikes deep. "Just because you're willing doesn't mean I have to feed."

"But you need—"

"Yes." I cut her off. "But I get to choose when and how. Being hungry doesn't strip me of that choice."

"Won't you starve?" Pyrah's eyes plead with me to see sense.

"Eventually."

"Then why…?"

"Because I want to find another way." The words spill out before I can stop them. "I'm tired of being a threat to you. Tired of wondering if this time I will take too much. If this time the hunger will win."

Her blue eyes flash in the darkness. "You haven't hurt me."

"Not yet." My voice rasps on the words. "But I won't gamble with your life every time I feed from you. I need to find another way. One that lets me love you without fear. You're precious to me."

"I'm not some delicate flower."

"Precious like a gemstone. Strong but still breakable."

She lets out a shuddering sigh, her resolve crumbling. "Rook…"

"The soulstone is our only chance at finding *kelrial*." I brush a lock of her fiery hair from her face. "Without finding equilibrium, my hunger will always be a threat between us. I must return to the castle."

"It's too dangerous." She catches me by the wrist and holds me there. "The queen's guards are everywhere."

"Which is exactly why I need to go now, before I'm truly starving. If I wait until hunger takes over, I will be a slave to desperation. I need to go while I still have my wits about me."

"Let me come with you."

"No." I shake my head. "Fuck," I add, for emphasis. "I won't bring you anywhere near the queen. Not after what she did to Lark."

"But—"

"No," I repeat, solemnly, and I hold her gaze in the darkness. "My mother's soulstone is hidden somewhere in that castle. Once I find it, we can create a more permanent bond together. Something that lets me feed without endangering you."

Her fingers tighten around my hand. "And what if you don't come back?"

"I will always come back to you." The promise aches in my throat. "But I need to do this. For us. For our future."

Her eyes shine with unshed tears. "I don't want you to go, but I understand why you need to do this."

I tilt her chin up. "Stay with Lark. She will keep you safe until I return."

She nods once, sharp and angry. "Just...don't die."

"I won't." I pull her close, breathing in her scent one last time. "This is the only way I can ensure I never hurt you. Let me do this."

"Go," Pyrah whispers.

And I must, before I lose my courage. I return to the campfire. “Lark,” I ask, “could you cast a portal to Netherhaven?”

Frowning, my sister pokes at the fire with a stick. “I thought you didn’t want to go back.”

“I left Bolt in a stable on the outskirts of the city. And I promised Pyrah that I would buy her some clothes of her own. Netherhaven has the biggest night market in Chymeria. Better to do my shopping there without being noticed.”

I don’t breathe a word about the soulstone. For the time being, that’s a secret between me and Pyrah.

Lark frowns at me as if doubting my intelligence. “Rook, you can’t wander through the night market in Netherhaven with black horns and silver hair and glowing red eyes.”

“I can wear my cloak. And gloves.”

She squints at me as if still unconvinced. “Should I come with you?”

I shake my head. “Stay here.”

“Rook, wait.” Pyrah stares up at me, and if I were a lesser man, her sad eyes would be enough to defeat me. Shivering, she rubs the goose bumps on her arms, despite the fire.

“Are you cold?” I ask.

“No,” she says, though I suspect it’s nothing more than a brave lie. “I have a terrible feeling in the pit of my stomach. Something is telling me that you shouldn’t return.”

I cup Pyrah's face between my palms, her skin warm against my cold fingers. The firelight catches in her blue eyes, turning them to liquid sapphire. My chest aches at the fear I see there.

"Listen to me." I brush my thumb across her cheekbone. "I have survived far worse than a trip to Netherhaven."

She grabs my wrists, keeping my hands against her face. "Please don't do anything reckless."

A smile tugs at my lips despite the dread trickling down my spine. "When have I ever been reckless?"

"Rook." Her fingers dig into my skin. "I'm serious."

"I know." I press my forehead to hers, breathing in her scent of clovers and dragonfire. "I will be careful. No unnecessary risks."

"And you will come back before dawn?"

"Yes." I kiss her on the cheek, a chaste kiss—a *safe* kiss. "Have faith in me. A few hours in Netherhaven won't kill me. I know every shadow and twist in the streets of the city."

"You might not believe it," Lark says, "but my brother is stealthier than he looks. He was something of a sneak thief when he was a boy, though he's too honorable to confess to any theft."

"It's true." I shrug. "An incubus is a creature of the darkness. This will be a return to the darkness of my childhood home."

Pyrah stands on her toes so she can curl her fingers around my horns. She drags me down into a fierce kiss. *Fuck*. It's so hard to kiss her back without devouring her. I let her take control, while I endure with equal parts torment and pleasure.

"Promise me you will come back," she whispers against my lips. "If you don't, I will hunt you down and murder you myself."

"You have my word." But then I smirk. "If you do murder me, though, make sure to claim the bounty on my head."

# CHAPTER TWENTY-ONE

ROOK

Lark casts a portal to the outskirts of Netherhaven. Beyond the portal, I can see gnarled trees shadow an overgrown graveyard. We both agreed this would be a strategic location, since it's just outside the city walls and yet unoccupied by the living.

Since I'm not a complete idiot, despite my sister's opinion of me, I put on my wool cloak and lift the hood. It does a halfway decent job of obscuring my face, though it's impossible to deny my horns jutting out through the slits in the hood. Luckily, I won't be the only demon in Netherhaven. Otherwise, this would be a fool's quest.

With the help of my teeth, I tug on leather gloves to cover my silver skin and black claws. Finally, I put on a mask, common enough in Netherhaven—those who survived the pox often wish to hide their scars. That should be enough to disguise my identity as the Gray Prince, though I won't be able to conceal my glowing red eyes if someone looks too closely.

Before I let Pyrah's sad eyes convince me to stay with her, I stride through the portal.

The magic hits me in the stomach. Acid rises in my throat. I brace myself against a tombstone and wait for the feeling to pass.

When I glance back at the portal, it's already gone. No more time for good-byes.

Keeping to the shadows, I creep through the graveyard. My feet wander as if compelled by magic. I can't help but linger by one of the graves. This plot looks less overgrown, as if it was unearthed not long ago. It has a simple tombstone, carved with one word: *Everhart.*

My father's grave.

I recoil from the sight of it. My boot crushes a plant underfoot. The pungent smell—bitter, stronger than sage—fills my nose. My stomach churns, the urge to vomit intensifying.

Wormwood. They planted wormwood at my father's grave.

*Fuck.*

My knees buckle and I collapse against the tombstone, the rough stone scraping my palms as I struggle to stay upright. The scent of wormwood floods my senses, dragging me back to memories I've tried desperately to forget.

Everhart always reeked of wormwood. He believed that this herb would protect him from vermin and disease. He had survived the pox as a child, though it left his face pitted with scars. While he was king of Chymeria, he ordered that wormwood be strewn throughout his bedchambers. The smell often foretold his arrival like a bad omen.

Who planted this wormwood? Or was this a sick coincidence?

He was never given a royal burial after Queen Dulcamara murdered him. By her command, she had his stallion drag his corpse through Netherhaven before dumping him outside the city walls. Someone took pity on him and buried him in this commoner's cemetery.

I never saw him after he died, since I had already fled like a coward, though they have whispered this story in taverns for years. My father would have been enraged by such disrespect.

Here in the graveyard, the stink of wormwood clings to my nose with every breath.

He's dead. He's gone. Nothing left of a proud king but bones. They already robbed his grave not too long ago. My sister's voice echoes in my mind. *Dulcamara brought me a baby boy, a pitiful little thing from some orphanage, and a finger bone dug from our father's grave.*

Perhaps there's nothing left buried in the dirt.

Whenever he worked himself into a rage, his voice would boom across the castle. Everyone in court would try to remain hidden and avoid his wrath.

Should I feel something for him? I'm too broken to care.

I still want to set this wormwood on fire and destroy the scent of him. That would be stupid, of course, since it would do nothing but attract the attention of guards. The bells in Netherhaven play their song before ringing the hour: two o'clock.

There's no time to waste. The night market closes at dawn.

Shaking, I abandon my father's grave.

Outside the graveyard, a night watchman wanders along the crooked street. The reek of alcohol trails behind him in the wind. When he stops to piss against the wall, I steal past him before he notices me.

Of the nine gates of Netherhaven, St. Kestrel's Gate is the easiest to enter. It's one of the oldest gates, the walls crumbling and shrouded by moss, and it's known for having underpaid guards with a fondness for gold.

I don't even need to bribe my way in, since the wall has fallen into further disrepair. My boots find footholds between the decaying stones. I scramble higher and vault over the rampart, then land in a crouch. I cling to the shadows and avoid the flickering torchlight.

Guards patrol the top of the wall. I wait for the nearest one to turn his back on me. Once he does, I jump off the wall and onto the roof of a nearby tavern. I run along the shingles until I can leap down to the ground. My boots skid on the muck in the gutter. Disgusting.

Netherhaven has gone to shit under the rule of Queen Dulcamara.

At least the locations of the streets haven't changed. I follow an alley down to a wider boulevard, then duck through an archway. It's late, but the city never sleeps. I avoid the townsfolk walking the streets.

At the heart of Netherhaven, I'm forced to confront the ruins of a temple. Candles drip melted wax into the broken marble, where plucked flowers wilt. Both must be tributes to the god of humans.

I linger in the darkness by the ruins. When I close my eyes, there's an image seared into my memory: Pyrah, kneeling in a wedding dress, forced to obey.

Scaldric would have married her if I had been a moment too

late. I interrupted the wedding just before he crowned her with a bridal crown. The ceremony broke into a battle, and the temple was destroyed.

I can't keep losing myself to memories.

I leave the ruins of the temple and journey into the night market. It takes place in the temple square, the space crowded with booths. Sizzling meat scents the air. Lanterns illuminate the night market both with candlelight and enchanted fireflies. It's brighter than I would wish, since I'm forced to leave the shadows.

I wander through the townsfolk until I find a merchant selling clothes. She's tiny, even for a human. Her stare travels from my boots to my horns. The top of her head doesn't even come to my chest.

The merchant blinks a few times as if she can't believe her eyes. "Haven't seen you around here before."

I shrug, hoping she hasn't seen me plastered on any wanted posters. "I'm looking for women's clothes."

"For a lady friend?"

"Yes." That's safer than explaining I'm mated to a dragon shifter.

She brings out a few dresses and hooks them over her arm to show them off. "Does your lady favor a color?"

"Amethyst purple." As if I could ever forget.

Choosing jewel colors seems to be a safe strategy. I select dresses in emerald green and ruby red. Surely these will please the covetous heart of a dragon.

It's still cold at night, especially in her cave in the mountains, so I get her a few pairs of woolen stockings.

Inevitably, I'm forced to ask, "Undergarments?"

The merchant opens and closes her mouth as if momentarily lost for words. "Will these be for yourself or your lady?"

I arch an eyebrow, since I own no undergarments. "My lady."

Her ears turn pink. "Of course."

The merchant ducks down, rummages beneath her booth, and finds several linen underpants. She discreetly folds them and slides them across to me as if we're making a black-market deal. I resist the urge to laugh. Silently, I count out the required coins and pay the flustered merchant. I stash my purchases in my pack before nodding in thanks.

After I retreat into the darkness once more, I stalk along the edges of the night market until something catches my eye.

Midnight plums, the same dark ones I pinched from the royal orchard when I was a boy. My claws close around one of the fruits, though I'm careful not to pierce the flesh. They have deep purple skin, red flesh, and a sweet yet sour flavor that makes my mouth water just from remembering.

I want to share this taste of my childhood with Pyrah.

"How much?" I ask the merchant.

"Twenty gold pieces each."

"Ludicrous." I fold my arms across my chest. "Ten."

"Fifteen, and not a coin less!"

I don't want to waste any more time haggling and risk blowing my cover. An unhappy merchant might call the guards. I grit my teeth and pay fifteen gold pieces for a plum, a king's ransom for a fruit.

These thoughts of castles and kings keep drifting through my head like smoke.

The castle looms over the city.

Beckoning me.

I can't walk away from Netherhaven without seeking the soulstone. I've spent far too long never dreaming of my future beyond surviving to the end of each day. I let hope dwindle inside me until it died to little more than an ember.

But Pyrah rekindled this ember inside me. For her, hope burns again. Without her, I have no reason to dream.

*Lirithel.* She is my dream.

I belong to this beautiful, fierce woman just as much as she belongs to me, and I want her to know it every moment. She deserves the soulstone.

I need to keep her safe—even from me.

And I want to marry her.

The truth of it sinks into the marrow of my bones. A weight lifts from my shoulders, and for the first time in a long time, I breathe a little easier at the path ahead of me. My exhalation escapes in a cloud of white.

I would be lying if I said I wasn't scared.

Not of marrying Pyrah, though perhaps I should be a little afraid. I'm scared of returning to the castle at Netherhaven. I haven't been back since my father died.

Queen Dulcamara must be waiting for me to blunder too close. She's lurking like a black widow in her spider web.

And I can't pluck a single thread without getting caught.

Netherhaven Castle was my home, not too long ago. It feels strange to return to a place shrouded by memories like years of neglected dust.

Once upon a time, the guards were playmates for the king's bastard son, who was kept hidden away from the world. I was that child. They trained me and taught me how to fight, since one day I would join their ranks and protect my father as part of the king's guard.

That day never came.

Tonight, I'm entering the castle as an enemy. I hope to God none of the guards have familiar faces.

The old library is located deep within the castle keep. No portals can be cast there, since an ancient magic imbues the stones of the keep and wards off any teleportation.

Luckily, I remember every secret passageway and hidden door in the castle. My sister and I played here as children, pretending to be travelers exploring a faraway realm, even though neither one of us had left the city yet.

The castle lurks on a hill above the city. Moonlight gleams on its white walls and towers. I creep around the bottom of the hill until I find a mossy boulder choked by ivy. Buried deep under the glossy leaves, there's a secret door carved from wood. Locked, of course, and I don't have a key.

Good thing I learned how to pick locks when I was seven.

The door creaks open to an underground passageway. It allows royals to escape if enemies invade the castle. I step inside, my horns scraping the stone before I duck down. It's cold and damp inside. The scent of earth and mushrooms clings to the air. I shut the door behind me, covering my tracks, and venture deeper into the utter darkness.

Stairs, carved from the bedrock, lead higher until I enter the underbelly of the castle. My breathing sounds too loud in my ears. My childhood fear still clings to me. I pause to catch my breath, willing it to slow to a quieter rhythm. This particular secret passageway opens to a closet in our mother's old bedchamber.

Has anyone else taken the room since she vanished?

I steel my nerves and open the door to the bedchamber.

Empty. Abandoned, in fact, with forgotten ashes in the fireplace and cobwebs shrouding the furniture. A dagger stabs her pillow—perhaps in warning. It's covered with enough dust that it must have been there for years.

Queen Dulcamara could have stabbed the pillow, though my mother was infamous for having a temper like a volcano. Slow to erupt but destructive when it exploded. I don't know how she reacted to my father's murder.

The library isn't far from my mother's old bedchamber. I keep my back to the wall and steal into the corridor. It's late enough that the servants must be sleeping, unaware that a monster is stalking through the castle.

Shadows and silence are old friends of mine. I learned from an early age when to hide or when to keep my footsteps quiet to avoid making anyone angry.

The library isn't locked. I lean my shoulder against the heavy door and push it open, slowly, to avoid the groan of hinges. Inside the library, silver moonlight pours through the windows. An army of books stands in neat ranks on shelves. I take a deep breath of the familiar scent of paper, leather, and beeswax.

But it's dangerous to succumb to the weakness of nostalgia.

I force myself to focus on my quest.

Where would our mother hide the soulstone?

I run my claws along the spines of books, not hard enough to hurt them. The royals keep a small collection of books written in Umbric, their titles glimmering in the moonlight as gilded runes.

I slide out *Legends of Elysium,* one of my mother's favorites, which is a collection of demonic fairy tales. Maybe one of the stories mentions soulstones and contains a clue she left behind for me or my sister to discover.

"Found you." A woman's voice cuts through the shadows of the library.

Fuck, I know that voice. I slam the book back onto the shelf and grab my sword. Before I can unsheathe the blade, she speaks again.

"Don't."

With a flick of her hand, blue magic flies from the darkness and locks around my wrist. It shackles me to the bookshelf, the enchantment as cold as iron.

The woman saunters into a moonbeam. Black hair, black eyes, and a smirk that says she's caught me. One of the queen's royal sorceresses, my least favorite.

"Zin." I growl out her name. "What the fuck do you want?"

"I was hoping for your sister."

"Lark?" I blink, clearly missing something important, while I tense the muscles in my arm against the magic. "Why?"

Zin sneers. "She hasn't told you?"

I need to keep her talking. "Enlighten me."

"Lark can't resist crawling back for more."

"More of *you*?"

"Don't look so shocked."

I wrench my wrist away from the bookshelf. The magic binding me shatters. Without hesitation, I free my blade and lunge into an attack before the sorceress can cast another spell.

Zin dodges my blade, the steel no more than a glint in the moonlight. And then she fights back. Her fingers twist the air, working magic, but I grab her by the wrist and wrench her arm to break the spell before she can finish casting it.

She scratches my arm with her human fingernails, which are too weak to do any real damage. I bring my claws to her neck and pin her against the bookshelf by her throat. I tighten my claws, just hard enough to break her skin. Her blood wells under my fingers.

"Don't." I echo her earlier command.

Zin swallows hard, her throat working under my fingers. When she spits in my face, I lift her higher. She's tiny compared to me. Her toes dangle above the floor. Choking, she struggles to pry my fingers from her neck. Her strength is nothing against mine.

I should kill the sorceress. Unless Lark has some...attachment to her.

Zin kicks against my knees, trying to push me away, but she remains trapped against the bookshelf. Her face starts turning purple.

Fuck.

I let Zin drop to the floor. Gasping, coughing, she crawls on her hands and knees. I loom over her with my sword menacing in her direction.

"Surrender," I command.

She speaks in a rasp. "Go fuck yourself."

Maybe her unwelcome interruption could prove useful. "My mother hid a soulstone in the library. Where is it?"

"What soulstone?" She bares her teeth in a sneer. "Oh, I see. Your sister wasn't stupid enough to take the bait, but you were."

Dread hits me in the gut like a fist. "You told her that?" She must have been trying to lure Lark back. "This was a trap."

"Not for you. I don't give a fuck about the Gray Prince." She laughs scathingly. "But the queen might."

Her hands flicker at the edge of my eyesight. I swing the pommel of my sword at her skull, ready to knock her out.

Too late.

She flings a spell at me, her fingers trailing black sparks, and the magic crashes into me. My skeleton locks up—she's hit me with a paralysis curse. My heartbeat pounds in my ears, an animal instinct to survive screaming at me. I battle the spell, but my muscles refuse to obey me. I can't breathe.

Zin staggers to her feet. She stands on her tiptoes and whispers in my ear. "Sleep."

When she kisses my cheek, I fall into oblivion.

# CHAPTER TWENTY-TWO

ROOK

Cold. Pain. Darkness, the kind that clings to me and keeps me from crawling into the light. I drift in and out of consciousness.

"Wake up."

When I fail to comply, someone slaps me across the cheek. The sharp sting brings me more clarity. I blink open my eyes, though they remain unfocused. I'm kneeling, slumped against a stone wall, my head bowed, my arms chained in front of me. I've been stripped naked, perhaps to degrade me.

Slowly, my bleary eyes focus on the person who hit me.

Fuck.

*Fuck.*

Queen Dulcamara.

The ruler of Chymeria has me in her dungeon, or wherever the fuck this place is. Down on my knees, I'm level with her eyes. They always look gray and empty like a mirror without a reflection. Soulless. Even the light from a torch grants her no warmth. My gaze drops to her dark hair, braided over her shoulder, easy to grab.

"Queen takes rook," she murmurs, as if playing chess.

Is this nothing but a game to her?

I lunge for Dulcamara, but my head jerks back and chains rattle behind me. Pain lances through the muscles in my neck. I grope overhead.

Shackles. They locked shackles around my horns so I couldn't move my head far from the wall.

Where the fuck am I?

This place looks nothing like the Forgotten Tower. I'm imprisoned in a gloomy chamber of stone. Words have been carved in the wall, but the letters keep swimming under my eyes. It's difficult to focus. I tilt my head to the right, as far as the chains around my horns will allow. Out of the corner of my eye, I glimpse a door wrought from iron. It's the only exit from this cage.

"Why are you here?" the queen asks.

I say nothing. If she doesn't know, that means Zin didn't tell her about the soulstone. There's a chance I might even live to see it one day.

Dulcamara's nostrils flare. She loathes disobedience above all else. "Answer me."

Still, I say nothing.

She slaps me again. Her leather glove stings my face; my skin heats in the shape of her hand. Of course she's wearing gloves. She wouldn't dirty herself by touching a filthy demonspawn.

"How can you be so ungrateful?" she asks, though it's not a question so much as a statement of fact.

"Ungrateful?" It's the first word I have spoken here, and my voice sounds rusty with disuse.

"I let you live." Disgust and hatred thin her lips into a white line. "You still breathe in this kingdom by my mercy alone. And yet you break into my castle, kill my knights, and ruin my temples."

"Temples?" I grunt. "Don't remember more than one."

"I could have you executed at my command."

I'm numb, distant, too far away for fear to touch me. "Why haven't you?"

"I'm not done with you yet." She sneers at me as if my question is stupidly obvious. "My royal sorceress told me you were looking for *this*."

A chain, fragile and golden, glints around her neck. She hooks her finger around it and lifts a pendant out from beneath the bodice of her gown.

Horror strikes me to the marrow of my bones.

My family heirloom, the last thing I have left of my mother, dangles around Her Majesty's neck.

She has the soulstone.

Fuck, this day just keeps getting worse.

I don't say anything out loud, since I don't want to betray how much my mother's soulstone means to me. Dulcamara will only wield my emotions against me, just like she always has, but I can't stop staring at the dark beauty of the soulstone. Even in this dungeon, the deep purple gem glitters with fire.

The soulstone means equilibrium with my mate.

Marriage.

*Everything.*

Dulcamara stares into my eyes without blinking, as if she sees the dilemma churning inside my mind like a storm. She's waiting for me to crumble.

"Where did you find that?" My voice rasps on the question.

"Your whore of a mother abandoned it." She twirls the soulstone between her fingers.

I ignore her insult. If my mother abandoned the soulstone, that implies she fled from the castle, not that the queen pried it from her cold, dead hands.

"It's a pretty little trinket, isn't it?" she asks.

She must be bluffing. She must know what a soulstone means to demons. Otherwise, she never would have kept it for herself, never would have brought it to the dungeon to taunt me.

"I don't wear jewelry," I say, which isn't a lie.

"Then you won't mind if I toss this into a cesspit? Lost forever in the piss and shit?"

"You wouldn't."

We lock stares for a moment, each daring the other to admit what the soulstone means to them. If the queen were stupid, this would be a whole lot easier, but unfortunately, she has always had a ruthless intelligence.

Her nostrils flare as if she smells a stink. "You guessed correctly. The soulstone has value to me." But she doesn't say why, or how much she knows about demons. Perhaps she believes the soulstone will tempt me.

"What do you want from me?" When she doesn't answer me, I ask another question. "Why would you ever dirty yourself by wearing demonic jewelry?"

The queen has always believed that demons are little better than filth.

"Because everything your mother once had now belongs to me." Her eyes glitter with cold disdain. "Even you."

"Don't forget my sister."

The queen scoffs. "Lark worked for me of her own free will. She was proud to become a sorceress for the crown."

Her words wouldn't sting so much if they weren't true, but I refuse to take the bait.

Dulcamara softens her voice, which somehow makes it that much more unnerving. A shiver crawls down my spine. "Lark's punishment in the Forgotten Tower should have corrected her rebellious nature. Eventually, she will come crawling back on her hands and knees, eager to serve me again."

Conveniently, she omits the part where Pyrah and I broke Lark out of the Forgotten Tower. I'm surprised she imagines Lark still has such loyalty to her. Is she truly so arrogant?

"That's why you haven't killed me yet," I say, calmly, keeping any emotion from my face. "You still believe I will surrender to your control."

"Dead, you are worthless."

*Worthless*. Like my father? She wouldn't even let his body rest in its shallow grave but had his corpse exhumed so she could steal one of his bones. She wanted to create an heir born of dark magic. Of course, Lark refused to cast the spell but that won't stop Dulcamara.

"Is that why you brought the soulstone?" I ask, pretending I don't know why she desecrated my father's grave. "Will you bribe me with it?"

"Bribe?" Spit flecks her pale lips. "How dare you suggest

such a thing? You should be begging for my mercy, not demanding payment from me."

"You still haven't answered my question. What the fuck do you want from me?"

When Dulcamara stares into my eyes, hers look so empty. "Tell me where she is."

"Who?" Maybe she wants Lark, too, so she can have the complete set of bastard twins.

"The red dragon, Pyrah."

Surprise jolts me, and this time, I'm unable to keep it from my face. Why does she want Pyrah? Her knights have been trying to slay the dragon, but I had assumed they only wanted the bounty on Pyrah's head.

Did Pyrah meet the queen before? When she was captured by Scaldric?

I should have asked her myself, but now it's too fucking late.

"Why?" I rasp, the gravel in my voice intensifying.

"Don't play the fool."

"Your evil plans make little sense."

"Evil?" Her eyes glimmer as if she has the right to act insulted. She always liked to cry on command. "I have sacrificed so much for the good of this kingdom."

"Every time you open your mouth, more shit falls out."

She slaps me yet again, hard enough that my head jerks to the side. An iron taste fills my mouth. My fangs must have cut the inside of my cheek.

"Tell me," she demands. "Where is Pyrah?"

I bare my teeth in a bloodstained smile. "Fuck you."

Dulcamara inspects me as if I'm a puzzle she wants to crack. "You have yet to learn the value of regret."

She exits the dungeon through the iron door. Where does the door lead? This godforsaken place could be one of the dungeons in Netherhaven Castle, buried deep in the bowels of the fortress, but I don't recognize it. I was forbidden from exploring the dungeons when I was a child.

A shiver passes over me. It's cold here, and I'm not wearing any clothing. I don't see any kind of bedding. There's nothing but a bucket to shit in.

Zin enters the room. Bruises darken the skin around her neck where I choked her before. The sight shouldn't gratify me and yet it does. She sneers with disgust at my naked body, her gaze lingering below my waist. The muscles in my back tense.

Torture. That's what I would expect.

She's carrying a cup in her hand, full of some dark liquid, and brings it to my mouth. "Drink."

"Poison?" I ask.

Zin rolls her eyes. "Why the hell would we poison you after we caught you?"

"I presume for an agonizing death."

"Trust me, Queen Dulcamara would watch. She isn't here right now, is she?"

I clench my jaw. "Why should I trust you?"

"For fuck's sake." She sighs. "If you don't drink this yourself, I will have to waste my magic on another paralysis curse and force it down your throat. I promise it won't make your dick fall off. I know how precious dicks are to an incubus."

"Tell me what the fuck it is first."

"It will make your sleep dreamless."

She must be telling the truth, since an incubus has the

power to enter the dreams of another. I will lose the ability to communicate with Pyrah.

I have no choice. If I fight, it's the paralysis curse again. With a grim nod, I surrender.

She brings the cup to my lips. The liquid drips into my mouth like oil, though it tastes bittersweet. I swallow every last damn drop.

The sorceress retreats out of my reach. Only then does she turn her back on me. She abandons me to my fate.

It's strange to sleep without dreams. I plunge into darkness and awake feeling empty.

A guard enters the room and brings me a bowl of gruel.

"Where are we?" I ask.

The guard says nothing, just slides the bowl across the floor to me. Some of it sloshes out onto the floor, slowly, oozing with disgusting thickness.

I wait until he has left before I figure out how to eat. The chains around my horns prevent me from bending down and devouring the gruel like an animal. With my arms chained in front of me, it's difficult to pick the bowl up, but I manage to bring it to my mouth.

Fuck, that's disgusting. Bland, thick sludge. At one point, it may have been oats.

When I stand to my full height, the chains rattle and tug against my horns. I'm unable to walk far from the wall. I lower my head and strain against the chains, until the muscles in my neck scream in protest.

Breaking my horns would be a permanent solution, since they grow from the bone of my skull. It would be bloody as well, since it would tear the arteries and veins inside my horns. I can't risk bleeding out. Whoever chained me to the wall by my horns knew my weakness.

Hunger gnaws, persistently, in my stomach. Food alone won't be enough to sustain me. Eventually, I will need to feed. My survival depends upon my devouring kiss. Regret strangles my throat. Perhaps I was a fool for refusing to feed from Pyrah one last time.

At the thought of my mate, my chest tightens as if crushed by an invisible fist.

Pyrah is alone. Vulnerable.

She has spent most of her life hunted by dragonslayers, hiding within her cave, without a single friend or ally. Even I was once her enemy. It's not unlikely that fears still live in the deepest shadows of her heart.

That she believes even her mate could abandon her.

She needs me.

And I don't know how long I can survive without her.

# CHAPTER TWENTY-THREE

PYRAH

In the darkness of my cave, my dragon's treasure glints under the pale glow of the mushrooms. I curl in the nest of pine boughs Rook built for me. Outside the mouth of the cave, moonlight colors the enchanted mist gray, still not yet darkened by his silhouette. I roll over with a frustrated sigh.

"You should rest," Lark whispers, lying under her blanket nearby.

"I can't." I breathe in Rook's scent, which still lingers on the pine boughs where he touched them. "Something feels wrong. In my gut, in my blood—I know he needs me."

Lark's eyes glow like embers. Sometimes she looks so much like her brother that it makes my chest ache. "Trust me, Rook has survived for this long on his own. He knows what he's doing."

But her words ring hollow. Dread grabs my ribs like a fist, squeezing my lungs until I can barely breathe.

"What if the queen catches him? What if—" My voice snags on the words. "What if I never see him again?"

"Pyrah." Lark's tone softens. "He will come back."

I swallow hard, fighting the urge to cry. Dragons rarely cry. But since I'm human, tears burn behind my eyes and threaten to overflow. If I let them, they will betray my weakness.

"We should have gone with him," I say, thickly, past the lump in my throat. "We could have protected him."

"While you can't shift? No. He made the right choice."

Yet another reminder of my current vulnerability. I miss the freedom of my wings and the power of my dragonfire. I'm trapped in this soft body, my blunt teeth and nails useless compared to fangs and claws.

"Gods." Lark's voice breaks the heavy silence. "I'm still hungry."

"You are?"

"Dinner wasn't enough. I can't survive on soup alone."

I prop myself up on one elbow. Across the cave, her eyes smolder. "Do you mean…?"

"The devouring kiss." She traces her lips with the back of her claws, as if remembering the taste of desires consumed before. "I spent much of my energy on magic. Tomorrow, I will hunt for prey. A succubus must feed every day to survive."

My heartbeat stutters. "Every day?"

"Yes." She hugs the blanket tighter to her body. "If I wait much longer, the hunger will start gnawing at me from the inside out, destroying my own body."

Realization settles over me like a shroud. Rook's tension at dinner. His refusal to kiss me with a devouring kiss. The way he pulled away when I offered to feed him...

"He lied to me." My throat tightens. "Rook said he could wait, that he didn't need to feed yet."

"My brother has always fought his own hunger as an incubus." Lark's voice carries a trace of sorrow. "He thinks he can deny himself through willpower alone."

"But why? Why wouldn't he just tell me?"

"To protect you. He would never harm you by choice."

He was starving himself to keep me safe. My heart aches at his steadfast devotion. All this time, he's been fighting his own nature, denying his needs. For me.

"I knew he was lying," I say. "He can be such a stubborn, infuriating, beautiful man."

She lets out a broken laugh. "You know him well already."

Lark falls asleep long before I'm ready, the rhythm of her breathing turning deep and slow. She looks so peaceful, even if that might not be the truth of how she feels. I envy her ability to rest. Perhaps her time in the Forgotten Tower taught her how to carve out tranquility from the threat of danger.

Stirring, Lark tugs her cloak tighter around herself. It gets cold at night up in the mountains. Her broken horn catches the glow of the luminous fungi. I wonder how long ago she was hurt.

My restless fingers fidget with the pine boughs. I strip needles from a branch and toss them away, a small act of destruction that distracts me. The bed Rook made feels empty without him.

I can't sleep—*won't* sleep—until he has safely returned.

I toss and turn in my bed of pine boughs, unable to stop, my body as uncomfortable as my mind. I barely spent any time at all in Netherhaven, when Scaldric brought me there, but I imagine the city and the castle. I think of all the dangers that could trap Rook there.

Nothing lasts as long as a night without sleep.

Outside the cave, the enchanted mist begins to lighten from gray to white. It's nearly dawn. I watch with rising horror as day breaks.

"Lark," I say. "Lark, wake up."

She blinks open her eyes. "What is it?"

"Rook never came back."

Lark sits upright, alert in an instant. Her gaze sweeps the cave as if hoping to find him lurking in some corner, but of course he isn't here. We are alone.

"He promised," I say. "He promised he would return by dawn."

"We should wait for him to return." She toys with a gold coin from my dragon's hoard. She turns it over and over between her fingers. "It's a long road from Netherhaven."

"He went to find the soulstone." The words slip out before I can stop them. "In the castle library."

Lark freezes, her face draining of color. Her fingers clench around the gold coin until her knuckles turn white. "What did you say?"

"The soulstone. He said it would help control his hunger, help us find our *kelrial*." I lean forward, caught by the horror in her expression. "What's wrong?"

"No, no, no." Lark drops the coin, pressing her palms to her temples. "Zin told me about the soulstone. She's the one who said it was in the castle library."

"Zin?" My blood turns to ice. "The queen's sorceress?"

"Queen Dulcamara's favorite." Lark's voice cracks. "We worked together when I was still a royal sorceress. I know Zin all too well. If Rook went into the castle looking for the soulstone..."

"It was a trap." The realization hits like a physical blow.

"Can't you make a portal into the castle?" My voice rises with desperation. "Like you did for Rook at the graveyard?"

Lark shakes her head. "The stones of Netherhaven Castle won't let me. They're imbued with ancient magic that repels portals and most spells. Even the most powerful sorceress in the Overworld can't breach those walls with magic."

I kick aside my treasure, sending gold scattering across the cave floor. The metallic clinking echoes off the walls, matching the chaos in my mind as I search for solutions.

"I can't stay here," I say. "Not while he's in danger."

Lark frowns. "Don't put yourself in danger."

"I don't care." My fingers curl against the stone wall, my nails feeble instead of claws. "I would fight for him."

"And how will you fight?" Lark's frown deepens. "Are you skilled with a sword?"

"No, but—"

"But you can't shift into a dragon. For how long? Days?"

Heat burns behind my eyes, though I refuse to let the tears fall. "Stop treating me like I'm helpless. I may be stuck in this form, but I am still a dragon. I've killed dozens of knights who thought they could claim my head as a trophy."

"And now you can't." Lark's words cut deeper than any blade.

"You sound just like Scaldric. Like I'm something to be protected and locked away."

"That's not what I—"

"I don't need your protection. I need your help before—"

I can't finish the thought. Can't breathe past the invisible claws of dread that strangle my neck. The cave walls feel like they are clamping down around me, this space shrinking until there's nothing left. I'm no stranger to this panic that overwhelms me, this animal instinct that screams to hide.

Last time I felt this way, Rook held me in his arms, his deep voice rumbling through my body, soothing me until the fear ebbed.

But this time, he's gone. He could be gone forever.

When I try to stand, my legs give out and I fall to my hands and knees. I'm pushed down by a phantom weight as my fingers are splayed on the stone. Black spots dance at the edges of my vision as I forget how to breathe. I'm trapped, trapped in this cave and in this body.

"Pyrah?" Lark's voice sounds faraway, underwater. "What's wrong?"

I can't speak, can't think.

Hands cradle my face, but they feel wrong somehow—too small, too soft. Not Rook's hands but his sister's.

"You're here with me," Lark says, her voice an anchor. "You're safe."

Cool magic seeps from her fingers into my skin, like mountain mist on a summer morning. Dread loosens its grip around my ribs, and I'm left gasping for breath as if I nearly drowned.

Lark lifts her hands from my face. "Better?"

I'm still shaking, my heart still pounding too hard against

my ribs like a trapped bird, but I can feel myself returning to solid ground. The cave no longer feels too small. "I think so," I say, my voice hoarse. "I-I'm sorry for getting angry with you."

"Fear and anger are two sides of the same coin. Often, one disguises the other." Her words carry the weight of someone who knows this truth all too well.

I think of my mother's death, of all the years of hiding in my cave, of all the dragonslayers who tried to kill me. My fingers trace the scars on my neck where Scaldric bit me, marking me as his mate. Even now, I remember the pain.

"Anger is better. I hate losing myself to fear." I hug myself, trying to stop the trembling in my body. In my dragon form, I have never felt this vulnerable—being a woman betrays every emotion, every weakness. "I'm not strong enough."

"You are," Lark says. "This doesn't make you weak."

"Who am I without the fear and the anger?" The question slips out before I can stop it. "Take them away, and I don't know who I am. If there's anything of *me* left. I have spent so long struggling to survive, I'm not sure I remember how to live."

"I know how you feel," Lark says, softly. "I don't know the answer."

I press my palms flat against the stone floor, grounding myself in this place. This cave has been my sanctuary for so long—my fortress against dragonslayers, my shelter from storms, my refuge from the world that wanted me dead.

But now the cold stone offers no comfort. The walls that once felt protective now feel like a prison. Every shadow reminds me of Rook's absence, every echo mocks the silence where his voice should be.

Then it hits me—bright and sudden as lightning splitting the sky.

"Zin." I grab Lark's arm. "We don't need to break into the castle. We need to draw her out."

"What do you mean?"

"If she set this trap, she must know where Rook is." My fingers tighten on her sleeve. "We could set our own trap. Catch her. Make her tell us what happened to him."

Lark's eyes widen. "You want to capture Zin?"

"You know her better than anyone. Know how she thinks, what she wants." I look into her eyes. "Help me trap her, Lark. She's our only link to Rook."

Lark's face relaxes as understanding settles in her bones. She paces across the scattered gold, her bare feet making soft clicking sounds against the metal.

"You're right." Her voice comes out as a husky whisper. "Queen Dulcamara would never kill him outright. She would want to make an example of him first. Which means..."

"He's alive." The words taste like hope on my tongue. "Somewhere."

"If Zin orchestrated this, she will know exactly where they're keeping him." Lark's fingers twist in her hair. "But catching her won't be easy. She's clever, dangerous."

"More dangerous than leaving Rook to rot in some godforsaken dungeon?" My hands clench into fists. "Than abandoning him to whatever tortures the queen and her sorceress have planned?"

The memory of Zin's magic crawling across my skin makes my stomach turn. But beneath the revulsion burns something hotter—rage at what she's done to Rook, to Lark, to me.

"We can't let them win," I say.

Lark traces patterns in the scattered coins, lost in thought. "I know how to draw Zin out."

"How?"

She rises, her red eyes smoldering. "There's something Zin wants more than anything. More than pleasing Queen Dulcamara. More than tormenting prisoners."

My skin prickles at her tone. "What is it?"

When she speaks, it's so quiet, almost a whisper. "Me."

# CHAPTER TWENTY-FOUR

ROOK

Pale, ethereal mushrooms sprout from the damp-slick walls of the dungeons. They caught my eye three bowls of gruel ago. Or was it four? Time has little meaning here.

The sight of the mushrooms twists something in my chest. Lark would be fascinated by this fungus, telling me about its properties, whether its flesh would hurt or heal.

I don't know if I will ever see my sister again.

My wrists chafe against the shackles, my shoulders screaming from supporting my weight. But I can't look away from the mushrooms. White spores drift through the stale dungeon air. Each speck glows in the torchlight before falling into the darkness and powdering the ground beneath my chains.

Even in this abysmal place, these mushrooms survive,

growing deep beneath the cracks in the mildewed stone. They persist despite this misery. Just as I must.

Eventually, the torches splutter out. I'm plunged into darkness for an eternity; the hours counted only by the snowfall of spores. When a guard's heavy footsteps echo outside my prison, the sound brings me something akin to hope. I hate myself for it. The guard replaces the torches before abandoning me once more.

Firelight slants across the wall, the illumination almost dazzling me. I stare at the words carved into the stone, not understanding them, until finally, they fall into place.

Umbric runes.

They are written in an ancient, formal dialect of Umbric, used by demons a thousand years ago, and I can understand some words and occasional phrases.

*...unlocked for me... from hell we come...*

Surprise jolts my blood, and my heart beats harder. The runes could only refer to the Demongate, the door between the worlds. Could this room be connected to it somehow? I don't know why else there would be ancient Umbric runes carved into the walls. I have never seen the Demongate myself, since it was both forbidden and impossible to find.

My mother knew all about it, but she never told me.

And now she's gone.

Whenever I think of her, I don't feel anything. Not the way I should. Mostly, I'm numb. I must do what's necessary to survive. There's no time for grief when it will only bring me closer to my own death.

But now, trapped in this prison, I'm forced to be alone with myself, and I'm often my least favorite person. I can't drown myself in either blood lust or carnal lust. There's no battle and no fucking here. Just silence and a choking sensation in my throat.

Am I…afraid? Yes, that's the best way to describe this emotion. Fear claws under my skin like a living thing. I want to pace back and forth, to release some of this energy but the chains around my horns prevent me from doing so.

I'm trapped in my own body, stuck inside my own head.

I force myself to breathe. To survive.

I wait for the queen to return.

I expect her to parade into this dungeon at any moment, ready to sneer at me and slap me until she's gratified by the bruises on my skin. My arms scream from the chains holding me up. The metal shackles bite into my wrists, though the chains on my horns force me to keep kneeling or standing.

The pale mushrooms, my only companions, drop another cluster of spores. I have counted twelve releases now. Each one seems to come about an hour apart, if my sense of time hasn't totally abandoned me in this stone tomb.

The mushrooms release another cloud of spores. Thirteen now. I wonder if Lark cultivated fungi like this one during her imprisonment, if she watched them grow to keep track of time passing. The thought of my sister enduring weeks in the Forgotten Tower makes my chest tight.

A drop of water hits my shoulder from a crack in the ceiling.

It traces down my bare chest, joining the rivulets of sweat and grime. I twist away from the unwanted contact.

Still Queen Dulcamara does not return.

I forgot how much I hate waiting to be hurt. It's almost worse than being hurt itself, to feel so sick with dread.

The guard brings me more gruel, the same thick sludge that may have been oats in another life. I force myself to consume it, though it fails to fill the void inside me.

Without Pyrah, I will starve.

The muscles throughout my body begin aching, though I'm unable to lie down with the chains shackled to my horns. They prevent me from doing anything but slumping against the stone wall.

The flickering glow of a torch creeps beneath the door.

Someone is coming.

A torch-carrying guard opens the door.

Finally, the dread in my gut turns into something akin to relief.

Queen Dulcamara strides into the room wearing a red gown. Perhaps to better hide bloodstains. A knife glints in her hand, not a proper dagger but a silver one taken from her dinner table. Was she feasting mere moments ago?

She slips an apple from her pocket and begins skinning it with the knife. Curls of peel drop to the floor. She might want me to eat them like a pig does scraps.

"Why haven't you tried to escape?" she asks. "Are you waiting for the red dragon to save you?"

There's no safe way to reply. I keep my eyes focused on the knife, ready to jerk away if she attacks. Not that I can go far.

"Rumors spread fast across the kingdom," she continues.

"Everyone knows that I captured the Gray Prince. If you mean anything to Pyrah, she will come looking for you."

Dulcamara intends to lure out the dragon. Am I nothing but bait?

"Why Pyrah?" I ask, speaking at last.

"One dragon isn't enough." She digs deeper into the flesh of the apple.

"Scaldric isn't enough?"

"She would have married him, before you destroyed their wedding ceremony."

"Against her will."

"You should know." Dulcamara grimaces at the apple as if she discovered a worm, though the fruit looks fine to me. "You have chained her in aellurium yourself."

I swallow hard, my mouth dry. I haven't had any water to drink since my capture. "I did." There's no use denying it.

"She can't truly care about you." Her lips curl into a sneer. "You're an incubus."

So many insults fit into that one word: I'm less than human, a predator, and a monster driven by the urge to fuck.

I have heard it all before. It's not difficult to fill in the blanks.

"She won't come," I say, not knowing if it's a lie. "You're wasting your time."

Dulcamara stares at me with her deadened eyes. "What happened after you stole her away from the wedding?"

When I shrug, the chains at my wrists jingle. "I'm an incubus. You already know."

She can imagine every depraved act she wishes. Her eyes narrow as she stares at me. "What did you do to her?"

I trace my tongue over the points of my fangs. "Pyrah *was* a virgin," I say, letting emphasis linger on the word.

Dulcamara stabs her blade deep into the flesh of the apple. She saws a slice free, though she doesn't eat it. "In this kingdom, do you know what we do to rapists?"

Disgust punches my gut like a fist. I always require explicit consent, but Dulcamara must believe that I forced myself on Pyrah.

The queen wants me to be the villain?

I can be her fucking villain.

I keep any emotion from my face. "Death, if I'm not mistaken. Though it seems to depend on who's doing the raping."

For the powerful, the law never seems to apply.

Dulcamara drops the apple. Before I can react, she holds the silver knife to my throat. The blade pricks my skin.

Undisguised hatred shines in her eyes. "I always knew there was something wrong with you." Her words taste like familiar poison, and it's too easy to drink them down. "Filthy cambion whore."

"Whore?" I grunt. "I would do it all again for free."

I want her to believe I'm nothing but a heartless bastard who could never love anyone. It's safer if she believes there's no true connection between Pyrah and me.

Let me be the only one she hurts.

The knife digs deeper into my throat. Heat trickles down my skin. Blood. Not enough to weaken me, nothing but a threat.

"It makes no fucking sense," I say, ignoring the sting of the blade. "Why do you need another dragon?"

"You're nothing but a cambion," she says. "Your seed is useless. Perhaps it hasn't occurred to you that two dragons can breed."

My stomach churns, the temptation to vomit increasing, but I won't give her the satisfaction. "And?"

"Imagine an army of dragons loyal to the crown."

I'm not arrogant enough to imagine such a thing. "Pyrah would rather kill Scaldric than submit to him."

"Where is she?"

I would rather die than betray Pyrah.

But the queen can't know the truth. "Who the fuck knows?" The lie rolls off my lips with ease.

Dulcamara lifts the knife from my throat, though it's only a temporary respite. The blade drifts lower down my body, not yet cutting me, before threatening my groin. It's impossible not to tense up under the cold steel.

It's better, in moments like these, to not inhabit my body. I want to be too far away to feel anything.

She lets the blade linger against my balls, as if pondering castration. Logically, distantly, I consider this mutilation. I could die from shock or infection. An ironic death for an incubus, just the kind of cruelty to suit the queen.

"You're a big bull of a man," she says, "though I have always found bulls less useful than oxen."

Death would be better than becoming her court eunuch.

With my hands shackled in front of me, and a knife at my balls, I'm left with few options. But I'm never helpless.

"Wait," I say. "Your Majesty."

Her gaze snaps to my eyes. "Are you ready to confess?"

It's just the distraction I needed.

I jerk my arms down and grab the blade in my left hand. It slices open my palm but pain means nothing. I wrench the knife from the queen and grab the handle in my right hand.

It takes her an instant to realize her mistake.

She scrambles away from me, screaming, "Guards!"

I lunge with the knife, aiming for her jugular vein, but I'm too ambitious. The chains around my horns yank my head back when she's already out of reach.

Guards swarm into the room like flies on shit.

I'm armed with a dinner knife while they have swords. Either way, I'm fucked, so I toss aside the blade.

That doesn't deter the guards. They punch me in the gut with their steel-armored fists. I take a blunt sword pommel to the jaw. Dazed, I stagger against the wall, while blows keep raining down on me. The iron taste of blood fills my mouth.

They keep shouting at me, words that don't make sense, until finally they kick my legs wider and chain my ankles to the wall. They unlock the shackles at my wrists, but a moment later, they lock my arms again.

I'm spread-eagled. Defenseless.

Dulcamara watches me bleed. Satisfied by the violence wrought upon me, she calls off her guards. As she exits, her command rings in my ears.

"Let him rot."

I'm left alone with pain as my only companion. It hurts even to breathe. The guards must have broken my ribs. One of my eyes has swollen shut, ruining my depth perception, and the taste of blood lingers in my mouth. Chained to the wall like this, I can do nothing but slump against the stones.

Was it worth it? I came so close to stabbing the queen in her jugular and watching her bleed to death.

Next time, I won't miss.

I drift in and out of consciousness, though I never sleep for long. Pain robs me of my slumber. The blood slowly drains from my arms, chained above my head, until they start to go numb. I fight the sensation by twisting against my shackles. How long can they keep me like this?

Lark's voice echoes inside my head. *Don't believe whatever you feel, but trust that you will make it through.* She was talking about magic, but her words have a deeper meaning to them. Right now, I feel despair, but I must believe that I can survive this moment and the next.

Night falls. The flickering glow of a torch heralds the return of a guard.

He's not alone.

I forget how to breathe until the woman steps into the light: Zin. She's carrying a glass bottle of liquid. It's too red to be the same potion as before.

She uncorks the bottle and pours a cup. "Drink."

"No." I have no reason to trust her.

"It's a healing potion."

"Why?"

"Nobody but worms will want you when you're dead."

She's not wrong. I allow her to bring the cup to my mouth.

The bitter sludge reminds me of my sister's own healing potions, so she must speak the truth. Slowly, the pain in my body begins to fade as it stitches itself together.

"Thank you," I mutter, since she didn't have to help me.

"You shouldn't thank me." Zin can't disguise a small shudder. "The queen prefers to heal her prisoners between rounds of torture, so they last longer. Many of her enemies have been locked away for an eternity."

"Where are we?" I ask.

"Nowhere."

I was a fool to have even asked. Zin would never tell me the truth.

When a dagger glints in her hand, every muscle in my body tenses. I would recognize that blade anywhere—it's one of my confiscated daggers. She takes a crystal bottle from her pocket. It's empty, unlike the bottles filled with potions, and that alone rings alarm bells inside my head.

"Zin," I say, "what are you doing?"

She brings the dagger to one of my wrists and lets it linger against my skin. My heartbeat hammers against my ribs as if it wants to break free from its cage. Still somewhat delirious from the pain, I can't stop staring into her eyes. They look darker than a night without stars.

"I thought you didn't want me dead," I say.

"I don't."

I hiss through my teeth when she cuts me across my wrist. The wound isn't deep enough to kill or even seriously injure me. She lets my blood trickle into the crystal bottle, drip by sickening drip, filling it with crimson.

Why does she want my blood?

Dread slams into my belly like a fist. I have royal blood in my veins. Dulcamara needs an heir. The queen knows that I'm sterile, incapable of fathering a child, but I'm still full of vitality and not yet rotting in the dirt. My blood could be a replacement for my father's bones.

An heir born of dark magic could be *my* child.

The pain in my heart hits the deepest. "Don't do this, Zin." I'm unable to keep a growl from roughening my voice. "Don't take this from me."

"It's just a little blood." Her words sound emotionless.

When the bottle overflows, my blood trickles over her fingers. She corks the bottle and pockets it. Grimacing, she glances down at her bloodstained hands.

"I know what you want," I say. "What the queen wants."

"I don't think you do."

I lock gazes with her, daring her to reply. "Tell me."

Zin picks at the blood beneath her fingernails. She must be feigning indifference while calculating her next move. Finally, she lifts her gaze to meet mine.

"The queen has many ambitions," she says.

"She wants an heir, doesn't she?"

Zin scoffs. "All rulers want an heir."

I have no patience for flippant remarks. "I will answer one of your questions if you answer mine."

"Where is she hiding?"

"Pyrah?"

"No, Lark."

"My sister?" Surprise jolts my muscles. "Why?"

She doesn't blink. "Answer the question."

It's too dangerous to give her Lark's location, even if she's hidden behind enchanted mist. "She isn't in the Forgotten Tower."

"Obviously." Zin curls her lip. "Never trust the word of a demon."

"It's still the truth."

"Not enough of the truth."

Unease crawls down my back like a creature with a hundred legs, a disgusting sensation along my spine. "I know of truths that I wish were lies. I know why the queen dug up my father's bones."

"Her Majesty would never dirty her own hands."

"Did she make you do it?" I fire back.

"Would it matter if I had?"

"You're nothing better than the queen's pawn."

"I know."

I bite my tongue between my fangs, just enough pain to keep me focused. Zin has always infuriated me with her sneering attitude. I can't stop her from taking my blood. I can only pray that my worst fears don't come true.

Finally, she takes a third bottle from her pocket. Thank fuck it's the sleeping potion. Without resistance, I swallow it down. There's no fight left in me tonight, and I welcome the oblivion of a sleep without dreams.

# CHAPTER TWENTY-FIVE

LARK

I trace my fingers along the stone walls of the narrow alley behind the apothecary shop, Morel & Sons, remembering nights spent here with Zin.

It's a cruel thing, memory, always reminding me what I have lost.

A cat slinks past, rubbing against my silver skin. Black as night, just a bit darker than the abyss of her eyes. Everything here whispers of her presence—the scent of crushed herbs, the flutter of crow wings, the way shadows seem to deepen in the corners.

The hidden staircase creaks beneath my feet, each step a memory of nights spent climbing to her door. Third board from the top still groans. Fourth step still wobbles. Some things never change.

My broken horn throbs. The pain feeds something darker

inside me, a hunger that coils and twists. Up here, the scent of dried herbs mingles with smoke from her eternally burning incense.

Her door. Plain wood, iron hinges. But the lock—that's pure silver, enchanted to keep intruders out. Has she changed the magic to keep me out?

My fingers shaking, I touch the silver, expecting pain.

But the enchantment recognizes me, warm against my skin. The door swings open to her sanctuary—bottles lined on shelves, grimoires stacked on tables, dried flowers hanging from the rafters. Everything exactly as I remember.

The hunger grows stronger. Here in her space, surrounded by pieces of her life, I feel my succubus nature rising. My skin grows hot, my breath quickens. The predator in me knows—this is where I'll find my prey.

"Come home to me, little bird," I whisper, using her words against her. The irony tastes sweet on my tongue. She kept me caged, fed me scraps of affection. Now I'll be the one doing the hunting.

I settle into her favorite chair, crossing my legs, letting my silver hair spill over my shoulders the way she always liked. The beast inside me purrs. Let her find me here, in her private space. Let her see what she created in that Tower.

I am no longer her pet songbird. I've grown talons and fangs of my own.

I trace my fingers along the dried herbs, remembering how we'd gather them together in the royal gardens. The nightshade blooms still hold their deep purple, even in death. Just like the bruises she'd leave on my skin.

"Such dangerous beauty," she'd whisper, those dark eyes consuming me. "Like you, my silver bird."

Chamomile dangles in delicate clusters. She'd brew it for me when nightmares kept me from sleep, adding honey and whispers of comfort. Strange how those gentle moments lived alongside the cruelty. Like the nightshade—beauty and poison intertwined.

"The deadliest flowers are often the most alluring," she told me once, crushing belladonna berries for her potions. The juice stained her fingers purple-black, like ink bleeding across parchment. She painted designs on my skin with those stained hands, marking me as hers.

My broken horn aches with the memory of her touch. Even now, after everything, my body remembers. The way she'd trace the curve of my horns, grip them to hold me still, use them to control me. The pleasure and pain she dealt in equal measure.

I shift in her chair, breathing in the herb-scented air. The hunger inside me grows stronger with each remembered touch. But I'm no longer the naïve creature who fell for her poisoned honey. I've learned to wield my own venom.

The shadows lengthen across the floor. Soon she'll return, expecting to find her domain empty and undisturbed. Instead, she'll find the predator she created, waiting in the dark.

The door creaks open. Zin freezes in the threshold, her dark eyes widening. The sight of her hits me like a physical blow—she's exactly as I remember, from her ink-black hair to the way she holds herself, like a drawn bow.

"You came back," she breathes. Her voice sends shivers down my spine.

My breath catches—she's still beautiful, still dangerous as nightshade. "I couldn't stay away."

I grip the arms of her chair, fighting the surge of memories.

Now she stands before me again, and I feel that same magnetic pull. My succubus nature responds to the familiar scent of her rosemary perfume. The hunger inside me rises, remembering how sweet her lust always tasted.

I remember the day she betrayed me like a scar carved into my soul. The way Zin's dark eyes held mine as she wove the portal spell, threads of magic wrapping around my wrists like chains. Her betrayal tasted like copper on my tongue.

"For your own good," she'd whispered, pressing one last kiss to my lips before the guards dragged me through. The Tower's darkness swallowed me whole.

But now, watching her approach, I let none of that show. Instead, I channel the hunger that's always there, just beneath my silver skin. Let her see what she expects—a succubus desperate for touch, for taste, for feeding.

"I tried to forget you," I breathe, rising from her chair. My fingers tremble as I reach for her face—not from desire but from suppressing the urge to tear her throat out. "Tried to hate you."

Her pulse jumps beneath my touch. Those dark eyes drink me in, and I feel her desire spark against my skin like static.

"But you couldn't," she murmurs, stepping closer. Her confidence makes my broken horn ache.

"No." I trace her jawline, remembering how she used to hold me down, control me, break me. "The hunger is too strong."

She smirks, thinking she's won. Thinking I'm still her tame little songbird.

I grab her hair and crush my mouth to hers. Pour all my rage into the kiss, let her mistake it for passion. Her lips part under mine and I devour her, teeth scraping, tongue demanding. Feed just enough to make her knees weak, to cloud her mind with lust.

She moans into my mouth, hands clutching my waist. The sound feeds both my hunger and my hatred.

This kiss tastes like vengeance.

I slide my hand under her skirt, fingers trailing up her thigh. Her skin feels like silk and memories flood back—nights spent tangled in her sheets, feeding from her endless desire. The familiar texture nearly breaks my resolve.

My succubus nature takes over as I deepen our kiss. I draw out her lust, drinking it like sweet wine. Her legs tremble. She clutches my shoulders, nails digging into my silver skin.

"Lark," she gasps against my mouth.

I could drain her completely. Take everything until she's nothing but an empty husk. The temptation burns through me, wild and fierce. My broken horn throbs with remembered pain, urging me to exact revenge.

But I need her. Need the information about Rook locked in that brilliant, cruel mind.

Still, I take more than I should. Pull the pleasure from her bones until she sways in my arms. Her dark eyes grow glassy, unfocused. The taste of her desire is intoxicating—spice and smoke and something darker underneath.

My fingers dig into her thigh, marking her pale skin. She whimpers, the sound shooting straight through me. Gods, I'd forgotten how responsive she is, how perfectly she yields to my touch.

The predator in me purrs. Here she is—the mighty royal sorceress, reduced to trembling need in my arms. I could keep drinking until she begs. Until she breaks. I pull back just enough to look into those dark eyes, clouded with desire. My silver fingers trail down her throat, feeling her pulse race beneath my touch.

"You always liked it rough," I whisper against her ear. "You liked taking what you wanted."

Her breath catches. "And you always gave it so sweetly."

The words spark rage in my chest, but I channel it into hunger instead. Let her mistake my aggression for passion, my hatred for need. My lips find her neck, teeth grazing the sensitive skin.

"I learned from the best." I bite down, not quite breaking skin. She gasps, arching into me. "You taught me how to take."

Her fingers tangle in my hair, trying to direct me. Still attempting to control, even now. I growl low in my throat and shove her against the wall, pinning her wrists above her head.

"No." I squeeze until she whimpers. "This time, you're my prisoner."

I press my thigh between her legs, feeling her heat through the thin fabric of her skirts. Her head falls back against the wall, exposing that lovely throat. Such trust from someone who never deserved mine.

"Please," she breathes, and the sound feeds something dark inside me.

I kiss her again, deeper this time, drawing out her essence with each stroke of my tongue. She tastes like spiced wine and desperation. Her desire floods my senses, as intoxicating as ever.

Rook would hate this—this taking without true consent. But Zin and I have never known anything else. We've always lived in shades of gray, in the space between yes and no. I feel no guilt as I drink deeper, pulling more and more of her energy into myself.

Her knees buckle. I hold her up, pressed between my body and the wall, as I devour everything she has to give.

Her dark eyes remain defiant even as she trembles against me. No trace of remorse crosses her face, no whispered apology falls from those cruel lips. Just hunger and need and that same arrogant tilt to her chin.

Something inside me withers. A foolish dream I'd been nurturing in secret—of reconciliation, of her falling to her knees and begging forgiveness for betraying me to the Tower. Of explaining it was all a misunderstanding, that she'd been forced to do it.

But there's only calculation in those obsidian eyes, even now. She watches me like a predator sizing up prey, despite being the one pinned to the wall.

"Did you think of me?" I whisper against her throat. "All those nights I spent chained in darkness?"

She laughs, breathy and low. "Every night, little bird. Every night I imagined breaking you further."

The words slice through my chest. I'd imagined our reunion so many times in my cell—her tears, her regret, her pleas for forgiveness. Such a child I was, even after everything.

"And here I am," I say, tightening my grip on her wrists until she gasps. "Still unbroken."

But something *is* breaking inside me—that last fragile hope that there might have been love beneath her cruelty. That we could somehow find our way back to those gentle moments between the pain.

Her lips curve in that familiar smirk. "Are you sure about that?"

I release her suddenly, stepping back. The loss of contact makes her stumble, catching herself against the wall. Without my touch, without the haze of feeding, I see her clearly at last.

There is no future here. No redemption. Only poison wrapped in honey, thorns hidden beneath rose petals. I was a fool to think otherwise.

I freeze, my fingers finding the dark bruises marring Zin's throat. The marks stand out like ink stains against her pale skin. My claw traces the edge of one particularly nasty bruise, and she flinches away from my touch. Pain flashes in those bottomless dark eyes.

Something twists in my chest. Despite everything between us, seeing her marked like this...

"Who did this to you?" The words come out rougher than I intend.

Zin's lips curl into a bitter smile. "Your brother."

The temperature in the room drops. My hand falls away from her throat as if burned. Rook did this? But looking at the bruises again, I recognize the pattern. The shape matches Rook's fingers perfectly.

The taste of her desire turns to ash in my mouth.

"Where is my brother?" The words tear from my throat, all pretense of seduction forgotten.

Zin's dark eyes widen with understanding. Her lips part, then press together in a thin line as realization washes over her face. "So that's why you're here."

"Tell me." I press closer, my silver fingers finding those bruises again. This time, I don't touch them gently.

Pain flickers across her features as I dig into the tender flesh. Her pulse races beneath my grip—not from desire now but fear. Good. Let her be afraid.

"You never came back for me at all," she whispers, and beneath the acid in her voice, I hear genuine hurt. Those bottomless dark eyes can't hide her disappointment.

I bare my teeth, letting her see the predator she helped create. "Did you really think I would? After what you did to me?"

Her breath catches as I tighten my grip. The bruises my brother left provide perfect targets for my fingers to press against.

"Tell me where he is, Zin. Now."

She tries to look away, but I force her to meet my gaze. Something breaks in those dark eyes—perhaps the last of her illusions about us, about what we meant to each other.

"The Forgotten Tower," she breathes.

Ice floods my veins. The words hit me like physical blows, each syllable a knife to my gut. I know exactly what awaits him there—the darkness, the chains, the endless silence broken only by guards' footsteps and distant screams.

My fingers spasm against her throat as memories overwhelm me—the weight of iron around my wrists, the bite of winter wind through barred windows, the crushing solitude that nearly broke my mind.

The moment of weakness costs me. Zin's hand flashes with dark energy, striking my chest. I stumble back, losing my grip on her throat. Pain blooms across my ribs as her magic burns through my defenses.

"Don't make me do this," Zin says, her voice soft despite the crackling power in her hands. "Please, Lark."

Another blast catches my shoulder, spinning me into her desk. Herbs scatter across the floor, their sweet scent mixing with the acrid smell of her magic. My broken horn throbs with remembered agony.

She advances, shadows wreathing her fingers. "I don't want to hurt you."

Rage burns through my paralysis. "You already did!" The words rip from my throat, raw and jagged. My voice cracks on the last word, and I hate how it betrays my pain.

My vision blurs, but I refuse to let the tears fall. Not here. Not in front of her.

Zin's fingers trace my collarbone, and before I can react, something cold presses against my skin. The aellurium jewelry gleams gold against my silver flesh. Pain lances through me as it fuses with my skin, spreading like molten metal through my veins.

"What have you done?" I stumble back, clawing at the metal that's now part of me. But it's too late—I can feel it coursing through my body, binding me to something. To someone.

"Now you'll understand." Zin pulls down her collar, revealing matching gold lines threading beneath her skin. "We're bound together. Your pain is my pain. Your life is my life."

Horror crashes through me as the implications sink in. I can't kill her without killing myself. The perfect trap—she knows my vengeful nature, knows I'd gladly sacrifice myself to destroy her. But not when it means leaving Rook alone in that Tower.

"This proves I never wanted to hurt you," she whispers, reaching for me. "Everything I did was—"

I stumble away from her touch, but something new floods my senses. Emotions that aren't mine wash over me—longing so deep it aches, twisted with a darkness I recognize all too well.

Desire and hatred tangle together like roses and thorns.

"You're lying," I snarl, but the bond betrays her truth. Beneath all her cruelty, all her calculated manipulation, there's something genuine—a hunger that mirrors my own.

I can't bear it. Can't bear feeling her emotions coursing through me, can't stand knowing that some part of her actually cares, even now. It makes everything worse somehow.

I flee, my boots clattering on the wooden stairs. She doesn't try to stop me. She doesn't have to—she's already won. We're bound together now, her poison running through my veins like liquid gold.

I stumble through darkened streets, my heart pounding against my ribs. The aellurium burns beneath my skin, threads of molten gold weaving through my veins. Each pulse sends new waves of foreign emotion crashing through me.

Ducking into a shadowed alcove, I press my hands against the rough stone and try to steady my breathing. The bond pulses, and suddenly I'm drowning in Zin's feelings—a twisted tangle of possession and need that makes me want to claw my skin off.

My fingers spark with magic as I tear open a portal, not caring where it leads. Anywhere but here. Anywhere but near her. The void swallows me, but even its emptiness can't silence the echo of her emotions.

Longing hits me like a physical blow. Not mine—hers. Pure and sharp as broken glass, cutting through layers of manipulation and cruelty. Behind it all lurks a desperate hunger that matches my own, a yearning so deep it threatens to pull me under.

I emerge in the forest, falling to my knees in damp leaves. The bond throbs and fresh understanding floods me. Every cruel word, every harsh touch—they were armor, protecting something softer underneath. Something that still remembers gentle kisses and whispered promises in the dark.

"No," I choke out, pressing my palms against my temples. I don't want to feel this. Don't want to know that beneath all her poison, some part of her still...

Hatred follows, dark and bitter as wormwood. But even that can't completely drown out the underlying current of desire. Of regret. Of something that might have been love, if either of us knew how to love without breaking things.

The truth of it tears through me—she wasn't lying. Not about this. The realization makes everything worse, turns all our shared cruelty into something more complicated than simple revenge.

I curl into myself, silver skin gleaming in the moonlight, as our twisted emotions tangle together until I can't tell which belongs to whom anymore.

I press my forehead against the cool forest earth, trying to sort through the storm of emotions coursing through me. The aellurium binding pulses beneath my skin, carrying echoes of Zin's feelings across our newfound connection.

Like a fool, I ran before confirming Rook's location. The Forgotten Tower... My hands tremble at the thought of those cold stone walls. But through our curse-link, I might have sensed if she had lied about keeping him there.

My fingers dig into fallen leaves, crushing them. I could go back right now, confront her again. The bond would reveal her true intentions, strip away her masks of deception. Every word, every claim about my brother's imprisonment—I would know the truth of it all.

But returning means facing her. Means standing before those bottomless dark eyes and feeling everything she feels. Means wrestling not just with her emotions but with my own tangled response to them.

The thought of stepping foot in that room again makes bile rise in my throat. Even now, I feel phantom chains around my wrists, hear the echo of her boots on stone as she approached my cell in the Tower.

Yet Rook needs me. My brother, who came for me when I was imprisoned. Who never stopped searching, never gave up hope of finding me.

The bond throbs, sending fresh waves of Zin's emotions washing over me. Longing tangles with possessiveness, desire with cruel satisfaction. She wants me back—wants to chain me again, this time with gold instead of iron.

I push to my feet, brushing dirt from my knees. Dawn approaches, painting the sky in shades of gray. I need to return to Pyrah, tell her what happened. We'll find another way to locate Rook.

I won't go back to her. Won't let her sink her claws into me again, no matter what truths the bond might reveal.

But guilt gnaws at my chest as I open a portal home. Am I abandoning Rook to the same fate I had suffered, just to avoid facing my former tormentor?

# CHAPTER TWENTY-SIX

PYRAH

I pace the cave restlessly, my bare feet sliding across cool coins. The emptiness without Rook feels like a physical wound. When Lark materializes through her portal, I rush forward, desperate for news.

But one look at her face stops me cold. Something's wrong. The silvery sheen of her skin seems different, threaded with thin golden lines that catch the firelight.

"What happened?" My throat tightens.

Lark's fingers trace the metallic patterns spreading across her collarbone. "Zin cursed me. When I confronted her about Rook..." Her voice cracks. "She bound our life-forces together with aellurium magic."

The word makes my skin crawl. Memories of cold chains flash through my mind—feelings of being trapped, helpless, forced into human form. "Aellurium?" My hands clench into fists.

"It's fusing with my skin." Lark pulls back her sleeve, revealing more golden veins spreading like a parasitic web. "I can feel her now, in my blood. In my thoughts."

Bile rises in my throat. The metal that took my freedom, now corrupting Lark from within. "We have to break this curse."

"I can't."

"All aellurium should be destroyed, buried in the deepest ocean trench where no one can ever use it to control another being again."

"I wish it were that simple." Lark's red eyes shine with unshed tears. "But our lives are linked now. If Zin dies, I die. If I die, she dies."

"She had no right! To take your choice away like that..." The violation of it makes my blood boil. No one should have that power over another.

Lark touches my arm gently. "We will find a way. But first, we need to save Rook."

I nod, but the sight of those golden lines spreading across her silver skin fills me with rage and horror. Aellurium—the metal of slavery and stolen consent. Now it has claimed someone else I care about.

I move to the cave entrance, tracking Scaldric's golden form through gaps in the clouds. "He's been circling for hours, waiting for me to break cover." My fingers trace the invisible barrier of Lark's protection spell. "Like a vulture."

"The enchanted mist is holding." Lark joins me, the golden lines on her skin catching the dim light. "He can't penetrate it."

"What if we didn't hide?" I turn to face her. "Could you cast something to knock him from the sky? Trap him like..." The memory hits me with physical force. "Like when Zin froze my wings midflight. I remember the ice spreading, the helpless plummet." My hands shake. "We could use her own tactics against Scaldric."

Lark's red eyes narrow as she considers. "It's possible. I know similar spells that could ground him. But..." She touches one of the aellurium veins spreading across her neck. "Taking on a golden dragon directly would be incredibly dangerous. Even with magic."

"I'm tired of cowering while others hunt us." The words come out as a growl.

"Rook would want us to stay hidden to keep you safe." Lark's voice softens. "Going on the offensive now, while you're unable to shift—"

"Don't remind me." I wrap my arms around myself, hating this vulnerable human form. "But we can't just wait here forever while Rook suffers in that dungeon."

Another shadow passes overhead. Scaldric's wings block out the sun for a moment, and I feel the weight of his presence even through the magical barrier.

"We could try," Lark admits. "But if anything went wrong, if the spell failed..." She leaves the rest unspoken.

"He won't kill me." I trace the curve of my neck where his claiming bite once marked me. "That's not what he wants."

Lark's expression darkens. "There are worse things than death, Pyrah." Her fingers brush the golden lines spreading across her skin. "Trust me."

The weight of her words settles in my stomach like lead.

Images flash through my mind—Scaldric's possessive grip, his attempts to force me to submit to him, the way he spoke of me like property to be claimed.

"I know what he would do." My voice comes out hoarse. "Lock me away in some mountain lair. Force more claiming bites. Try to breed me until..." I wrap my arms around myself, fighting back nausea.

"He's obsessed." Lark moves closer to me. "The way he hunts you, circles endlessly. This isn't just about dragon territory or mating rights anymore."

"No." The word tastes bitter. "It's about control. Punishment for daring to choose my own mate." I think of Rook's gentle touches, so different from Scaldric's crushing grip. "He would make me watch while he killed Rook. Then keep me chained in aellurium forever."

"Like a trophy." Lark's red eyes flash with understanding. "A reminder to other female dragons who might defy tradition."

My hands clench into fists. "I would rather die fighting than let him cage me again."

"He wouldn't let you die."

The truth of her words hits me like a physical blow. I sink down against the cave wall, caught between my need to fight and the reality of our situation. Scaldric wouldn't grant me the mercy of death. He would ensure I lived a long life of captivity and violation, all while Rook rotted in the queen's dungeon.

"We need to find Rook." I press my palm against the cave wall, drawing strength from the solid stone. "The Forgotten Tower could be another of Zin's lies."

Lark nods, the golden lines on her skin catching firelight.

"She has always played games within games. Even when we were..." She trails off, lost in memories I can't read.

"What about the curse binding you together?" My fingers trace patterns in the dust, trying to work through the puzzle. "Can't you sense where she is, what she's doing?"

"It doesn't work like that." Lark touches one of the metallic veins. "I feel her life-force, her magic. But not her thoughts or location."

"Then we're still blind. Still trapped while..." My throat chokes.

"There might be another way." Lark's red eyes gleam. "The queen would want to keep him close, under her direct control. The Forgotten Tower is too remote, too obvious."

"The castle dungeons?"

"Deeper." Lark's voice drops to a whisper. "There are secret chambers beneath Netherhaven. Places where my mother was kept, where the king..." She stops, shoulders tensing.

The pieces click together. "That's where they would hide a captured prince. Close enough for the queen to torment him personally."

"And far from prying eyes." Lark's hands clench. "Where screams echo through stone and never reach the surface."

My blood runs cold at her words, at the personal knowledge behind them. But at least now we have a real target, not just Zin's misdirection.

"We can't trust anything she tells us." I push away from the wall, new determination flowing through me. "But we can trust what we know of our enemies. The queen's pride, her need for control..."

"She would want him where she could gloat." Lark's expression hardens. "Where she could break him slowly, personally."

The thought makes my dragon blood boil, but I force the rage down. We need clear heads now. Strategy, not blind fury.

"Wait." Lark gasps. "This curse works both ways."

"What do you mean?"

"Zin thinks she's clever, binding us together. But she forgot what I am." Lark's red eyes gleam with dark promise. "A succubus can enter dreams, slip into minds like smoke through a keyhole. And now that we're linked..." She taps her temple. "There's nothing she can do to keep me out."

My heart pounds faster. "You can see inside her head?"

"Better. I can walk through her dreams, peel back every lie, every secret." Lark's broken horn catches the light as she straightens. "No matter how strong her magical shields are, she can't block me now. The curse made sure of that."

"So, we can find out if Rook is really in the Forgotten Tower." The hope rising in my chest feels dangerous, but I can't stop it.

"Exactly." Lark traces one of the golden lines on her arm. "Tonight when she sleeps, I will slip into her mind. She won't be able to hide the truth from me."

"How soon?"

"Dawn is coming. Zin will have to rest eventually." Lark's smile turns predatory. "And when she does, I will be waiting. She thinks she knows what it means to be haunted? I will show her true nightmares."

The vengeful edge in her voice should frighten me. Instead, it feels right. After what Zin did to Lark, to Rook, she deserves whatever horrors await in her dreams.

I lie in my cave, hating this weakness, this womanly frailty that keeps me trapped in flesh and bone. The bleeding has slowed but still persists, a constant reminder of my current powerlessness. My dragonfire stays locked away, unreachable.

"Come on," I mutter, flexing my fingers. Not even a spark emerges. The cave walls mock my earthbound state.

I pace the length of my cave, counting steps to keep my mind occupied. One, two, three... My muscles coil with unused energy. Twenty steps to the back wall. Twenty steps to the entrance. The monotony drives me mad.

A pebble skitters across the floor as I kick it. In my true form, I could reduce this whole mountain to rubble. Instead, I'm stuck here, bleeding, waiting for my body to remember its truth.

I press my palm against the rough stone wall, trying to draw strength from the mountain itself. Dragons are creatures of patience, my mother used to say. But I have never mastered that skill. Every fiber of my being screams to take flight, to hunt, to fight.

I slide down the wall, wrapping my arms around my knees. My body feels like a cage of flesh, worse than any aellurium chain. At least that I could rage against. This requires a different kind of strength—the strength to endure, to wait.

I close my eyes, focusing on my breathing. In through the nose, out through the mouth. Searching for that spark of dragon magic that usually burns so bright within me. It's there, just beyond reach, like starlight glimpsed through storm clouds.

*Just a little longer,* I think.

Finally, *finally,* the bleeding stops. A wild hope rises in my chest.

I reach inside myself, searching for that familiar spark of dragon magic. There, like an ember waiting to ignite, my power hides deep within my body. I grasp it with my mind, letting the heat flow through my veins.

The transformation ripples across my skin. Bones shift and stretch, muscles expand, and scales emerge, gleaming crimson. Joy surges through me as my wings unfurl, brushing the cave ceiling. I am myself again. Whole. Complete.

A rumbling purr builds in my chest. I flex my claws against the stone floor, relishing their sharp strength. My tail sweeps behind me, perfectly balanced. Every sensation feels heightened after being trapped in human form—the air currents dance across my scales, the subtle vibrations in the rock hum beneath my feet.

Tears spring to my eyes, steaming, nearly boiling in my dragon form. I was never truly weak. Even in human shape, dragonfire burned in my soul. I spread my wings wider, feeling the pull of the heavens. Battle sings in my blood. I am no helpless maiden to be protected, no prize to be claimed. I am a force of nature, as wild and fierce as the mountains themselves.

My fire builds, ready to be unleashed. I am exactly what I was meant to be—neither human nor beast but something greater than both. Something that bridges earth and air, flesh and flame.

I crouch at the cliff's edge in my dragon form, watching Scaldric's golden scales flash in the sunlight as he circles above. My claws dig into the rock, leaving deep gouges. Every instinct screams at me to take flight, to meet him in battle.

Through gaps in Lark's enchanted mist, I track his movements. Back and forth, back and forth, he's like a pendulum marking time. He knows I'm here. His roars of frustration echo across the valley, making the water ripple in the nameless lake.

My wings twitch with the urge to fight. I could match him flame for flame, claw for claw. But Rook's life hangs in the balance. If I reveal myself now, before Lark can find him through Zin's dreams, Queen Dulcamara might—

I shake my head, dislodging that thought before it can take root. The rock beneath my claws crumbles as I grip it tighter. I destroy the brink of the cliff instead of destroying him.

"Soon," I growl, smoke curling from my nostrils. "Soon I will tear your golden wings to shreds."

But not yet. I must be patient, must wait for Lark to uncover the truth. My fire burns hot in my chest, begging for release, but I swallow it back. There will be time enough for battle once we know where Rook is truly imprisoned.

I coil my tail beneath me and resign myself to waiting. Though restraint runs counter to dragon nature, I will conquer it for Rook's sake. We locate him first. Then we wage war.

I will wait with patient violence.

Scaldric's shadow passes overhead again. I crouch on the cliff, my muscles tensing, though the mist keeps me hidden. His frustrated roar splits the air—he knows I'm near, but he can't pinpoint my location through Lark's magic.

Let him hunt. Let him drain his power with his futile patrol while we prepare. When we strike, I will teach him the difference between a dragon ruled by greed and one driven by devotion.

# CHAPTER TWENTY-SEVEN

LARK

I slip into Zin's dreams like a shadow through silk. Her mind materializes around me—the familiar chambers of the Forgotten Tower where she once held me captive. How fitting that here, in sleep's domain, our roles reverse.

Her little bird has returned to trap her in a cage.

"You aren't where you belong." Zin's voice ripples through the dream, soft as silk and sharp as daggers.

I pause, uncertain. Does she sense my intrusion into her sleeping mind? The dreamscape wavers, stone walls bleeding into mist.

"But I am." I trace a finger along her jaw. "Your aellurium curse works both ways. Your mind is mine now."

She tries to back away but hits the stone wall. Dream-walls, dream-stones, all bent to my will. The tower chamber shrinks, pressing closer, trapping her here.

With a succubus invading her mind, she won't be able to wake.

"Get out of my head!" She claws at me without hurting me.

I circle her, drinking in her mounting panic. "You bound us together, remember? Your little aellurium trick?" I hold up my arm where golden lines spider across my silver skin. "Did you think I wouldn't learn to use it?"

Her dark eyes dart wildly as the tower walls press closer. Sweat beads on her forehead. Even in dreams, the human mind can only take so much strain.

"Where is my brother?" I lean close enough to kiss. "And don't bother lying. I will know."

"The Forgotten Tower, I told you—"

My cruel laugh echoes off the walls. "Wrong answer." The stones groan inward another inch. "Try again."

"You can't—"

"I can do anything here." I lean closer, drinking in her fear.

Zin snaps her fingers, her magic sputtering out before it ignites. Sparks scatter and fade like dying embers. Her power means nothing here—this is my domain now.

I touch the golden threads at my neck, marked even in this dream. "Why did you do this to me?" My voice escapes me as a hiss, my throat throttled by the pain of emotion.

"Because I want you back," Zin replies, as if it's the simplest thing in the world. "You shouldn't be an outlaw from the crown. You should join me as a royal sorceress again."

I bare my fangs at her. "Never."

I press closer, stoking her fear, her desire, her pain. Each emotion floods through our cursed bond, echoing between us like ripples in a pool tainted by poison.

"You think binding us together will make me want you?" My fingers trace her neck, still bruised by my brother's fingers. "After everything you did to me in that tower?"

"I always made sure you survived."

"Stop." I grip her throat, wanting to squeeze until the words die. But even this violence sends sparks of twisted pleasure through our connection. She feels this choke hold as if it were a caress. "You don't get to justify what you did."

"Then why are you here in my dreams?"

Because part of me still craves her touch. Because memories of our nights together in the tower still haunt me. Because her feelings seep through our connection like poison, threatening to corrupt my hatred into something else.

I jerk away from her, disgusted. "Tell me where Rook is. Now."

"Or what?" A smile plays at her lips. "You will hurt me? We both know you will feel it, too."

She's right. This curse binds us together—her pain becomes mine, her pleasure echoes in my bones. I hate her for doing this to me. I hate myself more for the way my body responds to her nearness.

"I don't need to hurt you." I lean close, letting my breath ghost across her lips. "I can do so much worse."

She shudders beneath my touch. "Lark."

"Surrender to me." I brush my lips against her ear. "Tell me where Rook is, and this ends."

"I can't—the queen will—"

"The queen isn't here. It's just you and your *little bird*." I whisper the last words, my broken horn scraping her cheek. "And I can keep you caged in this nightmare forever."

*Trapped*. Like she did to me.

Trapped in the dungeon, trapped by cursed aellurium.

*I hate her*. Hate that she wants me.

My fingers tighten around her throat, watching her dark eyes widen and her breathing quicken. "Last chance before I make this nightmare permanent."

"You wouldn't." But uncertainty creeps into her voice.

I press harder, feeling the echo of pressure around my own neck through our cursed bond. I can feel exactly how I strangle her, starve her of air. "Try me."

"The dungeons," she gasps. "He's in the dungeons beneath Netherhaven Castle."

"Which dungeons?" The castle has dozens of cells.

She tries to look away, but I force her gaze back to mine. "The oldest ones. Deep beneath the castle foundations. Built from the ruins of the Demongate."

Ice spreads through my veins. "The Demongate?"

"Yes." Her pulse races beneath my fingers. "The queen keeps her most dangerous prisoners there. Where the ancient stones still hold traces of demon magic."

I release her throat, stumbling back. Our shared pain eases, replaced by a hollow ache in my chest. Those dungeons were built from the shattered remains of the Demongate itself—a portal to the Underworld, my ancestors' homeland.

I have what I need from Zin. I know where to find Rook.

But still, I do not release my hold on her dream.

"Why did you never try to set me free?" My voice cracks. "Why did you let me rot in the Forgotten Tower for seven weeks?"

Pain flashes across her face, mixed with something deeper—regret? Fear? Her dark eyes swim with emotions I can't untangle.

"I couldn't," she whispers.

"But you could!" I grab her shoulders, claws digging into her skin. "You came to my cell every night. Fed my hunger. Held me while I cried. You could have—"

"Lark—"

"Don't!" I shove her away. "Don't say my name like that. Like you cared. If you cared, you would have helped me escape. Instead, you let them hurt me. And still you came each night, pretending to want me while keeping me caged."

A tear slides down her cheek. In this dream, I can't tell if it's real or manipulation. Everything about Zin is smoke and mirrors, truth wrapped in lies.

"I couldn't," she repeats, and I see that same complex emotion swimming in her eyes—the one I could never name during those long nights in the Forgotten Tower. Is it shame? Devotion? Both?

"Why?" I demand.

"I care about you too much," she says.

Her words hit me like a slap to the face. Worse—I feel the truth of them burning through our bond, scorching my silver skin with golden lines of connection. Her emotion writhes inside me like a parasite, trying to take root.

"Care?" I laugh, cruelly, the sound as brittle as breaking glass. "Was that what you felt when you watched the guards beat me? When you starved me until I begged?"

"Yes," she whispers.

"I don't believe you," I reply, and I release my hold on her dream.

Letting her dreams—and mine—dissolve like ashes in the wind.

# CHAPTER TWENTY-EIGHT

ROOK

When I wake, I'm down on the ground. They unlocked the shackles from my wrists and ankles, but my horns have been chained to iron bars embedded in the floor beneath me.

I stay down, my cheek flat against the stone, and watch a spider spin a web in one corner of the room. It weaves silk between the cluster of mushrooms that still endures in this dungeon.

Slowly, I brace myself on my elbows and crawl onto my hands and knees. I can't straighten any taller. I'm forced down on all fours like an animal.

This was done to humiliate me.

Soon I'm thirsty, my mouth parched. I haven't had anything to drink but potions since being imprisoned. When a guard brings me a bucket of water, some of it sloshes over the edges and seeps between cracks in the stone floor. What a fucking waste. A growl of frustration tears from my throat.

The guard backs out of the room and locks the door behind him. Kneeling, I drink from my cupped hands. Stale, brackish water has never tasted sweeter.

But all the water in this world can't quench my demonic thirst.

I can't survive without consuming lust.

Time melts together without a clock or a calendar to give it meaning. Sunrises chase sunsets, one after another, while my hunger sharpens to the edge of a knife.

It has been days since I last fed. Ever since I lost my childhood innocence, I have not been able to escape this hunger. It gnaws inside me like a living thing, burning through my blood, crawling through the muscles around my bones.

My own body betrays me. Whenever I wake, my cock is hard. I refuse to touch myself in the squalor of this dungeon, since the guards or the queen might enjoy my depravity. I clutch my arms with my claws, forcing myself to focus on the bright sparks of pain instead of the intense need inside me.

Without Pyrah, I am lost. We agreed to be mates. It would be a betrayal if I devoured the lust of a stranger.

*Promise me you will come back. If you don't, I will hunt you down and murder you myself.*

Why hasn't she hunted me down already? Has she been hiding alone in her cave, still unable to shift into a dragon?

I refuse to believe she might also be a prisoner—or worse, dead.

Every day, I carve the stone wall with my claws, the deep grooves a tally of each time I have survived. I'm careful to sharpen my claws rather than dull them, since I have no weapons beyond my body.

Every night, Zin brings me the same sleeping potion.

Tonight, I refuse to drink. "I want to dream." The rust of disuse roughens my voice.

The sorceress stares at me with her dark eyes. "No."

I can't even straighten to my full height. I have lost the ability to loom over the sorceress and intimidate her. "Seven days. That's how long it's been since you captured me."

"Are you starving yet?" Her voice lacks any trace of emotion.

"Would it please you if I answered yes?"

"Others might find your bravado amusing, but I merely find it annoying." She tilts her head, her stare merciless.

"Just give me the fucking potion and let me sleep."

She shakes her head as if I have somehow disappointed her already low expectations. Without comment, she sets down the potion on the floor and watches me drink it. I swig down every last drop and wait for the darkness to take me.

In this dungeon, it's my easiest escape.

Delirium infests my mind. Words start slipping away from me.

I'm left with the strongest few: *need. Want. Hunger.*

It's too cold in here, and I can't stop shivering. When Zin returns, she stares at me for a long moment. What does she want from me? I'm down on my knees, my muscles tensed and ready to lunge.

Feral instinct whispers to me, *easy prey.*

Without my consent, she casts a spell upon me. Paralysis locks every bone in my body. I can't even bare my teeth at her.

She touches her hand to my forehead, a gesture that feels grotesquely caring. "You feel feverish."

She grabs the shackles around my horns. Beneath her hands, the iron freezes and shatters into fragments.

Freeing me.

Why?

What's next? Torture? Death?

But Zin's behavior becomes increasingly more bizarre.

She slices her hand through the air and opens a portal. On the other side, the silver glow of the moon washes a forest.

Is this a fever dream?

The spell around me breaks. I fall onto my hands and knees.

Her heartbeat hammers even faster. I can *hear* it thumping inside her ribs. I inhale through my teeth in a hiss of breath, and she backs away from me.

If she runs, I won't be able to resist.

Fuck.

*Fuck.*

I don't want Zin. She isn't my prey. No matter how much my hunger screams at me to consume her.

The ragged edges of the portal shimmer. Sparks of magic fly

into the darkness before disappearing. I let them capture my attention long enough that I can focus. The portal must be a trap, but I can't tell how, and the urge to escape builds inside me until it's impossible to resist.

"Go," Zin says, but I'm already fleeing.

I hit the portal at a run and tumble into the moonlit forest. I hunch on the ground, my stomach clenching and my mouth watering. There's nothing left in me to vomit, not even human food.

I'm beyond hungry.

Ravenous.

The portal crackles shut behind me. Where the fuck am I?

I pace in a circle, as if I'm still a caged beast, before recognizing the edge of the forest and the lights of a distant town: Havenwold.

The nearest town to Pyrah's territory, where Zin attacked us for the first time.

Why would she release me here, so close to safety?

It's hard to focus, my thoughts flying through my mind like dark birds in the night, too quick to grasp.

I linger on the brink between civilization and wilderness. The monster in me knows that my prey lives in town, slumbering in their beds or wandering out of taverns after a long night of drinking. Sleeping or drunk humans make easy prey.

No.

I won't surrender. I'm not a predator, and I refuse to betray Pyrah.

I turn my back on the city and flee deeper into the woods. I stumble through the underbrush and break branches that claw against my skin. Am I being hunted by the queen? I'm being too loud, too obvious. I'm naked, barefoot, unarmed.

My breathing sounds ragged. I force myself to stop, bracing myself against a tree. My claws sink deep into the bark.

Pyrah.

I'm possessed by a fierce longing to find her and drink her down. It's been far too long since I tasted her sweet desire. She's *mine* and I need her now more than ever.

But I can't.

Not like this. Not while I can't control myself.

I shake my head hard, trying to clear my mind, and my horns gouge the tree by accident. I'm little better than a stag in rut. An animal driven by instinct.

It's not safe to stay here.

And so I run.

The first time I fled from the queen, I hid in Hexfall. I know the way to the castle ruins by heart.

The night melts into an endless memory of black shadows and silver moonlight. The Thornwood welcomes me back with open arms, the cursed brambles tasting blood from my skin. I'm a monster among monsters. This is where I belong.

I've been running for so long that my lungs burn and my legs ache. I'm nearing the end of my stamina.

The ruins of Hexfall gleam under the moonlight.

I stumble over a broken stone before dropping onto the ground. I roll onto my back and stare at the moon above me. I'm gasping for breath. My heartbeat hammers against my ribs.

Even exhausting myself could not purge my hunger. Pyrah dominates my memories of Hexfall. I can't stop thinking about gripping her hips and guiding her onto my cock for the first time. Or kneeling before the throne, where she sat like a queen, and licking the nectar of her arousal.

A deep groan escapes my throat.

My cock throbs, already so hard it hurts. I grip it in my fist, trying to calm myself, but that makes matters worse.

"Fuck." The word escapes through my clenched teeth.

My fist moves over my cock in sharp, savage jerks. I'm frantic, desperate for release. The muscles in my thighs tremble as my heels brace against the dirt.

I close my eyes and picture Pyrah in the bath, her cheeks flushed, her red hair wet and dark. My mate. All mine.

Shaking, grunting, I fuck my fist until my climax erupts. Blinding pleasure destroys all thought. My cock jerks in my hand and shoots hot jets of seed across my body.

Boneless, I sprawl in the dirt. The fog lifts from my mind, just a little, and I glance down at myself. Fuck, I'm filthy. I need a bath more than I have ever needed one in my life.

On unsteady legs, I drag myself to my feet and wander over to the abandoned royal baths. The moon peeks through the eye of the dome above. Overgrown moss and ferns do not entirely obscure the white marble of the room. In the center of the room, a pool glimmers darkly.

I wade into the cold water before swimming deeper. I scour all the filth and grime from my skin. I claw at myself until it starts to hurt.

It's a pity I can't scour my memories.

Clean at last, I stride out of the bath. Exhaustion turns my bones to lead. The soft moss underfoot invites me.

I have no clothes, no blanket, and I'm still dripping wet. It matters little to me. I curl upon the moss like a beast in its den.

It begins to rain, and the plinking of water in the pool lulls me to sleep.

It has been an eternity since I last dreamed.

I'm back in the prison, locked in shackles. Even my own mind believes I'm still not free. Disgusted, I take control of the dream and turn the chains binding me to ashes. They scatter into nothingness.

I stare at the iron door, wondering where it might lead, knowing that the journey would be nothing but a fantasy. I do not know what lies beyond the door in reality. When I open the door, I see nothing but darkness.

But I am an incubus, and the realm of dreams is my domain. They are mine to manipulate and control.

I close my eyes, focusing, and open them again. Dreams gleam like wet gems at the bottom of a dark river. That's always how they appear to me, whenever I hunt for them, though I have heard that other demons see them differently.

Only a few dreams lie within my reach. I'm deep in the wilderness of the Thornwood, and most of the dreamers sleep too far away for me to peer into their slumbering minds. Here and there, the dreams of dire wolves flicker, though I have never been able to enter the mind of an animal before.

"Where are you?" I murmur, though she can't hear me.

Sleep puts some distance between my body and myself. I'm

less bound by the needs of the flesh. My hunger no longer dominates my every thought, but I am still weakened.

I must feed.

*Find her,* my hunger urges me. *Find her, quickly.*

I wade into the dark river until the water laps at my mouth. Swimming now, I allow the current to carry me among all the fantasies and imaginings that don't belong to me. My incubus senses allow me to hunt down my prey with unnerving accuracy. Instinct guides me to my target.

My gaze locks on a dream of sapphire blue, lying deep in the river.

Pyrah.

I dive down and capture the dream in my claws. When I touch it, the world changes between one blink and the next. Such is the strange logic of dreams.

I'm standing in the mountains, the white snow almost blinding, on the edge of a cliff. The sky stretches, enormous, above me. I have never seen a sky so blue before.

Where is she?

Powerful wings pound the sky. I whip around just as a magnificent red dragon soars over the cliff's edge. She isn't looking down, because her neck is stretched out, straining for altitude. Her talons rush past my horns.

Breathtaking. My heart floats higher just watching her fly.

"Pyrah!" I shout her name into the wind.

She circles back before landing on the edge of the cliff. Her wings arch above us and capture the brilliant sunlight. Illuminated, they look like red stained glass.

"Pyrah," I say. "It's me. I'm here."

Her pupils narrow to slits. "No." She digs her claws into the stone. "I keep dreaming about you, night after night, but you're never real."

My throat chokes up at her pain. That must be a particularly cruel torment. "Pyrah, that wasn't me. I was unable to enter your dreams. They took me prisoner."

"They?"

"The queen and her sorceress. They captured me. Chained me." I swallow hard and decide to omit the details of my torture. "Drugged me with a potion of dreamless sleep."

She blinks, again and again, as if she wants to wake herself from this dream. "I know you aren't real. I'm only imagining what might have happened to you, hoping you aren't dead." Tears roughen her voice, though she does not cry.

I can't let her suffer like this. "I'm not dead."

"How can I believe you?"

"Let me prove it. Let me take control of your dream, if you will allow me."

Her tail flicks against the ground like that of a wary cat, but she says, "Yes."

When I take control, she gasps at the invasion of her mind. I'm gentle with her imagination, careful not to turn her dream into a nightmare. Slowly, I let the mountains and the vividly blue sky fade away. I bring her to Hexfall, where the red petals of roses drift like endless rain in the night.

She relinquishes the armor of her dragon form. When she shifts into a woman, she's shivering, her naked body pale and beautiful in the moonlight.

Every muscle in me tenses. I thought that I could hold my hunger at bay here, but it roars to life inside me.

Fuck, how much longer can I resist her?

"Pyrah." I growl out her name. "I haven't fed in over seven days."

"You must be starving." She searches my eyes, her own glimmering. "It's really you, isn't it?"

"Yes."

"Rook. Rook." She repeats my name as if she can't believe I'm finally here. "Where are you now? What happened to you?"

"I'm safe."

"But where?" She glances around the dream. "Hexfall?"

"Yes," I say again. "And you? Are you safe?"

"I'm in my cave. I don't know when I stopped being able to sleep alone, but it took me an eternity to fall asleep tonight. It's been so difficult every night without you."

"Are you still bleeding?"

"No."

My breath escapes me in a hard exhalation. "You can shift back into a dragon?" It would be safer that way, if she can defend herself.

"I can." Her throat works as she swallows. "Let me touch you. Please."

This is just a dream. I have to remind myself that I can't hurt her here.

When I release her wrist, she combs her hand through my hair. Her fingernails lightly skim my scalp. Shivers rack my body. She curls her hand around one of my horns.

"Pyrah." My breath shudders out of me. "I left you when you were vulnerable and in pain. I should have been there to protect and comfort you."

She shakes her head. "It wasn't your fault."

"I don't know if I should return to you."

Her blue eyes flash gold for a moment. "Why wouldn't you?"

"I would rather starve than hurt you." My words sound guttural, and I force myself to gentle my voice. "Even in this dream, I can feel my hunger taking control. Turning me into something monstrous."

"No." She challenges me with a defiant stare. "You are my monster. Devour me."

"I can't." My heart pounds like a hammer in my chest. "Not in a dream. Here, a kiss is just a kiss."

She stands on her toes, her hands hooked around my horns, and kisses me. Our mouths collide with an intensity that knocks the breath out of my lungs. Even though it isn't a devouring kiss, I'm overwhelmed by a rush of emotions too tangled and fast for me to name. I'm falling from a high place and might never hit the ground.

She breaks the kiss, her breathing a little shaky, and locks eyes with me. "I will find you in Hexfall. Don't you dare try to run away from me."

I admire her ferocity. "I won't."

"Time to wake up, Rook."

With a nod, I release my hold on her dream.

# CHAPTER TWENTY-NINE

ROOK

I jolt back into the waking world. I'm alone in the abandoned royal baths but not for long. She can shift into a dragon again, which means she can fly over from her cave and meet me here.

My muscles remain tense with unspent energy. I pace around the edge of the pool like a caged beast before jumping into the water. I wash myself again, trying to remove every trace of the dungeons from me, wishing I had a decent bar of soap.

I have nothing. All my belongings were taken from me. My daggers, my sword, my armor. My stomach swoops in an unpleasant lurch, reminding me of what I have lost. I never should have returned to Netherhaven. Never should have tried to find the soulstone for Pyrah.

What a fool I was, still clinging to hope. Queen Dulcamara's power crawls into every aspect of my life like a strangling vine.

Even here, I can't stop remembering what it felt like to be caged in her dungeon.

I hate that the queen holds so much power over me. I'm no longer a child, but it's all too easy to remember the choking sensation of dread that filled much of my childhood solely due to her reign over me.

My father, too, was to blame. Even being his son granted me no protection.

I lean back against a corner of the pool. Outside the eye of the dome, it's nearly dawn, the sky turning gray.

I focus on that hint of light. I force myself to count my breaths until the choking sensation loosens around my throat. The cold water of the bath embraces me and numbs me to my emotions.

I'm here. I'm safe.

Hexfall has always been a place of solace for me, my lair in the Thornwood. I often crave the scent of the cursed roses, for they remind me of safety.

Red flashes through the heavens, the color unmistakably familiar, brighter even than the crimson petals of the roses.

My pulse starts pounding. Hunger sharpens to the edge of a knife, the pain almost sweet in its intensity. I climb out of the pool, the muscles in my shoulders flexing, and my shadow wings burst free. They fling aside droplets of water.

I stride to the door and halt on the threshold. My tail uncurls from my spine and whips behind me, betraying my impatience.

Outside, among the cursed roses, a red dragon shifts into a woman.

Pyrah.

It's impossible to hide my arousal. My cock rises to greet her as the first rays of sun touch her beautiful hair.

She stares at me with eyes that still linger gold. Her gaze travels over my wings before dropping to my erection. My tail curls around my cock. Unable to resist, I stroke myself, an obscene gesture that drags out a slippery hint of seed.

"Fuck," she breathes. She's looking at my tail with obvious jealousy.

When she advances, I retreat.

"Wait." Gravel roughens my voice. I raise my hand to stop her, and I'm ashamed to admit it's shaking.

"What is it?"

"Pyrah." Her name comes out as a soft growl, a predatory snarl of anticipation. "We must be cautious."

Her throat works as she swallows. Her eyes have turned from gold to blue, no trace of the dragon remaining. I don't know what this means, but I watch her without blinking, desperate to understand her every move.

"Should I be afraid of you?" she asks.

I tell her the truth. "Yes."

Her sharp intake of breath betrays her fear. "How much?"

"I don't want to hurt you." It sounds like a threat, which wasn't my intent, and I grimace. "But the urge to devour you is…overwhelming."

"Rook," she says, her voice gaining certainty as she speaks. "Come here."

I stalk into the courtyard of the ruined castle. The claws on my toes dig into the moss beneath my feet.

"Kneel," she tells me.

I fall to my knees and await her next command. Lust clouds

my mind, and it's difficult to resist the urge to stroke my cock while she watches me.

"You told me once that devouring me is like drinking wine from a glass. Can you stop before you drain me empty?"

My tail curls behind me, unable to remain motionless. "That is my intent."

She hesitates. "Will you stop if I'm unconscious?"

Shame chokes my throat, making it hard to breathe. She deserves so much better than me and the curse of my demonic hunger.

"Without question," I reply. "I would never violate you like that. I need you to want me."

"You always care so much about consent and desire," she says, "but you rarely tell me what *you* want."

"I don't want to feel this way." My own confession shocks me into silence.

"Like what?" Her question holds no judgment, her eyes wondering, and she waits for me to speak again.

"Ashamed. Desperate. Afraid." I spit out each of the words like bitter seeds. "Ashamed of my own desires. Desperate to escape my own body. Afraid that I might lose control."

While I remain kneeling, Pyrah walks over to me. She places her hand on my cheek and I lean in to her touch. She's trembling.

"When we met," she says, "I was a virgin afraid of my first heat. You helped me through my own shame, fear, and desperation. You gave me everything I needed and more. Let me help you now."

"Pyrah."

I don't know what else to say. Words crumble away to dust,

unspoken, in my mind. I'm left with nothing but my body, though I know this language well. I'm an incubus, and I understand how to communicate through fucking.

My already frayed control snaps.

I'm wordless. Shaking. Nothing more than a wild animal.

With a feral growl, I drag her down to the ground and cage her between my arms. My claws bite into the earth, bracketing her face and trapping her there. My shadow wings arch above us and hide my prey from the sky. I cut off her startled gasp with a kiss.

*Fuck.*

She tastes like paradise. A hint of her desire flows into my mouth, as rich and thick as honey. With a soft moan, she melts under my weight. Her legs hook behind my hips and pull me closer. She welcomes me into her body. On the brink of penetration, though, I meet resistance. I stop, not wanting to hurt her, and consider what should happen next. I know exactly how to make her even wetter.

I trace my claws along the inside of her thigh, where her skin feels softer than silk. "Let me worship at the altar of your cunt."

Her lips round with shock and delight. "Yes, please."

Her belly flutters as her breathing turns shallow. I crawl down her body and bow my head to please her with my mouth. While I lick and suck and nip at her, she grabs me by the horns and holds on for dear life.

The nectar of her arousal tastes nearly as good as her desire.

Her fingers slip lower, to the roots of my horns, and I'm so on edge that I groan. My balls tense up with the urge to climax and make a mess all over her skin. My hips jerk, rutting against the air, my cock aching for more friction.

I want her to come first. My tongue and mouth alone might not be enough. I curse the claws on my fingers, too sharp and wicked for such delicate work. Instead, I slide my tail between her thighs and rub her with its hard, pointed tip. I torment her, circling her clitoris without touching it directly.

Her legs kick against the ground, her muscles trembling, and her thighs clench around me. I fuck her with my tail, pushing it deeper and deeper, curling it in just the right place until she breaks.

She cries out, shuddering, her whole body tightening like a bowstring. She throbs around my tail as she comes. Finally, the aftershocks of her pleasure fade away.

"Look at your pretty pink cunt," I say. "You're so wet for me."

I rear back onto my knees and grab my cock in my fist. When I stroke myself, a shimmering thread of arousal drips from the slit. She watches me, her eyelashes fluttering, still panting for breath.

"I want you wetter," I say.

My fist moves faster, the sound of skin against skin both delicious and obscene. I'm desperate for release. Pleasure curls at the bottom of my spine before it breaks loose in a flood. I grunt with every hard pulse of my orgasm. My cock jerks in my hand, shooting out jet after jet of seed, and I target her already wet cunt. She's drenched with milky white.

It takes me a minute to catch my breath, my chest heaving. "Perfect."

She touches herself between her legs as if fascinated by how filthy she has become thanks to me. Not nearly filthy enough. I'm not done with her yet.

"Why haven't you devoured me yet?" she asks.

Her question hits me like an arrow and pins me to the spot. My throat aches with emotion. "Because I'm afraid that if I do, I won't be able to stop."

"Rook." She strokes my cheek. "Trust yourself as much as I do."

Her words unlock a feeling deep inside me—a small, hesitant hope. It flutters through my ribs like a moth.

Slowly, I bring my mouth above hers, until we are separated by nothing but our breaths. She waits for me to close the distance, giving me the control I need and so desperately desire.

When our lips touch, her lust trickles over my tongue. It's good, so good, and a muffled grunt escapes me. She grabs my cock, still hard, and brings it to her slick, seed-drenched cunt.

The crown of my cock stretches her flesh before my blunt spikes demand entrance. When I thrust deeper, she takes me all the way to the hilt. My balls hit the curve of her ass. We both gasp at the intensity of sensation. It's a raw, primal kind of intimacy.

"Fuck me," she demands.

I'm not foolish enough to disobey.

I fuck her like a wild animal in rut, hammering inside her, harder and harder until she's writhing beneath me and clawing at my back with her nails.

While I'm fucking her, I devour her. Her pleasure floods my mouth and flows down my throat and fills me with such sweet relief that it overwhelms me.

She climaxes hard, her whole body shuddering, and I drink

down every last drop of her pleasure. It's the most delicious ambrosia I have tasted in all my life, and it satisfies me down to the marrow of my bones.

When she collapses beneath me, my heart stops beating for a few seconds. I wrench my mouth from hers. She's struggling to catch her breath, her eyes closed.

"Pyrah," I say.

"Wait," she gasps.

"Are you all right?"

"My mind melted a little." She laughs. "But I'm alive."

I exhale hard. "Should I stop?"

"No." She clings to my ass with both hands. "I love it when you devour me. I love taking you deep."

My heart aches with fierce pride and longing to please her more. She deserves the most exquisite ecstasy.

"I'm not done with you yet," I warn.

"Good."

I slide out of her only long enough to lift her into my arms. I carry her outside the royal baths and brace her back against the marble wall. Her feet can't reach the ground, since I'm so much taller than she is. She's at my mercy. I hold her by the hips, my claws indenting her flesh but not hard enough to hurt. She clings to me and surrenders all control.

I lock eyes with her when I penetrate her again, the intensity of it only heightening the intimacy between us.

"I wasn't lying when I said I wanted to worship at the altar of your cunt," I confess. "Your body is my temple. You are my goddess."

Her cheeks flush pink. "Me?"

"Yes."

"I'm anything but divine."

"I want to prove you wrong."

My wings encircle her, protecting her, and my tail coils around her ankle, possessing her. With every stroke of my cock, I bring her closer to bliss. She's on the edge. I can taste it and angle my hips until I hit the secret place deep inside her that unlocks her most intense pleasure.

Her climax hits her hard. She flings her head back and moans as she rides out wave after wave. I kiss her on her open mouth and swallow down her lust.

*Mine. All mine.*

I won't stop, can't stop, until I have satisfied my hunger. I have been ravenous for far too long, and my only solution is devouring her completely.

*Careful.*

In the back of my head, I know that I have to stop. An incubus can drain all the energy from their prey. But the temptation to continue is nearly impossible to resist. I'm fighting the primal instinct of an incubus by refusing to feed.

When I touch her neck, her heartbeat flutters beneath my fingers.

*Stop.*

I wrench my mouth away from hers.

But she's limp like a doll in my arms.

# CHAPTER THIRTY

ROOK

"Pyrah?" I say, urgency roughening my voice. "Talk to me."

"Fuck." She sighs out the word, though she doesn't open her eyes. "Don't stop. Keep devouring me."

"No."

It's the only acceptable answer. I have taken what I need from her, and it doesn't matter that I want more.

"Was I enough for you?" she asks.

"You are my everything."

Gently, I carry her to a patch of moss and cradle her in my arms. I clutch her to me and press my forehead to her cheek in a silent apology. Emotion rushes through me and grabs my throat in a choke hold.

"Rook," she whispers. "Are you crying?"

I have always believed myself to be the kind of man who never cried, but I'm defeated by the bittersweet potion of shame and relief. My tears keep falling upon her face, no matter how hard I try to stop.

"I'm sorry." I grit out my apology. "I went too far. I almost hurt you."

She tries to comfort me, her hand resting on my thigh, but her cool touch brings me back to the dungeon and the cold threat of the queen's blade.

My stomach twists from the sick memory.

I push myself away from the ground and start pacing through the ruins of the castle, acting little better than a caged animal. I'm shaking with unspent energy as a torrent of emotions overflows inside me.

"What happened to you in the dungeon?" she asks.

"Nothing they haven't done to me before."

She's silent for an eternity. "Who did this to you?"

"The queen. My father is dead."

"Rook…"

"I don't know what's wrong with me."

"No." She speaks with protective ferocity. "There's *nothing* wrong with you."

How can she be so certain? She knows little of the darkness in my past, and the shadows that still cling to me even now and cast doubt upon my feelings. Why am I crying, when I don't even deserve the luxury of tears?

"I'm not a good man," I say. "I'm not even a man. I'm a demon, a cambion, a half-breed bastard. There's a crack running through the middle of me, just like that fucking throne in the prophecy." The pain in my throat clamps down and strangles the rest of my confession.

Pyrah stares at me with what might be horrified fascination.

When she understands who I am, and how broken I am, she will know she has made a mistake.

"They hurt you," she says, and it isn't a question. "You're still hurting."

"They stripped me naked. I'm unable to hide my scars."

More than a statement of fact, these words fill me with a sense of rage and grief that threatens to drown me. I lean against the crumbling wall of the castle and press my forehead to the stone until the grit reminds me of reality.

*Queen takes rook.*

Dulcamara's sneering words echo through my mind, even now, and I want to claw them from my memories.

"Should I touch you or not?" Pyrah asks.

My claws gouge the stone of the wall. Fuck. She noticed when I flinched away from her hand on my thigh. My memories poisoned her tender gesture. I'm filled with a deep sense of self-loathing.

"The queen held a knife to me," I confess. "She threatened castration."

"Fuck," she whispers. "That makes me sick. I'm so sorry, I didn't mean to remind you of what happened."

"Don't apologize. You didn't know."

"Could I shift into a dragon? Would that be different enough?"

I swallow hard. "We could try."

When I turn around, she's already armored in red scales. Her skeleton melts into another shape. Fully dragon, she looms over me. She wraps one of her wings around me, a gesture in common with both dragons and demons. The fire in her belly heats us both. I surrender to her embrace.

My tears twist into ugly sobs that wrench the air from my lungs. Every day, every minute, every second of my time in the dungeon has been bottled up inside me like poison, until I cracked open and spilled everything out.

No, that's not true. I have more memories than those from the dungeon. I learned how to swallow down poison as a little boy. All the hatred and disdain from the king and queen filled me up until it became a part of me.

I have swallowed enough poison already that I could drown in it. I have been submerged in it for most of my life.

I can't let it all out. I don't know how.

After what might be an eternity, I'm wrung out, with no more tears left to shed. I'm empty of all emotion. Calm settles over me like a shroud. It's not the same numb feeling as before but a blissful absence of pain.

I lift my head from Pyrah's shoulder. We look at each other in silence. I never expected to find such comfort in a fearsome dragon's golden eyes.

"Thank you," I say at last.

She lifts one of her claws to my face, with utmost precision, though she stops before she touches me.

"Your eyelashes," she says.

"What about them?"

"They still have tears on them."

"I was crying." Gruffly, I rub them from my eyes. "And I never cry. Not since I was very small."

When tears always lead to punishment, even a child learns to control their emotions.

Her claws drift lower, to my jawline, where she traces the stubble of seven days. "You have a beard now."

"Just stubble." I want her to remember me how I was before, when we first met. "Unsurprisingly, they didn't allow me to have a cutthroat razor while I was locked in the dungeon."

"What happened?" She rests her head against my shoulder. "Tell me, if it's not too painful."

"You asked me not to go back to Netherhaven." I close my eyes for a moment. "I should have listened to you."

She says nothing, just stares at me, and I can't tell if she thinks I have been brave or the biggest fool alive. Shame creeps through me like a stain, an old, familiar feeling. My father never believed I was good enough, but I must believe that Pyrah doesn't see me the same way.

I swallow hard. "I went looking for the soulstone."

"Rook." Her voice snags on my name. "You did this because of me."

"Because of *us*." I look into her eyes. "Our equilibrium."

"*Kelrial*?" The Umbric word sounds strange in her voice, since she has never said it before.

"Yes. But the queen has the soulstone." My fist clenches at my neck as if gripping an imaginary pendant. "She dangled it in front of me while I was trapped in her dungeon."

"That bitch," Pyrah growls. "She deserves to die."

"I know."

"God, Rook, I'm sorry. We tried to find you."

"Your apology is unnecessary," I say, trying to be gentle.

"But, Rook, it was as if you had vanished from the Overworld." Her voice breaks before she takes a steadying breath, regaining her composure. "I refused to believe you were dead."

It hurts to meet her gaze and see the pain shining in her

eyes. This was my fault. I should have stayed with her. "I'm unworthy of such devotion."

"Why would you believe such cruel things about yourself?"

Because that was what I had been taught to believe since birth. Because all the people who had power over me wielded it to hurt me. When I was younger, I believed them without even understanding their cruelty.

I settle for a blunt distillation of the truth.

"The queen hated me," I say. "The king hated me more."

"Where was your mother? Why didn't she protect you?"

It's difficult to put into words, but for Pyrah's sake, I must try. "My mother belonged to the king. She was a succubus, a courtesan, and she had very little power. The court considered her a glorified whore. I was a whore's son, and some believed I should not have been born. What was worse, I had a twin. My sister was twice the proof that the king had sinned. Some in the court suggested that he should…correct matters."

Pyrah exhales a puff of smoke, a mere hint of her anger. In a true rage, she would unleash an inferno. "If anyone threatened my baby, I would destroy them." Not that it was ever in any doubt.

"My mother was furious but powerless." I frown. "Maybe we need to get the hell out of this kingdom."

"Where would we go?"

"Chymeria isn't the only kingdom in the Overworld. And there's the Underworld, though the Demongate has been closed for years. Lark still believes that our mother escaped, and she's waiting for us in the Underworld."

Pyrah searches my eyes. "What do you believe?"

"That the queen must have killed my mother and buried her

in a shallow grave." There's no bitterness in my voice, just the cold, hard facts. "Sometimes I doubt it ever happened. Sometimes I wish I had seen her dead, just so I would *know*."

"You never had the chance to say good-bye to your mother." She whispers it, her words almost lost in the wind. "I gave my mother a dragon's funeral, on a pyre, and my dragonfire helped her to the afterlife."

"How old were you?"

She shivers under my touch. "Not quite sixteen."

It's impossible not to feel for her. Her grief and loneliness must have been heartbreaking. "You should never have to feel such pain again. If I can protect you from it, then my life will have been worth living."

Her golden eyes glitter. "And you still believe yourself unworthy of my devotion?"

"Perhaps less unworthy." I glance down at my empty hands. "After what happened in the dungeon, I have nothing. Not even the clothes on my back."

"That's not true." She laughs as if she's delighted to surprise me with what she says next. "When we went looking for you, we found your horse."

My heart jumps. "Bolt?"

"She was in a stable outside Netherhaven, along with all her tack and everything in her saddlebags. We brought her back to Lark's cottage. She's getting fat and happy eating all the grass in the meadow."

Against all the odds, a smile shadows my mouth. "Good."

"Let me take you home."

*Home.* Such a simple word, and yet it carries so much weight. "Where?"

"My cave or Lark's cottage. Those seem to be our only options at the moment." Pyrah glances at my body as if remembering that I'm naked. "Sorry for not bringing any clothes with me. It can get cold up in the sky."

I glance around the ruins of Hexfall. "Give me a minute."

Years ago, when I fled from Netherhaven and hid in Hexfall, I discovered forgotten finery in the royal bedchambers. Perhaps by some quirk of the curse's magic, they remained untouched by moths and rot. Even better, there should be some swords that have not yet rusted in the abandoned castle armory.

It's a far cry from my own leather armor and blades, but I have little choice in the matter. I can't leave myself completely vulnerable to attack.

Pyrah glances at the sky, as if worried the golden dragon might swoop down from the heavens at any moment. Was Scaldric a problem while I was gone? I'm afraid to ask.

"Hurry," she says.

"You should shift back into a woman. You could hide more easily that way."

"I'm done hiding. I will stand guard while you go inside."

Rather than argue with her, I journey deeper into the ruins of the castle. Inside the old keep, it reminds me of my wintery dream, when I saw Pyrah holding our white-haired baby. But that was just a dream. There's no time for wonder when survival is required.

I enter the cobweb-tangled bedchambers that once belonged to my ancestor, King Mallex the Wrong. I have no qualms about looting the wardrobe of a dead king. His clothes have always fit me well enough. They are, I suppose, my inheritance.

I dress simply, all in black, and hurry onward to the armory.

My footsteps echo in the cavernous hall, where cursed roses snake through the windows and tangle with armor and weaponry abandoned a hundred years ago. The knights in this court wore chain mail rather than full plate armor. That might be useful, though I have never worn it before and it could slow me down. I tilt my head, considering.

Fuck it.

I grab a hauberk and slip it on over my shirt. The weight of the mail rests upon my shoulders like a reassurance, as if the ghosts of the past want to lend me strength. Finally, I grab a bastard sword, a brutal length of steel that still holds a sharp edge. I find this out the hard way when the sword nicks my thumb and tastes blood.

*A bastard sword for a bastard prince.*

I'm ready.

I exit Hexfall and leave the ruins of the castle and my memories here behind me.

Pyrah stands guard with her back to me, though she must hear me approach. When she turns around, her gaze travels over my armor before lingering on my borrowed blade.

"You found a bastard sword?" she asks.

I tilt my head at her reaction. "Yes, why?"

"It reminds me of the bastard sword *he* had." She shudders. "The dragonslayer who killed my mother."

She never told me this before. She never even knew his name before she burned him to ashes. If I could go back in time and slaughter her enemies for her, I would do it a thousand times.

"I'm sorry," I say. "It wasn't my intent to remind you."

"I know."

"We shouldn't linger here. It's not safe."

"Haven't you hidden in Hexfall before?"

"I wasn't being hunted before."

Her eyes glint with ferocity. "Queen Dulcamara must die."

It's foolish to disagree with a vengeful dragon, but it's even more foolish to attack the ruler of Chymeria. The queen has knights and royal sorceresses at her command. We are outlaws in her kingdom, without the armies or allies needed to defeat her.

And yet…

The prophecy keeps echoing in my head. "*The Gray Prince will sit on the ruined throne.*" When I speak the words out loud, a sense of destiny settles over me, stronger than any armor. "Maybe we were wrong."

Pyrah tilts her head. "Wrong about what?"

Restless, I pace back and forth through the forgotten castle. "Maybe the ruined throne was never in Hexfall. Maybe it was the throne in Netherhaven."

"The queen's castle?"

"Yes." From the ashes of despair, hope flickers inside me like a flame. "Perhaps I misunderstood my fate."

"But the throne in Netherhaven isn't ruined."

"Not yet." I lock eyes with her. "For you, I will let the kingdom burn."

Pyrah holds her breath for a moment. "The whole kingdom? Even a dragon can't burn the entire thing down."

When I stop pacing, I stand at attention as if ready for battle. "I am not the queen's victim to torment and discard. I am the Gray Prince. I am the one who will bring about her destruction." Realization falls over me like rain. "She never had the power to end my story for me."

"When you speak of endings, do you mean death?"

"I would die to protect you."

"I won't let you do that." Her eyes flash with defiant fire. "The prophecy never said you would sacrifice yourself."

"That would be my choice."

"You don't need to be the hero."

"You're right," I say. "I need to be the villain."

Her sharp intake of breath could be either fear or excitement. She looks at me as if seeing me for the first time. I'm overwhelmed by a fierce desire to protect her and prove myself worthy of her love. My shadow wings unfurl behind me and betray my fully demonic form.

"Rook," she says. "You're not the villain of this story."

"Whose story? In this kingdom, I have always been the villain. That's what the queen and all her human subjects believe about me. Do you know why they fear me? Because villains have power."

"I don't care what they believe about you. What do *you* believe?"

I bow my head while I ponder her words. "I believe that I have been on the run for far too long. That I have spent far too many years of my life hiding from the truth. That I was unable to accept the royal blood in my veins or the weight of the prophecy on my shoulders."

*Royal blood.* Unbidden, a memory darts through my mind—the dagger slicing my wrist and letting my blood flow. Why did Zin collect my blood? What dark magic has she wrought?

Pyrah's words bring me back to the present. "What would it mean for you to become the Gray Prince?"

"I can't be an outlaw any longer. I can't cling to an existence as a monster hunter in the shadows. My old life died back in that dungeon."

Her breath escapes her in a sigh. "I have never seen you so certain before. There's this undeniable confidence about you." She shakes her head. "Is this who you really are?"

"Yes."

There's nothing else to say. I'm standing in the ruins of a forgotten castle, a place once ruled by my ancestors. I should not have fought the prophecy for so long, though I wasn't ready to accept my role until now.

"What does this mean for *me*?" Her voice rasps with emotion.

"You would be my queen."

When I cradle her cheek in my hand, she leans in to my touch. She's silent for a moment before she speaks. "If we burn down the kingdom, we would rule over ashes."

"Sometimes things must be destroyed before they can be reborn."

The truth of these words sinks down to the marrow of my bones.

I am the Gray Prince, and this is my destiny.

# CHAPTER THIRTY-ONE

PYRAH

Rose petals drift through broken windows, piercing the crumbling defenses of Hexfall.

The sweet perfume of these blooms nearly overpowers my sharpened dragon senses.

"Should I shift back?" I ask. "Into a woman, I mean."

Rook looks into my eyes, uncertainty shadowing his features. I remember the pain that haunted him when I touched him before, and I don't want to hurt him again. I don't want to remind him of the dungeon.

He swallows hard, his throat working. "We can try," he says at last.

Relinquishing the armor of my dragon form, I shift back into a woman. My heart thunders inside my rib cage as I stand motionless. Rook's hand reaches out, trembling slightly before making contact with my shoulder. The touch is tentative, testing. I resist the urge to move, letting him set the pace.

A shuddering sigh escapes his lips, his shoulders falling with relief. He pulls me into his arms, crushing me against his chest. I rest my cheek against the cold steel of his hauberk. His familiar scent of pine and masculine warmth surrounds me as I melt into his embrace.

Here, wrapped in his strength, I allow my walls to crumble. My body softens, vulnerability seeping into my bones. His arms tighten, and for the first time since his imprisonment, I feel truly safe again. My eyes sting with unshed tears.

"I missed this," I whisper. "Missed being held by you."

His fingers thread through my hair, gentle despite his fierce grip. Even with his armor in the way, I can hear his heartbeat beneath my ear. The steady rhythm drowns out everything else—the whisper of falling petals, the sigh of wind through broken windows, even my own unspoken thoughts.

After a long silence, Rook speaks again, his voice solemn. "I thought I had lost this forever. Lost you."

I pull back just enough to see his face, though I keep my hands flat against his chest. His silver skin glimmers, lustrous, after his devouring kiss. But his eyes look shadowed. Something still troubles him.

"I'm here," I say. "I'm safe."

"You're not safe." He shakes his head. "The queen told me why she wants you."

My stomach knots. "What do you mean?"

"She plans to breed you to Scaldric." His words pierce me like arrows. "Create an army of dragons loyal to her crown."

I jerk back, acid rising in my throat. The thought of being forced to mate with Scaldric, to bear his children against my will...

"I would rather die," I spit.

"I won't let that happen." Rook's eyes flare with hellfire. "I swear it."

Horror clamps around my throat with its claws. I force myself to breathe past the choking sensation. Worse, he's not the only one who must confess. "There's something I need to tell you, too."

His shoulders stiffen. "What?"

"Something happened to Lark." I struggle to find the right words. "She tried to find you. She wanted to know where the queen was keeping you locked away."

Rook's throat works as he swallows hard. "What did she do?"

"She found Zin." The name tastes sour on my tongue. "I don't want to tell you everything—that should be Lark's choice. But Zin..." A shiver racks my body. "She did something to Lark. Cursed her with aellurium."

His eyes smolder with anger. "Fuck."

"She's alive," I add quickly. "But changed. There are these golden lines across her skin now, like cracks in silver."

"Fuck," he says again, softer this time. His jaw clenches, guilt etching deep lines around his mouth. "I should never have gone to the castle alone. This is my fault."

"No." I hold his face between my hands. "You were trying to protect us. To find the soulstone. None of us knew it was a trap."

Rook lets out a slow sigh. "Thank you for telling me about Lark."

"Your sister should tell you the rest herself."

"Where is she?

"Home. Her cottage," I add, since she's no longer staying at my cave.

"Let's go. Now."

But the weight of unsaid words sits heavy in my chest. We can't leave, not yet.

His eyes narrow as if he detects my hesitation. "What's wrong?"

"We need to be careful." I retreat from his embrace, wrapping my arms around myself. "Flying there might be dangerous."

"Why?"

The question lingers between us. Behind my closed eyes, I see the glint of golden scales. "Scaldric has been circling my cave for days now."

Rook's hand drops to the hilt of his bastard sword. "That motherfucker has been stalking you?"

"He never stopped." I lean back against the ruined stones of Hexfall. "Sometimes I catch his scent on the wind. Other times I see his shadow pass over the lake. He's been waiting for me to leave the protection of Lark's mist."

"You shouldn't have come here." A tendon leaps in Rook's clenched jaw. "Fuck, Pyrah. You risked everything—"

"To find you." I cut him off. "And I would do it all again."

Rook lets out his breath in a hiss. "Scaldric could have followed you."

"Don't worry, I was careful."

"Careful?" He frowns at me, probably convinced I was reckless.

"I was stealthy." I wander over to one of the broken windows. Through the jagged glass, I peer out at the twisted brambles of the Thornwood. "I walked through the enchanted mist on foot, as a woman, and didn't shift into a dragon until I was sure I was far enough away."

"Did Scaldric see you?"

My fingers find a shard of glass. It crumbles beneath my touch and shatters against the stones below. A shadow passes over the treetops, and my heart stutters, but it's just a cloud.

"No."

"Pyrah." Rook's hand finds mine on the windowsill, his touch strong yet gentle. "Are you certain?"

"No," I repeat, quieter. "I'm not."

"It may be time to end him." His voice drops to a low, dangerous murmur. "Make your choice, Pyrah. This is your decision."

"You want me to kill him?"

"Or I will. Just give the word." Rook speaks with such grim ferocity that I know he would relish slaying the golden dragon.

My heart pounds as I consider his words. The urge to shift and take flight burns through my blood—to meet Scaldric in battle, dragon against dragon. To finally hurt him more than he hurt me.

But Rook has a hollow look in his eyes, still haunted by his time in the dungeon, and he must be weakened. When he devoured my lust, the intensity of his hunger took my breath away. I came so close to blacking out, though I refuse to admit how shaky I feel even now.

We can't take any chances.

If Scaldric wins this fight, he would kill Rook and force me to be his mate.

"No." The word comes out barely above a whisper. I clear my throat and try again. "No. I'm not ready to face him. Not yet."

Rook dips his head in a curt nod. "Understood."

"We should go to Lark first." I glance down at myself, since of course I didn't bring any clothing. "Though I'm not walking there like this. Flying might be dangerous, but it's worth the risk."

"I'm not sure I agree."

"You want me to stroll naked and barefoot through the Thornwood?"

He lets out a noise between a growl and a sigh. "Could I convince you to wear some clothes borrowed from Hexfall?"

"I would prefer to be a dragon. I don't want to be powerless."

Rook tilts his head as if considering what I have said. "You believe yourself to be powerless when you aren't a dragon?"

I open my mouth to reply, then pause. The truth is, I do feel vulnerable in my human form. Soft. Like prey instead of predator.

"Most of us can't shift into another form," Rook adds. "Myself included."

"That's different. You have your skill with a sword."

"You could learn." He folds his arms across his chest. "I could teach you how to wield a blade like a true warrior."

The idea intrigues me more than I expect. I picture myself fighting like Rook does, moving with deadly grace through combat. But I know that it would take years of training to reach his level.

Our enemies won't wait.

"Maybe someday," I say. "For now, I will defend myself with dragonfire."

"Pyrah—"

"Besides," I cut him off, "you promised to teach me how to read first."

Rook shakes his head, fighting back a smile. "Books won't save us."

"Not this time." I stretch, already anticipating the shift. "We should go." I glance outside, where foreboding clouds have plunged the forest into shadow. "The sky looks dark. Like it's going to rain."

He nods. "Lead the way."

I walk into the overgrown courtyard of Hexfall, my bare feet crushing fallen rose petals. I close my eyes and coax out the dragon within me. Shivers rush over my skin, followed by the sweet ache of transformation. My bones lengthen and reshape into a bigger skeleton. Crimson scales armor my skin.

In moments, I'm towering over the ruins.

Rook rests his hand against my shoulder. It has begun to rain, and droplets cling to his silver hair. "Ready?" he asks.

"I am."

He swings onto my back and leans forward against my neck. His weight feels familiar already, as if he has always been there.

"Fly low," he murmurs. "Try to stay unseen."

"That might not be easy." When I snort, a puff of smoke curls from my nose. "I wish I weren't so red."

Rook's hand strokes my crimson scales. "You're beautiful."

His words warm my heart, though I still can't shake the lingering sense of dread.

My muscles tense before I lunge into the air. My wings thump once, twice, before they catch the wind. We soar over the castle ruins. Tilting my wings, I bank over the dark canopy of the Thornwood. I fly low over the trees, so low that I could reach out and pluck a leaf between my talons.

Thunder rumbles over the mountains as I slice through the darkening sky. The rain intensifies, pelting me, each drop a pinprick of cold on my wings. It's dangerous to fly in a storm, even for a dragon, but I need to keep going.

Out of the corner of my eye, a flash of gold makes me flinch. Just a sunbeam breaking through the clouds. But my pulse won't slow. Every glint of light, every shadow could be Scaldric.

Rook's arms tighten around my neck. "Steady," he says, though the wind nearly steals his words before they reach me.

Another flash of lightning, followed by the rumble of thunder. I bank hard to the right, my wing nearly clipping the trees. It sounds too much like a dragon's roar. My neck aches, the pain renewed where Scaldric bit me without my consent. The memory of his teeth in my flesh makes me sick.

Lightning tears open the heavens. For a heartbeat, everything turns blinding white. I blink fast to clear my vision. Stars dance in my eyes, a distraction, and I search the sky for any hint of gold.

Nothing. But he's out here. Watching. Waiting.

A shadow passes over us—just a cloud—but my muscles seize with terror. Last time I saw Scaldric's shadow fall across me like that…

I push myself harder, my wings carving the sky. I can't shake the feeling of being hunted. Every nerve screams that he's near, that powerful golden dragon ready to strike from the clouds, to pin me down, to force me to submit.

"There!" Rook shouts over the storm.

Through the endless rain, I spot the telltale shimmer of Lark's enchanted mist blanketing the meadow. My wings ache from fighting the storm, but sanctuary lies just beyond the forest.

We reach the edge of the Thornwood. Folding my wings, I dive into the mist and plummet toward the meadow. I'm plunged into a white oblivion where the rain still falls, though its fury has been lessened by magic. Outside the mist, the next rumble of thunder sounds muffled.

My wings snap open, scattering rain, and halt my descent. My claws sink into the wet earth of the meadow. The mist swirls around us, thick enough to hide us from even the keen eyes of a dragon. Here, at least, Scaldric can't claim me.

"Pyrah." Rook swings his leg over my back and leaps down. "You're shaking."

He's right. My body won't stop trembling despite the heat of my dragonfire. I'm panting for breath, my lungs still burning from my sprint.

I shift back into a woman, my scales melting away, until I stand naked and shivering in the rain. My legs buckle as relief overwhelms me, but Rook catches me before I fall.

"Easy," he says.

His arms wrap around me, and only then do I realize he's soaked. Water drips down his silver hair and the steel of his armor. Closing my eyes, I cling to him and drag air into my aching lungs. The rain feels so much sharper against my bare skin.

"Cold," I manage, through chattering teeth.

"Let's get you warm." He kisses the top of my head. "I swore I bought you proper clothes in Netherhaven. Even a midnight plum for you to eat. But..." His words fade away, and he must be thinking of the dungeon.

"I don't need any of that," I say, my voice raw with emotion. "I need you. Nothing else matters to me."

# CHAPTER THIRTY-TWO

ROOK

My arms tighten around Pyrah. *I need you. Nothing else matters to me.* Her words pierce my heart until it aches.

"That's sweet of you," I say, gruffly, "though we both know it isn't true. I won't let you freeze to death, woman."

She rests her cheek against my chest. "Keep me warm."

I arch an eyebrow. That's tempting, though she needs clothing. I can't shelter her forever.

Before I can reply, a whinny interrupts us. Bolt canters across the field with her tail held high. The black mare greets me by nudging my face with her nose. Reunited at last, I lean my forehead against her muzzle. When I exhale, she huffs, her breath sweet with hay. It's a familiar scent that inexplicably brings me close to tears.

"Bolt," I murmur. "It's been too long."

Leaning back, I stroke her neck. They braided her mane

while I was gone, and it looks prettier than any of my work. Bolt nudges my hand with her velvety soft muzzle, as if expecting me to have brought treats from the dungeon.

I smile. Her favorite sin has always been gluttony.

I haven't forgotten Pyrah, who's still shivering in the rain. I hook my arm around her shoulders, which shields her from some of the weather. "Let's get you inside."

We walk through the mist together. Bolt trots alongside us. The white vapor swirls away and bares Lark's cottage. I knock on the door, barely lifting my knuckles before it's yanked open.

Lark braces herself against the doorframe. "Rook!"

Her silver skin looks duller, some of the luster lost. Worse still, golden threads of aellurium crawl over her body, just as Pyrah said. This must be the curse from Zin.

My sister runs out to meet me and we collide in an embrace. She squeezes me with all the strength in her arms, despite the hard steel of my armor, the borrowed hauberk from Hexfall.

"You're alive," she says, her voice muffled against my chest.

"I am."

She pulls back to look at me. "What happened to you?"

"Long story." I shake my head. "Let's talk inside."

Bolt stands behind me and rests her muzzle on my shoulder. She's still begging for treats.

"Have you been spoiling my horse?" I ask.

"Blame Pyrah," Lark says.

"In my defense," Pyrah says, "Bolt deserved more than a little spoiling. She let me ride her all the way back. She even avoided some dire wolves along the way, so I rewarded her with carrots."

Dire wolves? Fuck, I can't help but think I should have been there to protect them. I was unable to do so while I was imprisoned in the dungeon. I never want to feel so powerless again.

We enter the cottage together. Rain drums on the roof, a comforting sound, and heat radiates from the fire crackling in the hearth. Lark must be baking bread again, judging by the delicious aroma that fills the air.

I'm overwhelmed by my memories of this place. My throat aches fiercely with emotion. It feels like an eternity since I was last here, surrounded by family. I never allowed myself to miss them while I was locked away, but at this moment, I miss what I have lost. Seven days of my time with them was stolen from me.

I pet Bolt one more time before closing the door of the cottage. I can still see her through the window. My mare trots off and begins grazing on the lush grass of the meadow. She looks plump and glossy, which is good. I want her to enjoy this moment of peace.

“Thank you for taking care of Bolt while I was gone,” I say.

“It was no trouble at all,” Pyrah says, which must be a polite lie.

"Lark, could Pyrah borrow some of your clothes?" I ask. “She's shivering.”

"Of course." Lark disappears into her bedroom, returning with a woolen dress and stockings. "These should fit.”

Pyrah puts on the clothes with trembling hands. Her wet hair clings to her face in dark tendrils. I guide her to sit on the rug before the fire, then kneel behind her. With gentle fingers, I begin working through the tangles in her hair, careful not to pull too hard.

Steam rises from my borrowed armor as it dries. The metal should be uncomfortable against my skin, but I barely notice the cold anymore. Perhaps it's the incubus blood, or maybe I'm still numb from my time in the dungeon.

"You both look frozen," Lark says, shaking her head. "I could make some coffee to warm you up."

"Coffee would be perfect," Pyrah says, rubbing the goose bumps on her arms.

I continue combing through her hair with my fingers, working out each knot. The fire's warmth seeps into her skin. Finally, she stops shivering.

Lark brews coffee in a pot over the fire. The bittersweet scent fills the cottage, mingling with woodsmoke and baking bread. My chest aches at the simple comfort of being here with my sister and my mate, safe and warm. How could I have forgotten this feeling?

But I already know the answer. In the dungeon, I had to be numb. Otherwise, I would not have survived.

I rest my mouth against the crown of Pyrah's head. Her hair is starting to dry, turning from deep crimson to bright flame in the firelight.

"Better?" I murmur against her hair.

She leans back against my chest. "Much better."

Lark pours us each a mug of coffee. I pull out a chair at the table, though I cradle the mug in my hands without drinking. Steam wisps from the black coffee. I stare into the dark liquid as if I might read my future there.

Pyrah gazes into the fire. She looks wistful, lost in thought, rather than on guard. Lark sits opposite me, and I know by the determined glint in her eye that she wishes to interrogate me. She deserves answers—they both do.

"Where were you?" Lark asks.

"One of the queen's dungeons." I sip the coffee to steel my nerves. "It wasn't the Forgotten Tower."

"We know."

Her words hit me like a punch in the gut. "You returned to that horrible place to look for me?"

"No. I entered Zin's dreams to find you." Lark's voice trembles. She rolls up her sleeves, and my blood runs cold at the sight. More of those golden veins of aellurium trace beneath her silver skin like a metallic infection.

"What did she do to you?" I grip the edge of the table, my claws leaving gouges in the wood.

"She bound us together with a curse." Lark traces one of the gleaming lines with her finger. "Our life-forces are connected now. If Zin dies, I die. If she bleeds, I bleed."

My shadow wings writhe beneath my skin, on the edge of betraying my emotion. "I will destroy her for this."

"You can't." Lark grabs my wrist. "Don't you understand? Any harm done to her happens to me, too. We're forced to be allies now, even though we're enemies."

I struggle to contain the fury building inside me. The queen's sorceress has trapped my sister in another prison—one made of magic instead of stone.

"There has to be a way to break it," I say.

"Maybe. But for now, we need her alive." Lark pulls her sleeves back down, hiding the evidence of Zin's betrayal. "We can't kill her without killing me."

The coffee grows cold in my mug as I process this cruel twist of fate. My sister, bound to her former captor and tormentor. The woman who helped imprison her in the Forgotten Tower now holds Lark's life in her hands.

"I should have been here to protect you," I say.

"You were in chains yourself." Lark's eyes soften. "None of this is your fault, brother."

"Where *were* you?" Pyrah asks.

"I don't know." I rub my thumb over the rim of my mug. "There were runes carved into the wall, Umbric runes."

Lark's eyes sharpen. "Umbric? What did they say?"

"It was an ancient dialect of Umbric. I couldn't understand all the words, but the rest of them are carved into my memory." I stare into the distance as I repeat them out loud. "*...unlocked for me... from hell we come...*"

"The Demongate?" Lark asks.

"That's what I wondered." I narrow my eyes, thinking. "Are we certain that the gatehouse of King Aurius was destroyed?"

"Yes."

"But we all know what happens to rubble—it gets rebuilt into new buildings. Nobody wastes stone, not if it's already chiseled into blocks. No wonder the Umbric runes were in pieces. That dungeon must have been cobbled together from the ruins of King Aurius's gatehouse."

"You never left Netherhaven," Lark murmurs.

Pyrah rises from the hearth. Her eyes meet mine, and the firelight turns them such a brilliant blue that I'm distracted for a moment. "How did you escape?"

"I didn't." I swig the rest of my coffee and frown at the dregs. "It was that sorceress."

"Which sorceress?" Lark asks.

When I glance at my sister, she's sitting extremely still in the chair. That alone tells me that she already knows who it was.

I pause for a moment before replying. "Zin." My sister

flinches, almost imperceptibly, but I still catch the movement. “She cast a portal and let me go outside the Thornwood. I don't know why she did it.”

“I don't trust that dark-eyed bitch,” Pyrah mutters.

“What did Zin tell you?” Lark grips the edge of the table until her knuckles turn white and her claws start digging into the wood. What isn't my sister telling me?

My chair creaks as I lean back from the table. “Zin claimed the two of you have a relationship that may not be strictly professional.”

“There's nothing between us, no matter how hard she tries to pretend otherwise.” Lark rakes her claws through her long hair, which has always been one of her tells. She's lying about something.

I tilt my head at her reaction, wondering what she isn't telling me, though I don't want to pry. “Regardless, why the fuck would Zin release me from the dungeon?”

Lark laughs, a bleak sound. “She never released me when I was imprisoned in the Forgotten Tower. She never even tried. Not even after the guards hurt me.” Her fingers flit over to her broken horn.

Why would she think Zin might free her? That implies there was some connection between them, maybe a twisted bond born of conflict.

“Did Zin hurt you?” I ask.

“No, not like that.”

*Not like that.* We both know there are so many more ways to hurt people than physical violence.

I lower my voice to barely above a murmur. “She cut me until I bled.” I rub the scab across my wrist.

"Rook," Pyrah whispers, and she lingers by my elbow, perhaps still unsure if it's safe to touch me.

Lark freezes as if petrified. I'm not even sure she's breathing. "She wanted your blood?"

"She bottled it."

"Oh," she says, little more than an exhalation from her lungs.

My stomach lurches as if I stepped over the edge of a cliff. "Tell me why." She must know the answer, and I need to hear the truth.

"To cast a tracking spell."

A sick mixture of dread and relief twists through me. Zin didn't need my blood to create an heir, but this was all an elaborate trap. I regret drinking any of the coffee. It rises in my throat with an urge to vomit that I fight.

"Our enemies can follow you right to my door," Lark says dully. "Not even the enchantment around my cottage can hide us forever. Not against the power of blood magic."

I shove my chair from the table with a terrible screech, and Pyrah winces at the sound. "We need to get the fuck out," I command.

Lark shudders. "It's too late."

"What?"

"I can feel her."

"Feel her? How?"

"Her magic." Lark closes her eyes. "She's here."

# CHAPTER THIRTY-THREE

LARK

The golden threads beneath my skin pulse with every heartbeat, quickening at Zin's proximity. I trace the metallic veins spreading across my wrists, an indelible reminder of the twisted bond she has forged between us.

She's here. Just beyond the enchantment that protects me.

"Where is she?" Rook asks.

"Outside the mist," I say. "Waiting for me."

He grips the hilt of his sword. "I won't let her hurt you."

"No." I catch my brother by the wrist, stopping him from charging into battle against my enemy. "You can't come with me."

"After what she did to you?" His eyes smolder with anger.

"That's why I need to do this alone." The aellurium pulses beneath my skin, urging me toward the door. Toward her. "If you hurt her, you hurt me."

Rook grimaces. “Don’t trust her.”

"I never did." My broken horn aches with phantom pain as I’m forced to remember my time in the Forgotten Tower. "Stay here. Both of you.”

"Are you certain?"

"Yes." My hand lingers on the door handle. "Whatever game Zin's playing, she can't kill me without killing herself. That's the nature of our curse."

“What if that’s what she wants?” Pyrah asks.

“Knowing Zin?” I exhale hard. “That’s not impossible.”

My brother nods grimly. "Be careful."

"I'll try."

I step outside into the cold mist. Rain falls hard and fast.

I lift my hands, unweaving the protective spell with a twist of my wrist. The mist swirls away, revealing Zin standing in the meadow. She's empty-handed, though of course a sorceress is never unarmed with the magic in her veins.

The aellurium sings in my blood, pulling me toward my enemy like iron to a lodestone. Golden threads beneath my skin shimmer brighter as I walk closer to the motionless sorceress.

"Zin," I say. "Why are you here?"

Her eyes look blacker than black. Unreadable. The connection between us hums with conflicting emotions—her determination wrestling with something that feels remarkably like regret. The golden threads under her skin glow in reaction to mine. Two cursed hearts beating in rhythm.

"I—" Zin chokes on her own words. "I'm here to surrender."

I hold my breath as she drops to her knees, her skirt pooling around her in the wet grass. Her gown is dark with rain. She must be soaked to her skin. How far did she walk to find me? How long was she waiting for me to come outside?

Through our curse, I feel her resignation wash over me like a wave. "Kill me if you want." Zin's voice cracks, though that could be a performance. "Lock me in your own tower. It makes no difference now."

"What are you talking about?" The golden threads beneath my skin light up in response to her turmoil.

"I helped your brother escape." She laughs, hollow and broken.

I take a step closer, unable to resist her raw anguish. "Why?"

"Because I couldn't—" Zin bows her head, her hair curtaining her face. "I couldn't let the queen kill him before—" She cuts herself off, but I already know the truth.

"You needed him," I say, "to find me."

"The queen will execute me for treason when she discovers what I have done." Zin lifts her chin, meeting my eyes, though I still can't read her gaze. "So do what you will with me. I'm already dead."

The golden threads pulse between us, and I taste the bitter tang of her despair on my tongue. After everything she's done to me, I should want her to suffer. But the curse shows me the truth beneath her mask, and I find myself frozen, caught between vengeance and something far more dangerous.

"You're lying," I say, but the words ring hollow.

The aellurium curse pulses between us, exposing the raw truth of her emotions. Every beat of her heart echoes through our connection, making deception impossible.

"You know I'm not." Zin remains on her knees, her dark eyes locked on mine. "The curse won't let me lie to you."

She's right. The golden threads beneath my skin burn with the authenticity of her confession. I feel everything—her fear of the queen's retribution, her conflict over betraying her ruler, and deeper still, the reason she helped Rook escape.

*She wants me badly enough to risk everything.*

"Why now?" My claws scratch at the curse marking my arms. "After everything you did to me?"

Golden lines shimmer across her skin, matching my own. The aellurium shows every crack in her walls of arrogance, every emotion she tried to bury beneath cruelty and duty.

"Because I—" The curse flares between us as she struggles to put her feelings into words. "Because watching you suffer was easier when I couldn't feel it myself."

I bite the inside of my cheek, focusing on the pain rather than letting myself cry. "You're a fool," I say, though my words lack true malice.

"And now I'm here, offering you what you've wanted since the Forgotten Tower—revenge."

But we both know revenge isn't what I truly want. The curse makes that truth impossible to deny. These golden threads are tangled with far more than simply hate.

"I should kill you," I say. "But I can't."

Rain streaks Zin's cheeks like false tears, though I have never seen her cry before. "Not without killing yourself."

"That's why you did this, isn't it? Why you bound us together?"

"No."

Her trembling fingers reach into the pocket of her skirt, withdrawing something that gleams in the rain. My breath catches as I recognize the deep purple crystal, the color richer than any twilight—my mother's soulstone.

"I took it from the royal chambers." Zin holds out the precious gem. "The queen...she keeps it on a chain around her neck while she sleeps. But I couldn't let her—" She shudders and hugs herself. "She was going to use it against you."

The aellurium threads beneath my skin pulse with her fear. Through our connection, I feel the truth of her words, sense the terror coursing through her veins at what she's done.

Zin's hand shakes as she offers it to me. "I can do one thing right."

When I reach for the soulstone, my fingertips glance against hers. The contact shivers through my skin in a way that I can't entirely blame upon the curse.

"Why?" I cradle the precious crystal between both of my hands. "Why would you risk everything?"

"Because I—" Zin's emotions flood through our bond—guilt, desperation, and something deeper that makes my heart stutter. "Because of you."

Her answer is everything and yet nothing at all.

"Get up," I command.

She obeys. "Do what you must."

My hands curl into fists. I battle to keep the emotions from my face, from my voice. "I must break this curse."

"You can't," she murmurs.

"I refuse to believe you."

Zin surrenders to us without a fight, not even struggling or protesting as Rook binds her to a chair with ropes. Grimacing, he checks the knots twice. Zin won't stop staring at me, no emotion glinting in the abyss of her dark eyes.

Through the curse, though, I can feel *everything.* And it hurts so badly.

"You imprisoned my sister." Rook paces the cottage floor, restless with anger. "She rotted in the Forgotten Tower for seven weeks."

"That was the queen." Zin keeps her head bowed, staring at her bound wrists. "That was never my choice."

"Your choice?" Rook snarls the words. "You never fought back. Not once."

"I couldn't."

The curse shimmers like spidersilk across Zin's skin. Through our connection, I feel her shame, her regret, and her overwhelming sense of dread. She risked everything to free Rook, to find me.

I stare at the gem in my hand. "She brought us the soulstone."

"Why?" Rook fires back. "Bribery?"

"No," Zin says, and her words from before echo in my mind. *She was going to use it against you.* What did the queen want?

"Tell the truth," Rook says. "If you even have the ability to do so."

I hold up my hand to silence him. "Zin can't lie." I kneel before our prisoner, bringing myself to her level. "Not to me."

Zin says nothing. She can't lie, but she can refuse to speak.

"Why did Queen Dulcamara want the soulstone?" I say,

speaking in a dangerous murmur, never looking away from Zin's eyes.

Zin's throat works as she swallows hard. She's still marked by the bruises of my brother's fingers, though they have faded with time. The aellurium curse isn't a truth serum, but I can sense her fear through our connection.

"The queen," Zin finally says, her voice barely above a whisper, "believes the soulstone can be wielded against demons."

Rook goes rigid beside me, every muscle tight with tension.

"How?" I demand, clutching the gemstone tighter.

"I don't know." Zin's dark eyes meet mine, unblinking. "But I believe she was speaking the truth."

The curse confirms her words—she truly doesn't know the specifics, but she believes what she's telling us. The golden threads beneath my skin burn with the weight of her confession.

"Tell me everything," I say.

Zin takes a shuddering breath. "Queen Dulcamara loathes demons. She wants you—all of you—erased from the Overworld."

"That's no secret," Rook mutters.

"No," Zin agrees, "but her obsession has grown. She speaks of demons as an infection from the Underworld, sent to corrupt the Overworld."

None of this surprises me. I narrow my eyes. "Where is the Demongate?"

"Beneath Netherhaven Castle." Zin's pulse spikes with fear, which intrigues me. "Below the deepest dungeon where they kept your brother. The door between worlds still stands, sealed but not destroyed."

Rook jerks his head in a nod. "That's why the stones had ancient Umbric runes. Built from the ruins of King Aurius's gatehouse."

"King Aurius tried to cage the Demongate," Zin says, speaking in a hollow voice. "Profit from a portal to hell."

"Dulcamara tried to destroy it," I say, "but she couldn't."

"She wants to destroy *you*. Both of you."

Rook bares his teeth. "She can try."

Curiously, Zin ignores my brother and looks at me instead. "Lark, you can't go to the Underworld alone."

When I jerk away from her, the golden threads of our curse pull taut between us. "I never said I was."

"Why else would you ask about the Demongate?"

I refuse to acknowledge her, to give her speculation any weight.

"You can't go to the Underworld without me," Zin continues. "The curse won't let us be so far apart. It would kill us both."

Horror smothers me like a hand over my mouth. I stare at her in silence, my mind racing through the implications. The aellurium binds us together, forcing us to stay close, to share each other's pain and death.

"Then maybe I should." The words slip out before I can stop them.

"You would die, too."

"Better dead than bound to you forever." But even as I say it, the curse reveals my lie. We both feel the falsehood burning through our connection.

"You don't mean that," Zin says, with a broken little smile.

I turn my back on her before I succumb to the urge to

scream. Unspent magic crackles between my fingertips. I need some air. Trembling, I flee from Zin and slam through the door of my cottage.

Rook follows me into the rain. "Lark."

I stare into the enchanted mist until my eyes swim. "I hate this. Hate *her*."

"I know." Rook shakes his head. "Fuck."

I fling my head back and stare at the clouds. There's still frustration trapped inside my chest. I fill my lungs before letting out a primal scream. The raw sound tears through my throat.

When my voice finally gives out, I'm left panting, tears mixing with the rain on my face. I don't feel relief. Not even a little. The aellurium curse still binds us together, unbreakable and unyielding.

"Feel better?" Rook asks, gruff yet gentle.

"No," I admit, wiping my face with the back of my hand. "I'm still bound to her. Nothing's changed."

The golden threads of the curse pulse beneath my skin like living veins. I can feel Zin's presence inside the cottage—her fear, her hope, her twisted affection for me. It makes me sick to think I will never be free of her, that her emotions will always be tangled with mine.

"I can't do this," I say, more to myself than to Rook.

"We will find a way to break the curse."

"She says it can't be broken."

"And you believe her?" Rook raises an eyebrow.

I hesitate. Through the curse, I felt Zin's certainty when she claimed the bond was permanent. But certainty isn't the same as truth. She could be wrong. She has been wrong about so many things.

"I don't know what to believe anymore." My hand clenches around the soulstone until the facets dig into my skin. I hold it out to my brother. "Take this. The soulstone belongs to you."

Confusion furrows his brow. "It belongs to both of us."

"I have no need for a soulstone." I soften my words. "Besides, I know you want to find *kelrial* with Pyrah."

His eyes widen. "How did you know?"

"She told me." I smile. "Besides, I'm your twin. I can read you like a book."

Rook's fingers close around the soulstone. "Thank you, Lark." His voice is rough with emotion. "Truly."

The sincerity in his words warms something inside me that even the curse can't touch. For a moment, it's like we are back at Netherhaven Castle, children again, before we had bounties on our heads.

"I will help you," he says. "With Zin, with the curse. Any way I can."

I shake my head. "You have enough problems of your own."

"Don't worry about me."

"Neither of us knows the ritual for *kelrial*."

Rook looks down at the soulstone, turning it between his fingers. "Perhaps the Underworld is the answer."

The rain seems to pause between us as I consider his words. "For both of us."

"What do you mean?"

"In the Underworld, we can learn the ritual for *kelrial*. You can find equilibrium with Pyrah." My heart beats harder as I continue speaking. "And I can find a way to break this curse."

# CHAPTER THIRTY-FOUR

PYRAH

When Lark screams, my heartbeat stumbles before pounding back harder.

The raw frustration and anger in her voice is all too familiar. I peer out the window, my cheek resting against the cool glass. Outside, Lark stands with her head flung back, staring down the rain.

Rook reaches for Lark's shoulder, no doubt trying to comfort his sister, though he doesn't touch her yet. When he speaks, his voice remains too quiet for me to catch any of the words. Some of the tension sags from Lark's body.

I turn my back on the window, since they need a moment alone, and my attention returns to our prisoner. Zin watches me silently. Golden threads of the curse run through her skin, matching the pattern on Lark's body.

"You're an evil witch," I say.

"And this surprises you?" Zin sneers at me as if unimpressed by my insult. "I never pretended to be anything I wasn't."

"What you did to Lark was unforgivable." I lean closer, letting her see the fire in my eyes. "You chained her life to yours."

"Even Rook chained you in aellurium."

I bristle at her words, though she isn't wrong. "That was different."

"Was it?"

I clench my hands into fists. "We were enemies."

"And Lark believes me to be her enemy."

I glance toward the window. "What you did to Lark is beyond cruel. You have forced her to feel what you feel, to die when you die. She will never be free."

When the door swings open, Lark storms into the cottage. Her gaze slides right past Zin as if she doesn't even exist. Lark starts looting books from a shelf, building a stack that towers on the kitchen table.

Zin leans back in her chair, her chin lifted with defiance. "You won't find what you're looking for there."

"Be quiet," Lark snaps. "There's always a countercurse."

"This curse cannot be broken."

"Don't make me hex you into silence."

Zin's mouth twists. "We would both—"

"I know."

Rook clears his throat behind me. I turn around and find him leaning against the doorframe. Rain clings to his long silver hair. He meets my eyes before tilting his head toward the outside.

"Pyrah," he says. "Come with me."

I glance between Lark and Zin. The tension in the room strains like a bowstring pulled too tight. I would be a fool not to take this chance to escape. As I pass Rook in the doorway, his hand brushes the small of my back. Though it's a simple gesture, it sends shivers down my spine.

After far too many lonely nights, I crave everything about him.

I follow him outside. The sweet scent of rain on grass fills the meadow. Bolt whinnies softly at Rook. There's a small stable at the cottage, nearly the size of a garden shed, though it's enough to shelter Bolt from the weather.

Rook finds his saddlebags waiting for him in the corner and digs through them. His movements are efficient. He must know exactly where everything is. When he pulls out a brush, Bolt's ears perk up.

"Hello, lady." Rook murmurs the words in a gruff yet tender way. Bolt pushes her nose into his chest, and Rook rubs her muzzle. "Missed you, too."

He starts brushing his horse in long, steady strokes. Mud and rain have matted her black coat, but Rook works through each tangle with infinite patience. She shifts her weight, leaning into his touch. Her tail swishes with contentment. His hair falls forward as he works, partially hiding his face.

"She carried me through three kingdoms when I was hunting a basilisk," Rook says, not looking up from his work. "Never complained once, even when we found the monster in a burrow choked with blood and bones."

"I believe you," I say, wondering how far he has traveled on his quests before. "Will you go back to hunting monsters?"

Rook's hands pause for a moment before continuing to

brush his horse. "No." He grunts. "Not unless I have no other choice. It's hard, dirty work, and none of it ever made me less of a monster myself."

He moves to Bolt's other side. There's something calming about watching him care for his horse. His hands move with practiced ease across her coat, brushing away mud until her dark coat gleams even in the dim light.

His horse nuzzles him as if thanking him. He kisses the white blaze on her nose, the shape reminiscent of a lightning bolt. He's such a sweetheart whenever he's with his horse, and she clearly loves him in return.

I comb some of his loose hair from his eyes. My hand drops to his jaw before running over the silver beard that has grown during his captivity. It softens the sharp angles of his jaw, making him look wilder, more dangerous—and somehow more vulnerable, too.

"I should shave," Rook says. "Need to get rid of this stubble."

"Beard," I say, correcting him, "and I think it looks good on you."

Rook's eyes shutter. "It reminds me of the dungeon."

My stomach tightens at his words. Every time he touches his face, he must remember his time imprisoned at the queen's mercy. The length of his beard marks the days of his suffering.

"I'm sorry," I say. "I didn't mean to remind you."

He shakes his head, his expression guarded. "No need for apologies."

"Could I help you forget?" I touch his jaw with tentative fingertips.

"How so?"

"With the shaving, I mean."

His eyebrows jump higher. "Have you done this before?"

Heat creeps into my cheeks. "Not yet."

"I can teach you." His mouth quirks with a hint of amusement. "I should have a cutthroat razor that will work just fine."

He unpacks his shaving things, then beckons for me to follow him. We wind down a path through ferns that drip with raindrops. By the river, a small stone building perches on the bank. Steam fogs the glass in the windows.

"The bathroom?" I ask.

Rook nods. "Not sure how we missed it that night. Too much demon wine."

The door groans open beneath his hand. My breath catches as we enter together. This doesn't look like any bathroom I have ever seen. Everything has been carved from gleaming white quartz, even what must be the toilet. The bathtub looks more like a fountain, with carved stone fish spitting water.

"The water's always hot," Rook says. "Magic."

I dip my fingers into the tub, marveling at the perfect warmth. "This is nicer than the royal baths at Hexfall."

"Don't let Lark hear you say that." Rook smiles. "Once she starts bragging about her magic, she won't stop."

Through the window, I watch rain ripple across the river while Rook prepares his shaving supplies. He kneels on the floor and arranges a cutthroat razor, a bar of pine soap, and a hand mirror. He lathers the soap and rubs the suds over his jaw in a well-practiced ritual. He's letting me in to this quiet moment of intimacy.

"Come here." He picks up the razor. "Like this."

His thumb presses into his cheek, pulling the skin taut. With his other hand, he shaves away the edge of his beard, revealing the silver beneath. He holds out the cutthroat razor to me and I take it by the handle.

"Now you," he says.

I kneel before him. My hands are trembling slightly. "I don't want to hurt you."

"I trust you," he says.

With my free hand, I press my fingertips against his cheek, trying to copy his movements. Slowly, carefully, I bring the razor to his skin. He doesn't even flinch, his breathing slow and even, as he allows me to shave him. I rinse the razor between strokes. My movements become steadier, more confident.

More and more of his silver skin emerges. More of the Rook I remember.

When I reach his throat, he tilts his head back, exposing the vulnerable line of his neck to the blade. I shave him with intense concentration, never cutting him, not even once, until finally he's rid of the beard.

"There," I whisper, setting aside the razor. "Like we first met."

He splashes water in his face, washing away the last traces of his time in the dungeon. "Thank you."

My fingers trace the strong line of his jaw, marveling at how smooth his skin feels now. I pick up the bar of soap and take a deep whiff of the spicy scent. "That's why you always smell like pines."

He catches my hand and presses a kiss to my palm. He reaches into his pocket and pulls out the purple soulstone Lark gave him. It catches the light, throwing violet reflections across the walls.

"I want you to have this," he says, rubbing the facets of the soulstone between his fingers. "Would you like to wear it? On a chain around your neck, perhaps?"

My heart aches at his words. I forget how to breathe. This moment feels significant, like a promise of our future together.

But I whisper, "I can't."

His brow furrows. "Why not?"

"I'm a dragon shifter." A broken little laugh escapes me. "My transformation would break the chain and lose the soulstone."

Understanding dawns in his eyes. "Of course." His fist closes around the soulstone. "We can't risk losing something so precious. Not until we find *kelrial*."

"Keep it," I say. "Wear it for me."

"For us both."

My eyes well with tears. "I love you, Rook."

He embraces me. Some things need no words.

Darkness falls and brings with it more rain that drums against the roof of Lark's cottage. The sound should lull me to sleep. Late at night, Rook and I lie together on the floor. The fire crackles low in the hearth. My fingers find Rook's hand in the shadows. I squeeze it tight, trying to comfort myself.

"Can't sleep?" His voice rumbles against my back.

"No," I whisper. "I can't stop thinking of Scaldric, no matter how hard I try." My fingers touch the scars on my neck. "Can't stop remembering the pain."

He lets out his breath in a rush. "I understand why you want to forget. You aren't ready to face him yet."

I'm silent for a moment, pondering his words. Thinking of Scaldric fills me with dread, but I have never been one to run away from my fears.

"No," I say softly. "I want to face him."

"When?"

"Sooner rather than later."

"Then we end this. Tomorrow."

I roll over to meet his eyes. "How?"

"We will return to your cave, near the lake with no name. I want you to shift into a woman and wander outside the enchanted mist. Wait for Scaldric to land on the ground by you. We lure him out with you as bait."

"Bait?" I repeat, and an involuntary shiver racks my body.

"Unless you are unwilling to do so."

My fingers curl into fists at my sides. I grimace at the thought of dangling myself in front of Scaldric like a scrap of meat. I will be all but helpless.

"I'm afraid," I confess. "But I trust you."

"I won't let him hurt you." His voice carries the weight of a vow. "Convince Scaldric to shift into a human. Do whatever it takes. While he's vulnerable, I will strike."

My hand tightens around his. "Will you kill Scaldric?"

"I will do what I must." His thumb brushes over my knuckles. "Ready to end this?"

"No more running. No more hiding." Determination steels my voice. "Let's finish the fight that Scaldric started."

Rook pulls me close, pressing his forehead to mine. His

shadow wings curl around us like a protective shroud. We share this moment of silence, our breaths mingling.

"Together," he murmurs, the gravel in his voice roughening.

"Together," I echo.

Morning dawns, cold and rainy.

We fly back to the mountains, where enchanted mist cloaks the land around my cave. Scaldric still circles in the sky, his golden scales glinting, but I land by the nameless lake before he can see my arrival. The mist welcomes us into its cold embrace.

I shift back into a woman. Naked, shivering, I stand ready. It has begun to rain, the water clinging to Rook's silver hair and his steel armor borrowed from long-dead kings.

Rook kisses me on the forehead. "You're stronger than you know."

"I hope so," I whisper.

With a silent nod, Rook vanishes in the mist. I turn my back on him and take a steadying breath. Behind me lies safety—ahead of me, danger. I start to walk along the lake.

I leave the safety of Lark's enchanted mist, each step carrying me farther from protection. The nameless lake stretches before me, its dark waters rippling under the onslaught of rain. My bare feet sink into the wet gravel of the shore.

My heart pounds so hard I can barely hear anything else. The muscles between my shoulder blades tense and twitch, anticipating the slash of claws or the rush of wings above. I scan the clouds, searching for that flash of gold.

The rain grows heavier, plastering my red hair to my shoulders. I continue walking the shoreline, exposed and naked and vulnerable in my human form. Every shadow makes me flinch. Every gust of wind could be his wings.

I know he's watching. Dragons are patient hunters—I should know. He will wait until I'm exactly where he wants me before he strikes. My fingers curl into fists at my sides as I force myself to keep moving forward.

A branch snaps in the forest to my right. I freeze but don't turn to look. Keep walking. One foot in front of the other. The gravel yields to pebbles that dig into my feet.

Thunder rolls across the mountains. Or is it a dragon's roar? My breath catches in my throat as I strain to tell the difference. The waiting is worse than any attack.

My heart slams against my ribs. He's coming. Any moment now, those massive talons will close around me.

I reach a jutting peninsula of rocks that forces me to wade into the shallows. The icy water bites at my ankles. I'm completely exposed now, away from the tree line, away from cover.

Defiant, I lift my face to the sky. "Scaldric!" My voice echoes out over the lake in a challenge.

Scaldric swoops down from the sky and plunges into the lake, spraying icy water everywhere. My heart stops. His massive golden form towers above me, water cascading off his scales. Steam rises from his flanks, his dragonfire hot within his chest.

"Pyrah." His voice rumbles through my bones.

I wrap my arms around myself, letting my vulnerability show. My tears mix with the rain on my cheeks. "You've been protecting me, haven't you? Following me, watching over me."

"Yes." His head lowers, his icy eyes studying my face.

"And you told me..." My voice breaks. I swallow hard. "You told me I would return to you. You were right."

The water ripples around my thighs as I take a step closer. My hands shake. "I'm ready now. Ready to be with you." The lie tastes like ash on my tongue. "But not like this. Not as dragons." I reach out, letting my fingers brush the scales along his neck. "I want to feel you as a man. To truly be your mate."

Surprise flashes in Scaldric's eyes. "You do?"

"I was wrong about the demon. Wrong about what I wanted." Tears spill freely down my face now. I pray he mistakes them for relief rather than revulsion. "Please," I whisper.

Scaldric shifts, his massive dragon form collapsing into the shape of a man. He stands before me, naked and proud, water streaming down his pale skin. My stomach churns at the sight of him, but I force myself to give him a false smile.

Let him believe that I am weaker than he is.

"Pyrah." Scaldric's cold blue eyes drink me in as he steps closer. "My beautiful mate." His fingers trace my cheekbone. "I knew you would come to your senses."

I tilt my face up to him, though every instinct screams to run. His lips crush against mine, possessive and demanding. I don't return the kiss but pretend to submit to him. My hands rest on his chest, feeling his heartbeat beneath my palms.

A twig snaps.

Scaldric breaks the kiss, his head whipping toward the sound.

But he's too late.

Rook bursts from the mist, his bastard sword gleaming. The blade arcs through the air with deadly precision. Scaldric throws his arm up to block the blow.

Steel bites deep into flesh and hits bone. Blood sprays across my face as Scaldric roars in pain, the sword lodged deep in his forearm. I stumble backward into the icy lake, my heart hammering. The water turns crimson around us.

Scaldric shudders, his skin patterned by scales. Shifting.

Rook yanks his blade from Scaldric's arm with a savage twist. Blood arcs through the rain as Scaldric's skin ripples with scales. His skin turns to a golden hue. But before he can complete the shift, Rook strikes again.

The bastard sword slashes across Scaldric's chest. Another blow opens his thigh. Rook moves like death incarnate, each strike precise and merciless. His shadow wings unfurl.

Scaldric tries to defend himself, but Rook is everywhere at once. The demon in him has awakened fully—his red eyes burn like hellfire, his silver skin gleams with an unholy light.

I have never seen Rook like this before. Gone is any trace of humanity. He moves with supernatural speed and grace, dealing death with every swing.

Blood flows freely from Scaldric's wounds. Each time scales begin to form on his skin, Rook's blade finds flesh. The water churns red around us. Blood mats Scaldric's hair to his face. Scaldric can't maintain his concentration long enough to shift—the pain keeps him locked in his vulnerable human form.

Scaldric's fist connects with Rook's jaw in a brutal crack. Rook stumbles backward, his boots slipping in the bloody water. My heart lurches as Rook's sword drops.

Golden scales ripple across Scaldric's skin. His wounds begin knitting together, flesh closing before my eyes, his healing accelerated. His spine elongates, horns bursting from his skull. The transformation has begun.

"No!" The word tears from my throat.

I don't think. I don't plan. Raw fury ignites in my blood. The shift rips through me like lightning, faster than it has ever come before. My bones crack and re-form. My skin hardens to crimson scales. Wings burst from my back as I unleash my power.

# CHAPTER THIRTY-FIVE

PYRAH

I launch myself at Scaldric before his transformation can finish. I'm already fully dragon. We crash into the lake, sending a massive wave across the surface. My claws tear into his partially scaled flesh. My jaws snap at his throat.

Scaldric thrashes beneath me, caught between forms. Blood clouds the water around us. I dig my claws deeper, pinning him down. All my rage at his possessiveness, at his violation of my freedom, at his attempts to control me—it all pours out in a savage roar that shakes the mountains.

My teeth clamp around his arm and bite until it severs. I taste his blood, metallic and hot. He screams, the sound caught between human and dragon. His partially formed claws rake my sides, but I barely feel it through my armor of scales.

This is what I am.

Not his mate.

Not his possession.

I will never submit to him again.

I fling Scaldric from my jaws. His body crashes onto the shore, blood staining the gravel beneath him. His transformation fails, leaving him naked and human, writhing in agony. Where his right arm should be, only a ragged stump remains. He clutches the wound, blood pulsing with every heartbeat.

Not even a dragon can heal from this wound.

Scaldric will carry it until his death.

Rook stalks forward, his bastard sword gleaming with Scaldric's blood. The blade kisses Scaldric's throat, drawing a thin line of red. Shadow wings spread behind Rook, casting darkness over Scaldric's broken form.

"Look at her," Rook's voice carries the weight of steel.

Scaldric's eyes meet mine. For the first time, I see fear in them. Gone is his arrogance, his certainty of ownership. Blood trickles from the corner of his mouth.

"Promise her," Rook says as he presses the blade deeper. "Promise you will never touch her again. Never hurt her again."

Scaldric's chest heaves with labored breaths. His golden hair is matted with blood and lake water. The mighty dragon reduced to this—a broken man on his knees before me.

I step closer, letting him see the strength in me that he tried so hard to crush. "Say it."

"I will never touch you again," Scaldric rasps, blood bubbling at his lips. "Never hurt you again, Pyrah."

Rook's eyes meet mine over Scaldric's kneeling form. His blade presses against Scaldric's throat, ready to end this. One nod from me and Scaldric's head will roll across the blood-stained shore.

But I can't.

Even after everything he's done, I won't become what he is —someone who takes a dragon life—any life—without mercy. The rain washes the blood from my scales as I shift back into human form.

"Leave," I command. "Leave this kingdom and never return. If I catch your scent here again, if I see one glint of golden scales in these skies, I will not show you mercy again."

Scaldric staggers to his feet, clutching the ragged stump where his arm used to be. Blood pulses between his fingers with each heartbeat. His proud shoulders slump as he stumbles toward the tree line.

I watch him disappear into the forest, still trapped in his human form. Whether he lives or dies now depends on how quickly he can find help. The thought doesn't bring me joy, but I feel no pity, either.

He made his choice when he tried to own me.

The rain washes away his bloody footprints, erasing all trace of him from my territory. Let him bleed his way to whatever fate awaits. I am done with him.

Rook paces across the cottage, his shadow tail lashing behind him with frustration. The soulstone gleams on the kitchen table, its purple depths holding untapped power.

"How does it work?" he demands.

"I don't know," Lark says.

"Ask Zin."

"Ask her yourself. She's not going anywhere."

With a growling sigh, Rook looms over Zin. "Tell me."

She stares up at him with haunted eyes. "Why would I know? The soulstone holds demonic magic. That's not my area of expertise. I have never been to the Underworld."

"Fuck," Rook grits out. "Pyrah, I'm sorry. I promised too much."

I shake my head. "It's not your fault."

I watch his frustration build, his muscles shaking with unspent tension. When he slams his fist on the table, a glass tips, spilling water across the wooden surface.

"No—" Lark says, too late. Water sloshes over the soulstone.

Purple light blazes from within the crystal, so bright I have to shield my eyes. The stone begins to hum, a deep resonance that vibrates through my bones.

The soulstone's glow spreads through the spilled water like ink, creating strange patterns that remind me of the Umbric runes Rook described from the dungeon. Even Zin's dark eyes widen as she twists against the ropes binding her.

The water ripples, spreading outward in unnatural patterns. A soft white glow emanates from the puddle, coalescing into the form of a woman with silver skin and a waterfall of pale hair. Graceful, wicked, black horns curl over her head.

My breath catches—she looks just like Rook and Lark.

"My children." Her voice echoes with an otherworldly quality. "You have found my soulstone."

Rook drops to his knees beside the table. "Mother?"

"I left this behind knowing you would find it someday. I

need you. Come find me in the Underworld. Please hurry." The image starts to fade. "I love you both."

The water stills, leaving only ripples from Rook's tears hitting the surface of the puddle. He grabs the stone from the water, but the enchantment has gone dark.

"All this time..." Lark sinks down beside her brother.

When he speaks, his voice with rough with emotion. "You were right. Our mother is alive."

Night settles over the cottage like a heavy blanket. Lark and Zin linger in her bedroom, their voices too quiet to make out any words. They have much to discuss in private. Rook and I sit by the hearth while the fire crackles and spits sparks.

*Such beautiful destruction,* I think, contented.

His eyes reflect the flames. "We need to destroy the castle."

"Destroy it?" I lean forward in my chair.

"Tear it down to its foundations." His voice sounds solemn with anger. "The Demongate lies beneath. It's the only way to reach the Underworld and to find our mother."

My heart pounds against my ribs. The thought of leveling an entire castle, of unleashing my dragon's fury upon stone and mortar, makes my blood sing.

But there's hesitation in Rook's face as he watches me.

"I understand if you don't want to come with me," he says softly. "Your treasure, your cave—I know what they mean to you. I won't ask you to leave everything behind."

I reach across the space between us, taking his hand. "My treasure means nothing compared to you."

"Pyrah—"

"No." I squeeze his fingers. "I would follow you anywhere. Beyond this world to the next. Whatever lies through that gate, whatever darkness we face—I choose you."

The tension melts from his shoulders. He brings my hand to his lips, pressing a kiss to my knuckles.

I study Rook's face in the firelight, the sharp angles of his cheekbones casting shadows. "What about the queen?" My fingers tighten around his. "Would you flee to the Underworld and leave her to rule over this kingdom?"

His fangs glint in a sneer. "I will destroy her throne."

"The prophecy says you will take back the throne."

Rook pulls away, pacing before the hearth. "I never wanted a crown. Never wanted any of this."

"But the people suffer under her rule."

He stops moving, his back to me. "You sound like Lark."

"Because she's right." I step closer, close enough to feel the heat radiating from his skin. "You can't abandon the people of Chymeria to Dulcamara's cruelty."

"They have abandoned me."

I press my palm between his shoulder blades, feeling the muscles tense beneath my touch. "They don't know who you are. Not yet. You just need to show them the truth."

Rook gazes into the embers of the fire. "They won't see me as their hero after we destroy the castle."

"But Dulcamara will be there," I say, already tasting victory.

He shakes his head. "She won't fight us herself. She will run to her knights the moment we attack. Hide behind their shields and swords while they do her killing."

My claws itch beneath my human skin. "Then we hunt her down."

"With what force?" Rook frowns, his eyes thoughtful. "The armies of Chymeria number in the thousands. Even with your dragonfire, we would be overwhelmed."

"Then what do you suggest?"

"We use the Demongate, right after we destroy the castle." His eyes glimmer with reflected flames. "We journey to the Underworld, find my mother, and raise an army of our own. An army of demons. Then at our hand, Dulcamara will meet her end."

A shiver crawls down my spine. "The Gray Prince," I whisper.

He embraces me in the darkness of his shadow wings. "And you, Pyrah, would be my queen."

**Rook and Pyrah's story will continue in *Deadly Reign*. While you wait, you can indulge in another dark fantasy romance with *Prince of the Undying*.**

# MORE BY KAREN KINCY

FANTASY ROMANCE

*Demonic Prince*

*Devouring Kiss*

*Prince of the Undying*

YOUNG ADULT PARANORMAL

*Other*

*Foxfire*

*Bloodborn*

YOUNG ADULT FANTASY

*Dragon by Midnight*

# AUTHOR BIO

Karen Kincy writes books when she isn't writing code. She has a BA in Linguistics and Literature from The Evergreen State College, and an MS in Computational Linguistics from the University of Washington.

Find Karen online at:

www.karenkincy.com
www.facebook.com/KarenKincyAuthor
www.twitter.com/karenkincy

www.ingramcontent.com/pod-product-compliance
Lightning Source LLC
Chambersburg PA
CBHW020249030826
48979CB00030B/2671/J
* 9 7 9 8 9 8 9 9 6 9 7 1 5 *